CAPITAL CRIMES

ALSO BY STUART WOODS

FICTION

Dirty Work†
*Blood Orchid**
The Short Forever†
*Orchid Blues**
Cold Paradise†
L.A. Dead†
The Run‡
Worst Fears Realized†
*Orchid Beach**
Swimming to Catalina†
Dead in the Water†
Dirt†
Choke
Imperfect Strangers
Heat
Dead Eyes
L.A. Times
Santa Fe Rules
New York Dead†
Palindrome
Grass Roots‡
White Cargo
Deep Lie‡
Under the Lake
Run Before the Wind‡
Chiefs‡

TRAVEL

A Romantic's Guide to the Country Inns of Britain and Ireland (1978)

MEMOIR

Blue Water, Green Skipper

*A Holly Barker Book
†A Stone Barrington Book
‡A Will Lee Book

STUART WOODS

CAPITAL CRIMES

G. P. PUTNAM'S SONS NEW YORK

DOUBLEDAY LARGE PRINT HOME LIBRARY EDITION

This Large Print Ediiton, prepared especially for Doubleday Large Print Home Library, contains the complete, unabridged text of the original Publisher's Edition.

G. P. Putnam's Sons
Publishers Since 1838
a member of
Penguin Group (USA) Inc.
Hudson Street
New York, NY 10014

Published simultaneously in Canada

ISBN 0-7394-3913-8

Printed in the United States of America

This Large Print Book carries the Seal of Approval of N.A.V.H.

THIS BOOK IS FOR
MARVIN GREEN

CAPITAL CRIMES

I

SENATOR FREDERICK WALLACE of South Carolina rose at dawn from the bed in the lakeside cabin that he had shared with his African-American lover for more than twenty years. He went into the bathroom and relieved himself noisily. His lover, Elizabeth Johnson, liked to sleep later than he.

Freddie and Elizabeth had produced two sons early in their relationship, both of whom were enrolled in Ivy League universities. Freddie's wife, Betty Ann, disliked coming back to Chester, their putative home, preferring the social life and shopping of Washington, D.C., which made it easy for Freddie to make weekend trips back to South Carolina, ostensibly for constituent services. He did a bit of that, of course, but mostly he and Elizabeth did each other. It was the only completely satisfying sexual relationship of his entire life, and he cherished it above everything else in his existence, except his status as a conservative Republican U.S. senator. Since he was a politician, the hypocrisy of his position weighed lightly upon him. Once, a couple of years before, someone had found out and had tried to expose the relationship, but Freddie had, by a previous plan with Elizabeth, denied everything and fought the rumor to a standstill. He had been unable to see her for three months, and that had hurt him badly.

TED, who had been sitting in the trees for more than an hour before first light, caught sight of the senator through the leaves, as he apparently relieved, then weighed himself in the bathroom. He didn't like the sight line—too many branches in the way—so he bided his time.

FREDDIE WALLACE tied his robe around him and walked into the kitchen. Since Elizabeth slept later, he always made his own breakfast. First, though, he attended to a little ritual that had been suggested to him by Harry Truman, a president whom he would not admit admiring. He went to a kitchen cupboard and removed a bottle containing an amber liquid, with a hand-printed label. It was a private-batch bourbon, 100 proof, that an old friend kept him supplied with, as many old friends kept Freddie supplied with many things, from suits to Cadillacs. He had once, in a reflective moment, calculated that if the value of all the gifts he received each year was made known to the Internal Revenue Service, the resulting income tax would exceed his income as a U.S. senator.

TED HAD HIM in the kitchen, now, and the line was good. He moved the tripod a couple of feet to his left, and sat down, cross-legged, behind it, tightening the mount adjustment and bringing the barrel to bear on the kitchen window. He had, on a previous visit, measured the distance from his present position to the center of the house, which came to three hundred and four yards, give or take, and he had already sighted in the weapon for that distance.

The appearance of the rifle, which he had

made himself, would have puzzled even an experienced shooter, since the weapon was bereft of any material that did not contribute to its accuracy—no walnut stock, just an aluminum rod; no trigger guard; no visible bolt. The long, fat flash suppressor and silencer would have seemed totally out of place; only the large, light-gathering telescopic sight would be familiar. Ted loaded a single, .22-caliber, long-rifle cartridge into the chamber and closed it, then took his first sight through the scope.

FREDDIE WALLACE POURED himself a jigger of the superb bourbon, then recorked the bottle and put it away. He tossed down the ounce and a half of spirits, waiting for it to hit bottom before he moved.

THE TARGET STOOD absolutely still for just a moment, and Ted, almost casually, squeezed off the round. The only sounds were the *pfffft* of the firing and the tinkle of window glass as the copper-jacketed round passed through it. Had he been inside the room, he would have heard a noise like a slap across the face as the bullet struck the senator's left temple, then the sound of his body collapsing like a sack of oranges onto the kitchen floor.

ELIZABETH JOHNSON was turning over in her sleep when she heard the noise. It was one she had heard only once before, but she had imagined it many times, the sound of a male body hitting the floor. Given the state of Frederick Wallace's health, she had been expecting it.

She got out of bed, picked up her robe, and walked toward the kitchen with some trepidation. "Freddie?" she called, but there was no answer. She continued into the kitchen and saw him lying there. It was not until she came near the body that she saw the hole in the temple and the blood and gore that the exiting bullet had taken with it. "Oh, shit, Freddie," she said, then she ducked down below window level and checked his pulse. There was none.

TED PICKED UP the rifle, with its tripod still connected, and walked off into the woods.

When the house had vanished behind him, he changed directions by sixty degrees, walked another five minutes, then switched back, avoiding any bare dirt or branches he might break along the way. After twenty minutes of walking, he could hear the traffic on the highway, and he approached the spot where he had left his other things. He knelt in the leaves, spread out a piece of army blanket, unscrewed the rifle from its tripod, removed the scope and the silencer, and packed everything into a camera bag and two fishing-rod tubes. He got out of his camouflage jacket, stuffed it into a back-pack, and donned his tweed jacket and matching hat.

He peeked through the underbrush at the traffic, waited until there was a lull, then ambled to his RV, parked in a little roadside rest area. He unlocked the cabin door, hid the camera bag and tubes in the places he had designed for them, got behind the wheel, and drove away at a moderate pace, not anxious to attract attention.

A few miles down the road, he parked in the lot of a fast-food restaurant, went to his laptop computer, adjusted the dish on the roof for contact with the satellite, logged online, using a program that took him through six portals before finally connecting, and went to Microsoft Front Page. He made some changes in the website, then logged off and went into the restaurant for a big breakfast.

ELIZABETH JOHNSON had gone through the house carefully, packing anything that might be linked to her into two large suitcases. She and Freddie had talked about this more than once, and his instructions had been explicit. She got the bags into the trunk of her car, then went back into the cabin and made another search for anything of hers. Finally, she went back into the kitchen, knelt next to the body, bent over, and kissed it lightly on the lips. "Goodbye, my sweetheart," she said, then she left the house with tears streaming down her cheeks and drove away.

When she was back in Chester, she pulled over, took out the cell phone that Freddie had given her, and dialed the sheriff's home number.

"Hello?" he said.

"Tom, you know who this is?"

"Yep, I do," he replied.

"You better get out to the cabin. Somebody shot him in the head about half an hour ago."

There was a stunned silence. "Was it you?" he asked finally.

"I was in bed asleep. I heard him fall."

"Anybody know you was there?"

"No, and I cleared out everything of mine. I'm on my way home."

"Don't you talk to nobody about this, you hear? I'll let you know what I find out after I find it out."

"Goodbye." She hung up, started the car, and drove to her little house. She went inside, lay down on the bed, and let herself cry some more.

2

THE PRESIDENT OF THE United States, William Henry Lee IV, sat on the edge of his bed and contemplated his toenails. His wife, Katharine Rule Lee, came out of the bathroom and stopped.

"What are you doing?" she asked.

"I hate clipping my toenails," he said. "Tell me again why I can't have pedicures."

"Because the Republicans would find out about it and cast you as an effete, liberal snob. And I'm not going to clip them for you. I have a very important meeting in less than an hour, and I have to get dressed." Katharine Rule Lee was director of Central Intelligence, appointed to that post by her husband, after an act of Congress had allowed him to do so.

"I know you have an important meeting,"

Will said. "I expect to be there, too, since you and the director of the FBI and the military are briefing me."

"Oh, yes, I forgot you'd be there."

The telephone rang, and Will picked it up. "Will Lee," he said.

"Sir, this is the White House operator."

"Good morning, Inez," Will said. "What's up?"

"We just had a phone call from a Sheriff Tom Stribling, of Chester, South Carolina."

"That's where Senator Wallace lives, isn't it?"

"Yes, sir. Sheriff Stribling asked that we inform you that Senator Wallace was shot to death less than an hour ago."

Will took a quick breath and tried not to think about the ramifications of such news. "Any details?"

"The sheriff said he is at your disposal, if you want to call him."

"Thank you, Inez," Will said, then hung up.

"What is it?" Kate asked.

"Freddie Wallace is dead. Somebody shot him early this morning."

"Anybody we know? I'd like to send him a box of chocolates."

"I hope to God it was a Republican."

"Well," Kate said, "it would be interesting to sit around and speculate about who did it and why. Heaven knows there are enough people with enough cause, not to speak ill of the dead. But, as I said, I have an important meeting to go to."

"I remember," Will said, picking up the phone.

"Put down the phone for a minute," she said.

Will put down the phone. "What?"

"I'll tell you something you don't know about Freddie Wallace, if you won't ask me how I know."

"Why can't I ask you how you know?"

"Because I'm the director of Central Intelligence, and how I know is classified."

"Am I not cleared at that level?"

"Maybe. Let's call it need to know."

"Tell me."

"For more than twenty years, Freddie has had an African-American mistress, with whom he is—was—deeply in love. They have two sons, one at Brown, one at Harvard."

"Holy shit. I thought that was just a canard."

"It wasn't."

"How do you know this?"

"You promised not to ask me."

"No, I didn't."

"Your promise was implied as part of an oral contract."

"Now you're talking like a lawyer."

"I am a lawyer."

"I forgot. I always think of you as a spy."

"I think I rather like that," she said, walking over to him, raising his chin with a finger, and kissing him.

"Maybe tonight we can find time to discuss at some length why you like that," he said, reaching for her ass and missing as she stepped away.

"I very much doubt it," she said. "We have a very important White House dinner this evening, and we'll both be worn out by bedtime."

"I could cancel it because of Freddie's death," he said hopefully.

"I don't think that the prime minister of Japan would think that appropriate, and since he's the guest of honor—"

"All right," Will said. He picked up the phone again. "Please get me Sheriff Tom Stribling, in Chester, South Carolina," he said. He loved never having to find a pencil to write down a phone number; all he had to do was speak a name, and he was connected to anyone, anywhere. It was one of the better perks of being president.

A few seconds later, the operator said, "You're connected, Mr. President."

"Sheriff?"

"Yes, Mr. President, I'm right here."

"Tell me what happened."

"I'm at the scene now, sir," the sheriff said. "The senator took a small-caliber bullet through the left temple and died instantly, far as we can tell. Nobody heard a gunshot."

"Who was with the senator?"

"No one, sir, he was alone."

"Then who didn't hear a gunshot?"

"Ah, well—"

"I know about the black lady, Sheriff." It was worth a shot.

Stribling let out a breath, as if he had been holding it. "She was here, sir. She heard him fall to the floor, but she didn't hear a shot."

"Is she still there?"

"No, sir, she's at her home, and so are all her things."

"I take it she's not going to be a part of any public announcement or inquiry."

"No, sir. The senator left very clear instructions about that a long time ago."

"Have you given this to the press yet?"

"No, sir. I expect it will be close to noon before we're finished with the crime scene. I'll fax an announcement to the Columbia papers and the AP after that."

"I see. Have you spoken to Betty Ann Wallace?"

"Yes, sir, a few minutes ago."

"How did she take it?"

"Hysterically."

"She's in Washington?"

"Yes, sir."

"I'll call her," Will said. "Thanks for letting me know, Tom."

"I'm glad to be of service, sir."

They both hung up.

Will got the operator back. "Get me Senator Wallace's wife, at their Washington home." He waited while he was connected, dreading the conversation ahead.

3

WILL WAS IN HIS LITTLE STUDY off the Oval Office at eight-thirty, and his secretary, a tall, thin African-American woman named Cora Parker, was waiting with his schedule and a number of other items.

"Good morning, Mr. President," she said, taking a seat next to his desk and setting the folder on his desk.

"Good morning, Cora," Will replied. "There's some news: I just learned that Senator Freddie Wallace was shot around dawn this morning. He died instantly."

"Oh, my God," Cora said, putting a hand to her mouth.

Since nothing ever fazed Cora, Will looked at her closely. "I know you're from South Carolina, but I wouldn't have thought that

Freddie's death would upset you all that much."

"No, sir, it doesn't, exactly," Cora replied. "I was just thinking about—"

"Cora, do you know about the senator's friend?"

"What friend would that be, sir?"

"The lady friend."

She sighed. "Yes, sir, I know. I'm from Columbia, but I've got a first cousin who lives in Chester, and she and the lady are friends. That's how I know her."

"What's the lady's name?" he asked.

"Elizabeth Johnson. She's a widow."

"And they had two sons together, is that correct?"

"Yes, sir, George and Johnny, named after her two brothers. Their last name is House, Elizabeth's maiden name."

"Do the boys know who their father is?"

"I believe they do," Cora replied.

"Is there anything else I should know about all this, just to keep from putting my foot in it?"

"Not that I can think of, Mr. President. Do they know who shot him?"

"No, not yet. This isn't going to be announced until around noon today, so keep it to yourself until you hear it on the news."

"Can I call Elizabeth?"

"Not on a White House phone," Will said. "We don't want that call logged, and don't use your staff cell phone, either. Wait until you can get to a phone outside somewhere."

"Yes, sir."

"Now, I spoke to Mrs. Wallace a few minutes ago. She wants two funerals, one here and one in Chester. She wants me to give the eulogy at the one here, in the National Cathedral."

Cora produced a leather-bound diary. "When, sir?"

"She wants it on Wednesday. Do we have anything that can't be canceled that morning?"

Cora consulted the diary. "Nothing I can't move around, sir."

"Coordinate that with the appointments secretary, then call Mrs. Wallace and confirm a time with her and let the Secret Service know about it."

"Yes, sir. Is there anything else?"

"We'll talk after my national security briefing," Will said. He went through his day's schedule, made a few phone calls, then got up and went into the Oval Office. Everyone present stood.

"Please be seated," he said, looking around. He saw his wife, representing the CIA; the director of the FBI, James Heller; the chairman of the Joint Chiefs of Staff, General Marvin Moore; his National Security Advisor, Alice Ramirez; and the vice president, Howard Kiel. Other presidents had been briefed by one agency at a time, but Will preferred having them all in the same room at the same time, since it promoted interagency information sharing. "Good morning to you all," he said.

There was a murmur of greetings in response.

"Let's get started. General Moore?"

The chairman of the Joint Chiefs of Staff leaned forward in his seat. "Mr. President, it was a fairly quiet night. We have a helicopter down in Afghanistan, but it looks like mechanical problems. One injured, none dead. The chopper is being repaired. Nothing else of note."

"Thank you, General." Will went from person to person until everyone had reported.

"Thank you, all. Jim, would you and Kate stay?"

The FBI director kept his seat, and so did Kate.

When the others had cleared the room, Will spoke again. "Jim, Senator Wallace of South Carolina was murdered this morning in Chester, South Carolina."

"What?" the director asked, looking alarmed.

Heller always said "What?" to anything put to him. Will let it sink in. "Get in touch with the local sheriff down there, Tom Stribling, and get some of your people up there from Columbia or Atlanta, or wherever's closest, and start an investigation."

"Mr. President, murder is not a federal crime," Heller said.

Will sighed. He had inherited Heller from the previous administration, and he found him barely competent and, sometimes, a little dense. He had not replaced him on taking office, because he felt that the position of FBI director should not be a political appointment, subject to change with every administration. But now, having worked with the man for a year and a half, he had decided to replace him at the first reasonable opportunity. "Murder of a federal official is a federal crime," he said, trying not to sound impatient.

"Oh, of course," Heller said, turning a little pink. "Any details?"

"The sheriff will have them. All I know is that he was shot and killed instantly."

"Any suspects?"

"Jim, I don't know. Ask the sheriff. Kate, do you have any information that might be useful to the director?"

"I'll check with my staff when I get to Langley, Mr. President," she said. She always addressed him formally when doing government business in the company of others.

"I think we're done, then," Will said.

"Mr. President, may I have a moment?" Kate asked.

"Of course. Goodbye, Jim. Brief me personally when you have a grip on the Wallace murder."

"Yes, Mr. President," the director said. He got up and left.

Will went and sat by Kate. "Are you going to tell Heller about Freddie's little indiscretion?"

"I don't think so, unless it turns out later to have some relevance to his murder," she said.

"I think that's just as well."

"However, the indiscretion reminds me of something that you and I should discuss."

"Shoot."

"I expect you remember Ed Rawls."

"I believe I do," Will said dryly. Ed Rawls was a disgraced former CIA operations officer, who had sold information to the Russians a few years back. He had been one of the Agency's top operatives and Kate's mentor there, until, largely through her efforts, he had been exposed, tried, and convicted. He was now doing twenty-five years to life at the Atlanta Federal Penitentiary.

"I have a lot to tell you about Ed Rawls—things I had hoped you wouldn't have to know. Freddie's death has dredged it up."

"You sound as though I'm not going to like this," Will said.

"You're not," Kate replied. "Neither do I. But it's time you knew."

4

KATE TOOK A DEEP BREATH and began, using the voice she used when briefing the president, not the one she used when giving her husband bad news. "Christmas three years ago, when you were deciding whether to run, we were in Delano with your folks. Do you remember that I had to go somewhere on business?"

"Yes, you took the car, and I thought it was very odd, but I've been trained not to ask questions when you say 'business.' "

"The business was Ed Rawls. I had a letter from him that morning, addressed to your parents' house, asking me to come to see him at the Atlanta Federal Penitentiary."

"And you went to see him?"

"Yes."

"Why on earth did you do that? It would

certainly be against Agency policy, wouldn't it?"

"Not if I reported the visit, and I did. Something in the letter made it necessary."

"What was in the letter?"

"He knew about Joe Adams."

Adams had been vice president at the time, and only the day before, he had invited Will and Kate to Camp David for brunch and told them that he was in the early stages of Alzheimer's disease.

Will was stunned. "Jesus, you and I had only known about it for twenty-four hours, and I thought we were the only ones. How could a man in prison get that information?"

"He wouldn't tell me. He did say that all sorts of things went on there that no one on the outside could imagine. He said there were prisoners there with cell phones. For all I know, he might have been one of them."

"I'm glad you didn't tell me at the time," Will said.

"There's more. Freddie Wallace also found out about Joe's condition and leaked it to a columnist, probably Hogan Parks."

"Why didn't Parks use it?"

"Because Ed somehow got to Freddie and threatened to expose his relationship with the black woman, if he let Parks run the story."

Will shook his head. "This is insane, all of it. A man in prison knows the most intimate secrets of the vice president and a United States senator?"

"You have to remember who Ed is, or rather, was. Of all the people I knew in the Agency, Ed had the widest range of contacts in government and the press. In those days, he could find out anything, track down any rumor, scare anybody to death, if he had to. He was not the sort of man you'd want for an enemy."

"I suppose not. But why are you telling me all this now?"

"Because of the real reason Ed wanted to see me in Atlanta."

"Which was?"

"He wanted a presidential pardon, and he thought if he helped you win the election you might come through for him."

"This is the craziest thing I ever heard of," Will said.

"Except that he did help you get elected. In fact, you could say that without his help, you would not have been elected."

Will blinked. "By dealing with Freddie about Joe Adams?"

"Exactly. He got a letter to Freddie, threatening to expose his relationship with the woman if he used the information about Joe's health. Freddie somehow figured out where the letter came from and had Ed thrown in some dungeon part of the Atlanta pen for a week, but when Ed got out, he managed to convince Freddie that he had the wrong man, and he continued to write to him, having letters sent from other places. He kept his foot on Freddie's neck for months."

"And he expects me to pardon him for that?"

"He does."

"And how do you feel about this?"

"At the time, I thought he was crazy, and I told him so, but he actually did the things he said he would do. Think back: During the summer before the election, after the president's stroke and Joe's becoming acting president, what would have happened if Freddie had managed to expose Joe's illness and the fact that Joe had told you about it? I'll tell you: Joe would have been forced to resign, you would have been disgraced, and the speaker of the House—your opponent in the race—Eft Efton, would have become president."

Will thought about that. "I suppose you're right."

"So, looking at it from your point of view, and incidentally, mine, Ed Rawls performed a valuable service for his country by keeping that shit Efton out of the White House."

"You have a point," Will said. "Was Rawls the one who leaked the story about Freddie and his lover later on?"

"Yes, but he did it with a light touch, so that it could never be substantiated. Freddie denied everything, and it all went away."

"And what would the CIA's position be on a pardon for Ed Rawls?"

"Until recently, dead set against it, but that position is softening."

"Why?"

"Because Ed still has friends at the Agency, and because I'm now director of Central Intelligence."

"So you're sympathetic?"

"Ed is not well. He's had some health problems, and he's seventy now. He still has that house on the island of Islesboro, in Maine—

you remember, I went to visit him and his wife there once?"

"Yes, vaguely."

"He says he wants to die there. If it were up to me, I couldn't deny him that."

"Kate, I might as well pardon Aldrich Ames or that FBI agent who was selling stuff to the Russians for years and years. It would be worse than that stupid pardon that Bill Clinton granted that fugitive in Switzerland on his last day in office."

"Will, I can't tell you that this is politically feasible; all I can say is that, if you felt grateful enough to Ed to pardon him, I could make it all right at the Agency. Certainly, you couldn't do it during your first term. You could pardon him on grounds of ill health. All I ask is that you think about it. Neither of us has to mention this to anyone else."

"All right, I'll think about it," Will said.

There was a sharp rap on the door, and Cora Parker stuck her head in. "Mr. President, CNN has something on Senator Wallace's death," she said. "Shall I turn it on?"

"Please, Cora."

There were four television sets in the Oval Office, tuned to the three major networks and CNN. Cora switched on the CNN set.

A reporter was standing a few yards from a rustic cabin beside a lake. ". . . and the senator was standing in the kitchen, only a few feet from the window." He pointed, and the camera zoomed in on a smashed windowpane. "What has a lot of people in Washington worried is that Senator Wallace was rumored to have kept extensive files on various people in government and that the information in those files might find its way into the media. According to the rumor, only J. Edgar Hoover had more dirt on more important people. Now back to the studio."

"You think that's true?" Kate asked.

"I wouldn't put it past Freddie," Will said. "And next week, I'm going to give a funeral oration for a man who did everything he could to destroy my political career and my reputation."

"If Freddie kept files like that, who would have them?"

"I haven't the faintest idea," Will said.

IN CHESTER, South Carolina, Elizabeth Johnson opened a desk drawer in the den of her home and took out a key. She went down the stairs to her basement and to a pile of boxes in a corner. She moved one, exposing a small filing cabinet, the kind that holds index cards. Tentatively, she inserted the key into the little cabinet and pulled open one of the four drawers. She switched on a light, illuminating a row of precisely filed cards, all of them labeled with the neatly printed names of some of the best-known, most powerful people in the country. Freddie had always been a splendid record keeper.

Elizabeth had meant to look through them, but instead, she stared at the cards as if they were a poisonous reptile. She closed the drawer, locked the cabinet, and went back upstairs. Instead of returning the key to the desk drawer, she went into her bedroom closet and pushed aside the clothes hanging there. She opened the wall safe that she had bought to keep the jewelry that Freddie had given her over the years, then she put the file cabinet key inside, closed the safe, and returned the clothes to their original position.

She would wait awhile, until the furor over Freddie's death had died down, then she would burn all those index cards in her fireplace.

5

JAMES HELLER, BACK in his office at the Hoover Building, called a meeting of the half-dozen highest-ranking people at the FBI, all of them men.

"Gentlemen, I have some news for you," Heller said, self-importantly. "Senator Frederick Wallace of South Carolina was murdered this morning." He waited for a response.

"Yes, sir," the deputy director for criminal investigations said. "It was on CNN a few minutes ago."

Heller blinked. "But the president himself told me about it only a few minutes ago. He got it from the sheriff down there." He somehow viewed this as a personal betrayal by CNN.

"Yes, sir," the DDCI said.

"Bob," Heller said, fixing the DDCI with his gaze. "I want you to call the agent in charge of the Columbia office on the phone right away and have him get some men over to Chester and talk to that sheriff."

"I have already done so, sir," the DDCI replied.

Heller blinked. "Oh." He took a deep breath and tried to think. "As I'm sure you know, the murder of a federal official is a federal crime—"

"Yes, sir, I know that."

"So we're taking over this investigation. This small-town sheriff isn't going to have the resources to properly investigate this killing."

"I have already given those instructions to the AIC in Columbia," the DDCI said. "The investigation is ours now."

"Good. So, what do we know so far?"

"I spoke to Sheriff Stribling, and he tells me that Senator Wallace was shot through a kitchen window by a sniper, who was probably three hundred yards or more away, since the land around the cabin was cleared to that distance, affording no hiding place for a shooter. A single twenty-two-caliber bullet struck him in the left temple, killing him instantly."

"Good, good. And what have our people turned up there?"

"Sir, Chester is more than an hour's drive from Columbia. They would have left Columbia no more than fifteen minutes ago."

"Do we have any suspects?"

"Sir, as you know Senator Wallace was a very popular man on the right wing of the Republican Party."

"I didn't know there was any other wing of the Republican Party."

"Be that as it may, sir, the senator was very unpopular with almost everybody to the left of him. He was a very skillful obstructionist in the Senate, managing to block many pieces of legislation and judicial appointments, some of them sent up by Republican presidents. He had many enemies, and the first assessment of people with motive to kill him would run into the hundreds, perhaps thousands. By the time we eliminate everyone who could not have been in Chester, South Carolina, this morning, we may have pared the list to dozens.

"It's possible that he was killed for political

motives, but it's just as possible that he was killed because of some personal grudge, by someone in his own hometown. We expect Sheriff Stribling to be valuable in that part of the investigation, so I've told our AIC to leave the sheriff in charge of the local investigation, liaising through one of our agents, who will be assigned to assist him."

"So you're telling me we don't have a clue as to who killed him?"

"Sir, we've known about the murder for less than half an hour. It's a bit early in the investigation to begin drawing conclusions."

"Well, let me give you my take on this, Bob," the director said.

"I'd very much like to hear that, sir," the DDCI replied without apparent irony.

"I think what we've got here is a vast left-wing conspiracy to eliminate a senator who has driven the left nuts for decades."

"Sir, with respect, I don't think we've had a vast left-wing conspiracy in this country since the forties, maybe as far back as when Stalin and Hitler signed a nonaggression pact, which caused a lot of American communists to leave the party."

"Are you suggesting a communist conspiracy, Bob?"

"No, sir, I am not," the DDCI said, rather desperately.

"So, you think it's a vast *right-wing* conspiracy?"

"I have not formed that opinion or any other opinion, sir. I think we have to wait until we have some evidence upon which to base a judgment, and that may take days or weeks, assuming there *is* any evidence."

"There's always evidence, Bob," the director said.

"Usually, sir."

"We won't have any trouble tracking down this sniper, I'm sure of that."

"Sir, may I point out how long it took to catch Eric Rudolph? And we got him only because a cop got lucky. A lone perpetrator, especially one with a support network, is a very difficult man to catch."

"Yes, yes, Bob, I understand that, of course. But I hope you understand that we're going to be under enormous pressure to come up with a suspect and make an arrest."

"We're always under pressure in a high-profile crime, sir. My people are accustomed to it."

"Well, that's good, Bob. Now, I'm calling a

press conference this afternoon timed to make the national TV news shows this evening, announcing progress in the investigation, so you get down to Chester, South Carolina, right now and get me something to announce."

"Sir, I think it would be a mistake to schedule a press conference when we don't yet have anything to announce. We could make fools of ourselves."

"Well, you just get yourself down to Chester and call me when you're on the ground there, and we'll figure out something for the press conference."

"Yes, sir," the DDCI said.

"Don't sound so morose, Bob," the director said. "We're going to crack this one, you and I."

"Yes, sir," the DDCI said, even more morosely.

6

Robert Kinney, the FBI's deputy director for Criminal Investigations, looked out the window at the piney woods below him and searched for the airport.

The airplane was an elderly Lear, and since Kinney was six feet five inches tall and weighed two hundred and sixty-five pounds, it was a tight fit for him.

The airplane suddenly banked left, and Kinney, to his relief, saw the Chester airport. It had three runways, in a triangular pattern, and one of them had *X*s at either end, indicating that it was closed. The place looked like a World War II–era training airport, a great many of which dotted the American countryside. Before the airplane made its final turn, Kinney could see a single car parked on the parking ramp, and it had a big star on the door.

THE AIRPLANE taxied up to the ramp, and the copilot opened the door for Kinney, then carried his luggage down the airstairs. A man in a business suit walked up and stuck out his hand. "Agent Kinney? I'm Ralph Emerson, AIC Columbia."

"Afternoon, Ralph," Kinney replied. "Call me Bob, please." Kinney had served with a lot of agents in his twenty-seven years with the FBI and knew a lot more, but he had not met Emerson before. The man's personnel file, however, had spoken well of him.

Emerson took Kinney's luggage and stowed it in the open truck of the sheriff's patrol car. "Bob, I'd like you to meet Sheriff Tom Stribling, of Chester County."

Stribling, a wiry man in his fifties, pushed off the car where he had been leaning and stuck out his hand. "How you doin'?" he said.

Kinney shook the hand and looked into the tanned face and bright blue eyes. "Good to meet you, Tom. We appreciate your help on this one."

"And I appreciate yours," Stribling said,

glancing at Emerson. He didn't sound as if he appreciated it. "You want to go out to the cabin or would you rather go to your hotel?"

"Let's go out to the cabin," Kinney said, getting into the front passenger seat of the car.

"How was your flight?" Emerson asked as they drove away.

"Awful," Kinney replied. "That airplane is the size of a coffin."

Stribling said nothing, just drove. After twenty minutes he turned left on a smaller paved road, then ten minutes later turned right on a dirt road. They came to a steel gate, which was open but guarded by a deputy. Stribling didn't even slow down, just waved. The road led into the woods, and a couple of minutes later they were driving down the shore of a lake of about a hundred acres.

"The senator owned about four hundred acres here," Stribling said, "including the whole lake and the cabin. It's the only house on the lake."

"He liked his privacy, I guess," Kinney said. Kinney wondered what land cost in Chester County and how Senator Wallace could afford so much of it.

"I guess he did," Stribling replied.

They drove around to the opposite side of the lake and through another steel gate, this one without a guard. Shortly, they pulled up in front of the cabin, which had yellow crime-scene tape strung from tree to tree, encircling the structure.

Kinney got out and looked the place over. "Nice," he said. There were window boxes planted with geraniums on the front side of the house. Kinney walked around to the back and saw the shattered windowpane.

"I reckon the shooter stood over yonder, just in the woods," Stribling said.

"You find any shell casings or footprints or other traces of him?" Kinney asked.

"No, sir," Stribling said. "I got a couple of old bloodhounds we keep for when somebody busts out of the county camp, and we took 'em out there a couple of hours ago. According to the dogs, our man zigzagged through the woods and came out in a little rest area on the main highway, about three-quarters of a mile away."

"Any car tracks?"

"Nope, the rest area is paved. I talked to the State Patrol and got hold of the man who patrolled that stretch of road this morning. He had a look in the rest area about six-forty-five this morning, and there were no cars in it."

Kinney nodded. "Can we take a look inside the cabin?"

"Sure," the sheriff said, leading the way to the back door of the cabin.

Kinney looked at the spot where the body had been found and lined it up with the broken window, then he walked into the single bedroom. The place was attractively decorated, with photographs and watercolors on the walls. He went to the bed and turned back the bedspread. The sheets were clean and ironed. He looked in the closet and found some clothes that looked like they were the senator's.

Kinney walked back into the kitchen and opened the refrigerator door. Inside were some fresh vegetables that appeared homegrown, not being in supermarket bags, and a plate of fried chicken and some cooked vegetables, all sealed with clear plastic wrap.

"Ralph," Kinney said to the agent, "will you give the sheriff and me a minute?"

"Sure," Emerson replied and walked out the front door.

"Tom, did Mrs. Wallace spend a lot of time here?"

"Nope," the sheriff replied. "She never came down here at all that I know of. The senator liked to be alone out here."

"We both know that's not true," Kinney said.

"Do we?" Stribling asked.

"It's pretty obvious that a woman spent a lot of time here," Kinney said. "All the decorating looks feminine. And who fried that chicken and cooked those collards in the fridge? Come to that, who put freshly ironed sheets on the bed that the senator got out of this morning? And one more thing, who called this in, a passing stranger?"

The sheriff gazed out the window toward the lake. "Okay, Bob, I guess I'm going to have to tell you about this and trust your judgment on whether to pass it on to your people and the press." He told Kinney about Elizabeth Johnson and the senator's relationship with her.

"I see," Kinney said. "Let's go talk to Ms. Johnson."

7

THE MEN WERE ADMITTED TO Elizabeth Johnson's home and were invited to sit down in the living room. Kinney had left Emerson in the car.

Ms. Johnson was an attractive woman with café-au-lait skin and carefully coiffed hair, and she seemed puzzled by the visit. "What's this about, Sheriff?" she asked.

"Mr. Kinney, here, is with the FBI in Washington, Elizabeth, and he's investigating the death of Senator Wallace."

"Oh, yes," she replied. "Such a tragic thing."

Stribling took a deep breath. "Mr. Kinney knows, Elizabeth. He just wants to talk to you about what happened this morning."

Her shoulders sagged a bit, and she looked out the window. "Well, I guess this had to happen," she said. "What do you want to know, Mr. Kinney?"

"How long had you and the senator been at the cabin on this occasion?" Kinney asked.

"Since yesterday afternoon around two," she said.

"Did anyone call to see either of you while you were there? Were there any telephone calls?"

"No one came to the house, and there is no telephone in the cabin. The senator turns—turned off his cell phone when he was there, unless he wanted to make a call."

"What did you do last evening?"

"I cooked us dinner, and then we talked for a while and played Scrabble. There is no TV in the cabin."

"What time did you go to bed?"

"Around eleven o'clock."

"Did you or the senator wake up during the night?"

"The senator tended to wake me up once or twice when he went to the bathroom. When he was back in bed, I would go to sleep again."

"Tell me about the events of this morning."

"The senator always woke earlier than I,

and I would wake up for a minute, too, then I would fall asleep again. It was that way this morning, then I woke up when I heard the sound of him falling."

"Did you hear a shot or hear the window break?"

"No. I've heard the sound of him falling before, when he had a heart attack last year, so I guess I was kind of on the alert for that."

"What happened then?"

"I went into the kitchen and found him there. I couldn't get a pulse, so I guess he died quickly. I gave him CPR when he had the heart attack, but when I saw the wound in his head, I didn't try that. I sat with him for a minute, then I did what he had always told me to do if he died. I got my things packed up and got out of the house. On the way home I called the sheriff."

"Did you see or hear anyone outside the house?"

"No, no one."

Kinney stood up. "I thank you for your time, Ms. Johnson. This conversation will not go into my report nor will I tell the press about it."

"I thank you for that," she said, sounding relieved.

Kinney turned toward the door, then stopped. "Sheriff, could I have a moment alone with Ms. Johnson, please?"

"Sure," the sheriff said, and stepped outside.

"Just one more question," Kinney said. "Ms. Johnson, the senator apparently kept some personal files at one of his residences. Are you aware of any file drawers or cabinets or files anywhere in the cabin?"

"No," she replied, "I'm not."

"Thank you," he said. He shook her hand and went out to the sheriff's car, where Stribling and Emerson waited for him.

"Get what you need?" Stribling asked.

"Yes, but it wasn't much," Kinney replied. "I'm going to want to go back to the cabin alone tomorrow."

"I'll fix you up with a car," the sheriff said. "You want to go to your hotel now?"

"Yes, please." Kinney looked at his watch. It was after five, and he had not turned on his cell phone since leaving the airplane.

"It's more of an inn, I guess," the sheriff said. "Widow lady runs it. She's only been open a couple of months, but it's the best we've got around here."

"I'm sure it will be fine," Kinney said.

• • •

THE CAR STOPPED before a large Victorian house, freshly painted and with a carefully tended lawn. A sign out front said Kimble House.

Mrs. Kimble met them at the door, and Kinney was impressed. She was fortyish with long, dark hair and lovely skin. Her clothes did not hide her very impressive body.

"Mr. Kinney? I'm Nancy Kimble. Welcome."

"Thank you, Mrs. Kimble. Ralph, are you staying here, too?"

"No, Bob, I have to drive back to Columbia," Emerson replied.

Kinney shook his hand and that of the sheriff. "If you could have a car for me at nine tomorrow morning, Sheriff."

"Will do." The sheriff got into his car and drove away.

"Let me show you to your room, Mr. Kinney," she said.

"It's Bob, please."

"And I'm Nancy." She took him to a large bedroom with a four-poster bed, a fireplace, and a comfortable sofa. "I hope this will be all right," she said. "Oh, I almost forgot, you have some messages." She reached into her pocket and produced half a dozen pink message slips.

Kinny glanced at them; they were all from the director.

"I can offer you dinner, if you like," she said. "You're my only guest tonight."

"I'd like that very much, Nancy," he said. "Perhaps you'd join me?"

"Thank you, I will."

"I'd better return these calls now."

"Seven-thirty all right?"

"Perfect."

She closed the door behind her.

KINNEY CALLED Washington and got the director on the phone.

"So, what have you got?" Heller asked anxiously.

"Senator Wallace was killed instantly by a single shot from a sniper outside his lake cabin. The perpetrator was tracked back to a rest stop on a highway nearly a mile away, but he left no footprints, tire prints, shell casings, or anything else that might help us find him."

"That's it?" the director asked, incredulously. "That's all you've got for the press conference? We're on in an hour."

"Sir, I'm afraid I'm in a small town in South Carolina, and I don't have access to television broadcasting facilities. You'll have to carry the ball, I'm afraid."

"But what am I going to say?"

"I've told you everything I've learned," Kinney lied.

"But I can't go on national television with just that."

"Sir, you may recall that I was opposed to the idea of a press conference, until we have something to report."

The director made a noise and hung up.

AT SIX-THIRTY, Kinney switched on the television in his room and tuned in a network news show. The director made his appearance during the first five minutes. He repeated verbatim what Kinney had told him, then added, "Of course, our investigation has only just begun, and we expect to begin developing suspects shortly."

"Then you're going to have to develop them yourself," Kinney said to the TV, "because this shooter is not going to give us anything." He switched off the TV, unpacked his clothes, and began to change for dinner. He was looking forward to dining with Nancy Kimble.

8

WILL LEE SWITCHED OFF the TV after the FBI director's press conference and turned to half a dozen of his staff who had been watching with him. "Do you think if I call him now he'll be able to tell me anything else?" he asked the group.

Kitty Conroy, his chief of staff, spoke up. "If he had anything else, he'd have said so on television, and I very much doubt if he expects to have suspects soon. He's just waffling, which is what he does."

"Makes you wonder why he bothered to call a press conference, doesn't it?" Will said.

"Makes me wonder why he's still director," said Tim Coleman, the press secretary.

"Don't start, Tim," Will said. "You know that's on my list of things to do."

"Do you want us to start developing a list of possible replacements?" Kitty asked.

"I've been thinking about it," Will said, "and I'm inclined to go a different route than in the past."

"How do you mean?"

"The past few directors have been federal judges or U.S. Attorneys, like Heller, and frankly, I don't think those jobs particularly qualify a person to be director of the FBI. I'd rather have somebody like a police chief who's done a good job in a big city, somebody who's run a large law enforcement agency and who has a background as an officer himself. Or herself."

"You think the FBI is ready for a female director?" Tim asked.

"I don't think the FBI will *ever* be ready for a female director, but I'm willing to give them one, if the right woman comes along."

"What about promoting from within?" Kitty asked.

"I tend to think that we need somebody who can shake up the FBI culture, make it more responsive to other agencies, and, for that matter, to me, and that would most likely be an outsider. But if you can find a superbly qualified senior man in the Bureau who hasn't been tainted by Waco or Ruby Ridge or the Richard Jewel mess or some other debacle, then I'll consider him." The president stood up. "I think that's the day," he said.

The group broke up, and Will, accompanied by a Secret Service agent, made for the elevator to the family quarters of the White House.

BOB KINNEY, freshly showered and shaved and dressed in a blue blazer with an open-necked shirt, left his room and wandered through the public rooms of the apparently deserted inn. It was handsomely decorated, he thought, and he hoped Nancy Kimble would find enough guests to make a go of it. He walked into a nicely paneled library, spotted a carved mahogany bar in a corner, and made for it.

"Can I buy you a drink?" she asked from the doorway.

"Let me buy you one," he said, slipping behind the bar.

She walked across the room toward him, tall, leggy, dressed in well-cut black trousers and a white silk blouse. "All right," she said. "I'll have a Laphroaig."

"A what?"

"Single-malt Scotch," she said, pointing. "On the rocks."

"I think I'll try one, too," he said. He found a pair of glasses, filled them with ice, and poured the amber liquid.

They touched glasses and sipped.

"Mmm," he said. "That's remarkable."

"I always think I can taste the peat from the Scottish soil," she replied.

"So you're new to the innkeeping business?" he asked.

"Yes. My husband dropped dead of a heart attack at his desk seven months ago. He was with a brokerage firm in Charlotte, and we had just finished decorating this house."

"How old was he?"

"He was fifty-two. How old are you?"

"Fifty-four and a half," he replied.

"I'm forty-four," she said.

"You don't look it."

She smiled for the first time. "That's just what you were supposed to say. I've never met an FBI agent before. Are you typical of the breed?"

"No, I'm larger, smarter, and more ornery. I've never met an innkeeper before, except across a check-in desk."

"Are you married?"

"Separated, pending divorce," he replied. "It'll be final next month."

"Kids?"

"Two, both girls, both all grown up and married. One of them is going to present me with a grandson in a couple of months. How about you?"

"Childless. We tried, it didn't work. It's probably just as well. I'm not sure what kind of a mother I would have been. Do you like veal?"

"Yes."

"Good, because we're having blanquette de veau, whether you like it or not."

"A blanket of veal?"

"It's a stew, and it covers the rice, like a blanket."

"Sounds great."

"I thought you might like something other than southern cooking, so I sent the cook home."

"I like southern cooking, too."

"Stick around a couple of days, and you'll get plenty."

"I'm going to do everything I can to stick around for at least a couple of days," he said.

"Good. Who shot the senator?"

"We've narrowed the list of people with a motive to about ten thousand."

She laughed aloud. "Add me to the list," she said. "I hated the bastard and his politics."

"What kind of shot are you?" he asked.

"I've never fired a gun of any kind."

"Where were you at dawn this morning?"

"Showing the cook how to scramble eggs *slowly.*"

"Well, you have a motive, but no means or opportunity," he said. "You're officially cleared."

"Aw shucks. I was hoping to be more thoroughly investigated."

He peered at her over the rim of his glass. "I didn't say you weren't going to be investigated," he said.

She smiled a little. "Oh, good."

9

KINNEY WOKE UP AT EIGHT and reached for her; she was gone, and the covers were cool. He sighed. It had been a memorable night, the kind he had not had since the first year of his marriage. He had to get moving.

He showered, dressed, and went looking for Nancy Kimble. He found a table set for one in the dining room, settled there and waited, sipping the glass of freshly squeezed orange juice that had been left for him.

Nancy soon came through the kitchen door with a plate heaped with scrambled eggs, bacon, and sausage and set it before him. "Good morning," she said. She sat down and poured herself a cup of coffee from the pot on the table.

"I appear to have taken advantage of you last night," Kinney said.

"On the contrary, it was I who took advantage of you. Here I was, alone in this house for the first time with a big, handsome man, and an FBI agent on top of that. I just couldn't help myself."

"I guess I'm pretty much an opportunist myself," he said. "It was the nicest night I've spent in living memory."

"You're sweet," she said, smiling. "What are you doing today?"

"I have some work to do out at the senator's lake cabin, and it will take me all day."

"You'll be back for dinner?"

"I will, but unless I get lucky and there's another serious federal crime in the area, I'm going to have to go back to Washington tomorrow."

"Well, there's always tonight," she said.

KINNEY WAS SITTING in a rocker on the front porch when the sheriff's patrol car pulled up to the curb, followed by a deputy in an unmarked car.

Tom Stribling got out and handed Kinney the keys. "All yours," he said. "Need any help?"

"Nah, this is going to be mostly repetition," Kinney replied. "What shall I do with the car when I'm done?"

"Leave it at the airport when you go," Stribling replied.

"Tom, I've made it clear to my people that you're in charge of the local investigation. We're just there to offer support—prints, lab work—anything you need."

"I 'preciate that," Stribling said. "I'm afraid I don't have anything new for you."

"That doesn't surprise me. This is going to be a tough one. Thanks for your help." The two men shook hands.

Stribling got into into his patrol car with his deputy, waved, and drove away.

Kinney started the car, drove to Main Street, and found a hardware store. He purchased some tools, then drove out to the senator's cabin. A deputy waved him through a gate, and then he was alone in the house.

He started with a thorough room-by-room search of every drawer and closet, every nook and cranny. That done, without success, he started on the floorboards, looking for loose ones or boards that were too short or out of place. When he found an interesting one, he used a prybar to lift it, then hammered it back into place when he was done.

He broke for lunch, heating up the fried chicken and vegetables still in the fridge. Man, that woman could cook! He worked for another four hours in the afternoon, until he was certain that nothing of interest could possibly be hidden in the cabin. Finally, he took a walk around the perimeter of the house, looking for a toolshed or other structure that might hide a filing cabinet. Finding nothing, he cleaned up after himself in the cabin, then drove back to Kimble House.

Nancy met him at the door. "You look tired," she said, "and a little disheveled. What have you been doing?"

"Investigating," Kinney replied. "It can be hard work."

She went and poured him a stiff Laphroaig. "Here," she said, thrusting it at him. "Drink this while you soak in a tub."

He did so, and was the better for it.

The following morning, she walked him to the door. "You still haven't investigated me," she said.

"What was that I was doing for the past two nights?" he asked.

"I mean *really* investigated me."

"I think I will need all the facilities of the Bureau's headquarters for that," he said. "Can you come to Washington soon?"

"Yes," she said.

"I have a place you can stay. It's very nice."

"As long as it has a bed."

"It does."

She pulled him back inside the door and kissed him properly, then he put his bags in the car and turned it toward the airport. Then he stopped. He made a U-turn and drove to Elizabeth Johnson's home.

She met him at the door. "What can I do for you today, Mr. Kinney?"

"Ms. Johnson, you may not believe this, but I'm here to do you a favor."

"How's that?"

"I'm here to take those files off your hands." He quickly raised a hand before she could speak. "Please hear me out."

"I don't have any files," she said adamantly.

"Please, Ms. Johnson, let me explain. The senator had a lot of enemies, some worse than others. If we interview every one of them, it will take us months, maybe years, to develop suspects." He took a deep breath and told the lie. “Now, I think it’s very possible that, somewhere in those files is the name and the motive of the man who murdered the senator, and I can’t believe that you would do anything to stop us from finding out who that is. I’ve already searched the cabin thoroughly, and the only other place the senator would have felt comfortable leaving those files is here.” He stopped and waited, watching her think.

“I hadn’t thought about the killer being in the files,” she said finally. She turned and started into the house. “All right, come on in.” She got the key from the safe, led him down to the basement, moved some things out of the way, and pointed at the index card files.

Kinney dug them out and tucked the little four-drawer cabinet under his arm. “Thank you,” he said.

She led the way back to the front porch. “You know, Mr. Kinney,” she said, “I expect there are a lot of things in there that would hurt people. The senator had a mean streak. I wouldn’t like to think you were going to use those files to hurt anybody.”

“Only the man who killed him,” Kinney

replied. "Thank you again." He got into the car and drove to the airport, where the Lear was waiting for him.

BACK IN THE Hoover Building, Kinney made room in his office safe for the little filing cabinet, set it inside and locked the safe, then he went to see the director.

"Sit down, Bob," Heller said, "and tell me what you've got. Tell me everything."

Kinney sank into a chair and crossed his legs. "We've got what I told you yesterday," he said, "and nothing more. There isn't anything more. The guy is a pro."

"You mean a hitman?"

"Sort of. I don't think the Mafia did it, if that's what you mean, but I think I can tell you something about the shooter."

"Please do."

"He's a loner, but maybe with a support network. He probably learned to shoot in the military. He's driving a nondescript vehicle—an SUV or a pickup or an RV—something that would blend in without attracting attention. It may not be the first time he's killed somebody, but he only kills people when he feels some moral justification. He's between forty-five and sixty-five. He's well-educated, with at least a bachelor's degree, maybe even with some graduate work. He's not a hired killer or a sociopath, he's doing this out of conscience. He's methodical, patient, and cool-headed, and he's going to be nearly impossible to catch, unless he makes a mistake next time, or the time after that."

The director looked alarmed. "You think there's going to be a next time?"

"There's an outside chance that he bore some personal grudge against Senator Wallace, but I doubt it. He's on a crusade, and he's only just begun."

"How do you know all of this?" the director asked.

"I don't *know* any of it," Kinney replied. "I worked in profiling for a while, and I'm an intuitive investigator, that's all."

"So you're guessing?"

"You could call it that, but if I'm guessing, then I've guessed my way into this job."

The director was turning red in the face. "Well, you listen to me, Kinney. You'd better stop guessing and come up with some real evidence that will help me catch this man, and you'd better do it quick, or I'm going to find myself a new deputy director for investigations."

Kinney stood up. "No, you listen to me, Mr. Heller. I've got twenty-seven years on the job, and I could retire tomorrow and quadruple my salary in the private sector. I know that, because I've had offers, so there's nothing you can do to scare me. In fact, you're the one who ought to be scared, because you're hanging on by your fingernails, and chances are you're not going to be around long enough to fire me. Until you do, I'm going to run this investigation as I see fit, which is a hell of a lot better than you or anybody else in this organization can do, so stop trying to pressure me. When I have something more concrete, I'll tell you. Until then, stay out of my way."

Kinney, feeling enormously relieved, walked out of the director's office, leaving the director agape, and went to his own office down the hall. Only twice before in his career had he spoken to a superior that way, and never to a director, but he was beyond caring now, and he was going to work his own way or not at all.

• • •

He stayed late at the office, went to another floor and copied the senator's files, two index cards to a sheet. He placed the copies in a shopping bag and went home to the residential hotel where he had been living since his separation from his wife. There, he locked the copies in his personal safe. He was too tired to read them.

10

THE PRESIDENT AND the first lady got out of the presidential limousine, shook hands with the bishop and the greeting party, and walked into the National Cathedral.

Will had been in the building many times, usually for funerals or memorial services, and he was always impressed with its size. It was said that the Washington Monument, laid on its side, would fit inside the nave. He followed a priest down the center aisle and, before he took his seat, he and Kate went to Betty Ann Wallace and murmured words of consolation.

Freddie Wallace's corpulent body rested in a mahogany coffin so large that it reminded Will of Napoleon's casket in L'Ecole de Militiare, in Paris. He hoped the gravediggers in South Carolina had been warned.

The service began briskly and got slower, with each speaker taking more time than had been allotted, drawing out the sound bites for the media, who were represented by a pool camera set up to one side of the coffin. Will was the last speaker on the program, and finally, his turn came. He stood up and walked to the pulpit.

"I have known Freddie Wallace since I came to the senate to work for Senator Ben Carr, more years ago than I like to think about. The very first thing I remember about him was that he knew my name the second time I saw him. I was flattered, because I didn't know at the time that Freddie had a prodigious memory, that he never forgot a favor or a slight, or the name of anyone who might be useful to him at some later date.

"Freddie and I spent the entire length of our acquaintance on opposite sides of nearly every political question that came our way, and yet he found time, even when I was a lowly senate aide, to share with me his extraordinary command of senate procedures. I confess I learned more about parliamentary obstruction than progress from

Freddie, but that has its place in the senate, too." He paused for a chuckle from the audience.

"In spite of our political differences, Freddie became my friend, in his way, and when I was elected to the senate he became a fount of good, if sometimes dangerous advice. I had to be very careful about taking Freddie's advice, and careful if I didn't, too, since Freddie was likely to take umbrage. Freddie's umbrage was to be avoided.

"There are many in Washington, perhaps more than a few in this audience, who will not miss Freddie, but I am not among them. I will miss his personal warmth and his wit, and especially, his advice, which often pointed the way to a good decision, in either the positive or negative sense.

"Kate and I send out our hearts to Betty Ann, and our condolences, too." Will returned to his seat and sat down.

As they made to depart the building after the service, Will made one more move to console the widow. Betty Ann grabbed him fiercely by the elbow and drew his ear to her lips.

"I have his files," she hissed, "and I'm going to use them." She released him and turned to the next mourner.

"What did she say?" Kate asked.

"I'll tell you later." Will looked up to see James Heller in his path and offered his hand. "How's the investigation going, Jim?" he asked quietly.

"Just great," Heller replied. "I've put the Bureau's very best man, Robert Kinney, deputy director for Criminal Investigations, in complete charge of the case."

Will thought he had heard the name, but he wasn't sure. "Good," he said. "Tell Kinney to keep me posted." He didn't believe for a moment that Heller would do that; the director would preserve his own channel to the president, and he wouldn't want a subordinate horning in.

"Yes, sir, I will," Heller replied, then went on his way.

Back in the limo, Kate spoke up. "So, what did Betty Ann have to say?"

Will pressed the button that rolled up the partition between the front and rear seats. "She said she has Freddie's files, and she's going to use them."

Kate laughed. "I wouldn't put it past her."

"Nor would I."

"You think those files are as dangerous as rumor has it?"

"I think they're dangerous to those Freddie didn't like and maybe to a few he did like."

"Like you?"

"I'm fortunate in having fewer secrets than a lot of people, and most of them have to do with what you and I do together in bed."

Kate laughed. "You think Freddie knew about that?"

"I hope to God not," Will replied. "One or both of us could end up in jail."

11

AS THE MEMORIAL SERVICE for Freddie Wallace proceeded, Ted drove the RV across one of the Potomac bridges into Virginia. He found the office building in downtown Arlington, then drove around the area for a couple of minutes before he found a legal parking spot two blocks from the building. He slipped into the rear of the RV, pulling a curtain behind him to prevent being seen through the windshield, and got into a necktie and jacket.

He checked the device once more—every connection, every component, especially the squat switch—and found it in good order. He removed his aeronautical charts and books from their container—a salesman's catalogue case—carefully slipped the device inside, and snapped it shut. Then he left the RV and walked briskly back toward the building, scanning the street for police cars, security guards, or anyone else who might take note of him.

He reached the office building and walked down the drive past the automated gate and into the parking garage. He kept up his pace as he searched for the car—a black Mercedes S600, with a vanity plate reading right. He found it closer to the elevators than he would have liked, but of course, Van Vandervelt would have a prime parking spot. Right Radio took up two floors of the building, spewing venom from a dozen shock jocks twenty-four hours a day, and Van Vandervelt was their star—the most popular right-wing talk-show host in the country.

Ted heard a car coming, and he devoted half a minute to inspecting the building directory beside the elevator until the car had left the garage. When all was quiet again, he walked quickly to the driver's side of the Mercedes and checked the door lock. The button was up, the car unlocked, but Ted knew that, in the Mercedes, the alarm would go off at a predetermined interval after the door had opened, unless the key was inserted into the ignition lock. He reckoned he had at least a minute. He set down the catalogue case, unsnapped it, and had one more look around the garage. Still quiet.

He opened the car door and dropped to one knee. Carefully, he slid the device, which was no more than two inches thick at any point, under the seat and pushed it well out of sight of the driver. Then he pulled off the tape that held down the squat switch, closed the door, picked up the catalogue case, and walked quickly toward the exit. He was nearly out of the garage before the car alarm went off, but it was unlikely that anyone would report it, since people had grown so accustomed to car alarms going off randomly in big cities.

The device consisted of twelve ounces of his own homemade plastic explosive and nearly a quart of gasoline in a flat, plastic bottle, along with the requisite electronics, all mounted on a quarter-inch steel plate that would have the effect of directing the force of the explosion upward.

Ted reached the sidewalk and turned back toward the parked RV. From half a block away, he could see a policeman trying to look through a curtained window into the vehicle. He continued straight past the RV, while reaching into his pocket for the little remote control that he always carried with him when leaving the vehicle. It was good for up to a mile, and the entry of the code into its keypad would set off an explosion that would reduce the big RV to ashes in a matter of minutes. He turned left at the next corner and, without looking back, walked out of sight of the RV.

He was not particularly concerned that the policeman was interested in the interior of his rolling home; people were always trying to look inside, to see how it was furnished. He went into a little news shop, bought a *Washington Post* and sat down on a bench outside to read it. After ten minutes he folded the newspaper, tucked it under an arm, picked up the catalogue case, and walked back the way he had come.

The cop was nowhere in sight, and Ted got into the RV, started the engine, and drove away, switching on the radio, which was already tuned to Right Radio.

"Well, my friends," Van Vandervelt was saying, *"thus ends another two hours of deep-frying liberals in their own juices, of telling the truth for all America to hear. I thank you for having the good taste and*

judgment to tune in today, and I look forward to having you back tomorrow, when I will puncture the myths surrounding Social Security and tell you how Franklin D. Roosevelt nearly wrecked the country when it was recovering on its own from the Great Depression. See you then. Isn't it great to be RIGHT?"

Ted switched the radio back to FM and National Public Radio. He stopped for gas, took off his jacket and tie, then headed for the beltway and points north.

VAN VANDERVELT swept his notes off the console into a trash can, got into his jacket, which had been made entirely by one man in Naples, Italy, who made only ten suits a year, two of them for Vandervelt, then he walked out of the studio and back to his office. His secretary followed him inside and closed the door behind him.

She was a tall, leggy girl with high breasts and full lips. "Just a few phone messages," she said.

"Fuck 'em," he said. "Come here."

She walked over to him and put her arms around his neck. "Anything special?" she asked, kissing him and letting her tongue play around his lips.

"Just your specialty," he said. "I've got a tee time in an hour."

She pushed him backward into a chair, dropped to her knees, unzipped his fly, and performed her specialty.

In less than two minutes, he was begging for mercy.

Thus refreshed, Van Vandervelt took the elevator down to the garage, got into his car, and turned down the street toward his golf game. He drove out to Burning Tree and parked the car in the lot near the locker room entrance to the clubhouse. He got out of the car, unknowingly releasing the squat switch, which his own weight had compressed, and before he could close the car door, the Mercedes became a huge fireball. The combination of the plastic explosive and the gasoline, plus what was in the car's tank, propelled the flaming body of the shock jock nearly thirty yards, where he landed, already dead, just outside the locker room door.

People ran toward the car from all directions.

• • •

As THE PRESIDENTIAL limousine returned from the memorial service and pulled to a halt under the portico of the West Wing, one of the phones in the armrest rang. Will picked it up. "Yes?" He listened for a moment. "When? Thank you." He replaced the handset.

"You look odd," Kate said. "What's happened?"

"Somebody put a bomb in the car of Van Vandervelt, the radio guy."

"Did it go off?"

"Yes, and he was killed instantly."

She looked at him closely. "You think this is connected to Freddie's death?"

"I don't know, but you have to wonder."

TED PARKED the RV in the parking lot of a fast-food restaurant off I-95, then he pulled the curtain and went into the rear of the vehicle. He switched on the laptop, aligned the satellite dish, and went to the website. He made a change or two to the content, then switched off the computer, locked the RV, and went inside for a bacon cheeseburger, his favorite.

12

BOB KINNEY ARRIVED at Burning Tree a little more than an hour after the bomb had gone off. The Arlington fire department and police were on the scene and Kinney found the detective in charge of the investigation talking to the fire department's arson investigator.

"Thanks for the call," Kinney said, shaking the hands of the two men. "We're happy to help. There's a vanload of people from our lab right behind me. Tell me what you've got so far."

The arson investigator led him over to the parking lot. "That used to be a Mercedes," he said, "but, as you can see, not anymore."

The car was a black hulk, still smoking. Not a single panel of the bodywork was still attached to the frame, and the engine rested a good twelve feet from the bulk of the car. Half a dozen other cars in the lot had been destroyed to varying degrees.

"We found the driver over there by the locker room entrance," the detective said.

"How did you identify him?"

"The caddy shelter is over there about fifty yards," the detective said, pointing, "and one of the caddies had been booked by Vandervelt. He saw the man get out of the car and was walking toward him when the car blew. The blast knocked him off his feet but didn't hurt him."

Kinney turned to the arson investigator. "Have you made any determination about the bomb?"

"It was under the driver's seat, probably detonated by a squat switch, since it didn't blow until Vandervelt got out of the car, but before he closed the door. And it was the work of a very sophisticated pro. That's about it. I hope your people can learn something more from the pieces. How can we help?"

"I'd like you to assemble your people and have them do an inch-by-inch search of the parking lot and the area around it. Have them flag any spot where any piece of debris is found, but I don't want them to touch what they find. Then my people can inspect each piece and determine what will be useful to the investigation."

"Okay," said the detective, "I'm formally handing off to you. I'm happy for my people to be of help, but the responsibility for this investigation is now the FBI's." He consulted his watch. "From this moment."

"We'll accept that," Kinney said.

"I've got just one question."

"What's that?"

"I know what you do at the Bureau. Why are you dealing with this personally? Is it because Vandervelt was a celebrity?"

"No, it's because this case may be connected with another case that we have under investigation."

"Senator Wallace?"

"I can't go into that."

"You think they were both killed by the same perp?"

"I hope not," Kinney replied.

"Why do you hope not?"

"Because if it's the same man, he's exhibiting all kinds of new skills, and that worries me."

The detective nodded. "For what it's

worth, I checked with Right Radio, and Vandervelt's secretary said he finished his show and left his office about forty-five minutes before the bomb went off, saying that he was rushing to make a tee time. If it was detonated by a squat switch, then the bomb was probably put in his car in the parking garage of his office building, since he probably wouldn't have stopped on the way here."

"That's good work. Thank you," Kinney said. "Anything else?"

The detective shrugged. "The man had a wife. Since you're running the case, you get to break the news to her." He handed Kinney a sheet of paper. "Here's her name and address."

"I'll take care of it." Kinney put the paper in his notebook.

TWO HOURS LATER, Kinney rang the bell of a Watergate apartment. A maid admitted him and showed him into the living room.

"Mrs. Vandervelt will be with you in a moment," she said. "Please have a seat."

Kinney walked over to the window and

took in the panoramic view of the Potomac River and the woods beyond.

"Mr. Kinney?"

He turned to find a woman standing in the doorway to the living room. She was of medium height, her hair was very blond and carefully coiffed, and her breasts were large.

"Yes. Mrs. Vandervelt?"

"You're with the FBI?"

"That's correct." He walked over and showed her his ID.

"What's going on? Why are you here?"

"May we sit down?"

She sat on the sofa, and he took a chair.

"Mrs. Vandervelt, I'm very sorry to tell you that there has been an attempt on your husband's life. He didn't survive."

She sat, staring stonily at him, quiet for a long moment. "When did this happen?" she asked.

"About three hours ago. I was unable to leave the scene until now."

"How did it happen?"

"Someone placed a bomb in your husband's car, probably in the parking garage of his office building. It went off when he got out of the car at Burning Tree. The car was destroyed and your husband was killed instantly. He never knew what happened, never felt anything."

"Well," she said, "I'm glad of that." She looked out the window for a moment, her face now drawn and sad. "Do you have any idea who did it?"

"Not yet, but if you're feeling up to it, I'd like to ask you some questions."

"Please go ahead."

"Did your husband have any enemies that you are aware of?"

She suppressed a laugh. "About half the country," she said.

"Did he ever receive any threats here, at home?"

"Not that I'm aware of," she said. "It was known that we live in the Watergate, so he got a fair amount of mail here, mostly fan letters, but occasional critical letters, too. I read many of them, but I don't remember a death threat."

"Who might have benefited from your husband's death?"

"Well, I suppose I'm your first suspect," she said. "Van was quite rich, and I stand to inherit most of it. He made a new will less than a month ago. We were married six weeks before that."

"Was your marriage a happy one?"

"We didn't really have time to get unhappy. I'm not sure where it would have gone. We were starting to get on each other's nerves."

"That happens to a lot of married couples."

"I suppose so. If it helps, I don't know how to make a bomb, and I don't know anyone who does."

Kinney got to his feet. "Thank you for your help, Mrs. Vandervelt, and I'm very sorry for your loss."

"Thank you," she said.

He gave her his card. "Please call me if you think of anything else."

"I will."

"And for what it's worth, you're not a suspect," Kinney said kindly, though it was not entirely true. She would be investigated very thoroughly indeed.

13

KINNEY WENT BACK to his office and called a meeting of half a dozen of his top people, including his assistant deputy director, Frank Coram.

"Gentlemen, I'm personally assuming responsibility for the investigations of the murders of Senator Wallace and Van Vandervelt," he said. "Frank, you'll be acting deputy director for investigations while I'm on this."

"Any idea how long this will be, Bob?" Coram asked.

"Until we wrap up the investigation. I'll meet with you once a week to talk about current investigations, but for the most part, you'll be on your own, and that includes administrative matters. Check with me on transfers of investigators, though."

"All right."

He handed Coram a list. "I've picked a few men to help me, and they'll be detached from their regular duties for the duration."

Coram read the sheet. "That's everybody in this room but me."

"That's right. My secretary will be with the group, too, serving all of us."

"Anything else, Bob?"

"Only that, if you run across anything in another investigation that pertains to my work, let me know."

"Of course."

"That's all, Frank. The rest of you remain with me for a few minutes." He called his secretary and asked her to come in. Helen Frankel, two years from retirement and imperious, came into the room and took a seat.

"All right," Kinney said, "we're the Group, that's the only name we'll have. We're an informal task force and we'll have priority for any technical services we require."

Someone raised a hand. "Sir, is there some relationship between the two cases? They seem very different on their faces."

"There are two connections: One, the two victims were spokesmen for the same set of political views; two, I think both murders were committed by the same man."

"Any suspects?"

"No, and we're not likely to have one anytime soon. The man we're looking for is extremely proficient in at least two disciplines—shooting and bomb making—and probably in many more. He leaves as little as possible behind, and we're not going to apprehend him unless we get lucky. Of course, the harder we work, the luckier we'll get.

"Harry," he said to the man who had asked the question, "it occurs to me that the sort of man we're looking for might very well work or have worked at a place like the FBI. I'd like you to take charge of investigating every retired technical officer who might have the skills exhibited in these two murders. Any one of them who isn't in a hospital bed is a suspect, until he's cleared. You can pick two agents attached to headquarters to help you."

"Yes, sir," Harry replied, taking notes. "Should we investigate retirees from other agencies, as well?"

"First us, then them. Start with Alcohol, Tobacco and Firearms when you're done here. Tommy, you're in charge of coordinating technical reports, starting with the Vandervelt killing. We've got all we're going to get from the Wallace case, and it's next to nothing, but this bomb investigation should turn up some bits and pieces for us to look at."

"Yes, sir," Tommy replied.

"The team at Burning Tree will be back in-house by the end of the day. Don't wait for their report to get involved. Look over their shoulders."

"Yes, sir."

"That's all for the moment. I want to hear from anybody with a theory or an idea on how to proceed. This is wide open, and you're all invited to contribute in any way you can."

Everybody shuffled out. "Helen, would you stay for a moment, please?"

"Yes, sir." She stayed in her chair.

When the room had been cleared he got up and opened his safe. "You and I are going to work together on a special part of this investigation," he said, placing Senator Wallace's index cards on his desk.

"In addition to my other duties?" she asked.

"Get somebody to cover the phones and do the ordinary secretarial work."

"All right. May I ask why you chose me instead of an agent for this assignment?"

"You're near retirement, and you have no political ax to grind. You're not bucking for promotion, and you won't take this to the tabloids. Frankly, I expect you to take it to your grave, and I think, based on past experience, you're perfectly capable of doing that."

Something like a blush appeared on Helen's face. "Thank you, sir. What are these files?"

"These are index cards kept by Senator Frederick Wallace for, I don't know, forty years. They are the equivalent of Director Hoover's fabled files, and I'm sure they contain dirt on many prominent people. I know you understand how explosive these files could be if anyone in the press became aware even that they exist, let alone their contents."

"Of course," she said.

"I'd like you to begin by making a written summary of the cards, in the order that the senator kept them, so that I can refer quickly to various people and to what the senator thought was important about them."

"Where shall I work?"

"Lock the outer doors to my conference room next door and work on the table there. I don't want even the cleaners in there, so you'd better have the locks rekeyed. You keep one key, and I'll keep the other."

"All right. Am I to draw any conclusions from what I learn?"

"I'll go over your summary myself. Until I do that, if you discover anything that you think might make one of these people a suspect in either of these two murders, I want to know about it immediately."

"Yes, sir."

"Thank you, Helen, now you can get to work."

He watched her ramrod-straight back retreat from his office, then returned to work.

14

JAMES HELLER, bone-tired, dragged himself out of his car and into the kitchen through the door from the garage. His internal security people insisted that he never get into or out of a car at his home, except in the garage.

His wife was not in the kitchen, and her car was not in the garage, so he assumed she was out. He hoped to God she would bring something home for dinner, because he loathed her cooking, not that she cooked very often. He walked into the central hall of the house and stopped, listening. The only sound in the house was the clicking of a keyboard, and it came from the little room under the stairs, where his fifteen-year-old son James Jr. had made himself a computer room. He walked down the hall, stopped at the open door and looked inside. For the life of him, he could not understand why a teenager would need three computers, two printers, a scanner, and God knew what else, all crammed into the tiny space. It was much neater than the boy's room. "Hi, Jimmy," he said.

"Hey, Dad," the boy mumbled, not looking up from the monitor.

"What's up?"

"Not much." He began typing very fast.

So much for the father-son relationship, Heller thought. He walked back down the hall and into his mahogany-paneled study, opened a cabinet door designed to look like a bookcase, filled a glass with ice, then filled it with twelve-year-old Scotch. He sank into a leather armchair, propped his feet up on the ottoman, found the remote control, and switched on the TV.

"FBI sources tell us that the Bureau believes that the murders of Senator Frederick Wallace and talk-show host Van Vandervelt may have been committed by the same man. Asked what the connections between the two killings were, a spokesman declined comment. The investigation is being run by the Bureau's top investigator,

Deputy Director for Criminal Investigations Robert Kinney, who has assembled a small group of senior agents who will work only on the two murders."

"Jesus," Heller muttered. "I didn't know that, but CNN has it?" He switched off the set in disgust and pulled on the Scotch, closing his eyes and leaning his head against the rear cushion. He had just dozed off when he jerked awake. "What?" he said.

"You gotta see this, Dad," Jimmy was saying.

Heller leaned his head back again. "Not now, Jimmy, I'm really beat."

"Daaad," the boy whined. "This is important. It's Bureau stuff."

Heller didn't understand. "On the computer?"

"On the Internet. Come on, you gotta look at this."

"Jimmy, can you give me just fifteen minutes to get my strength back?"

"Is that what whiskey does? Gives you your strength back? Forget it." The boy left the room in disgust.

Heller tried to go back to sleep and failed. The tone of his son's voice had cut him like a knife. "Oh, all right," he said, struggling out of the chair and bringing along his Scotch. He walked down the hall to Jimmy's computer room. "What is it?" he asked.

"I don't want to bother you," Jimmy replied. "Maybe tomorrow you'll feel up to it."

"Come on, Jimmy, I got up and came down here. What's going on?"

"Just something I came across on the Internet."

"And what would that be?" He pulled at the Scotch.

"Just something about those murders you guys are trying to solve."

"Murders? You mean Senator Wallace and . . . that other guy?"

"Van Vandervelt. He was cool. I listened to his show all the time."

It irked Heller that his son thought a jerk like Vanderevelt was "cool," but he tried not to show it. "Doesn't his show come on when you're in school?"

"Yeah, but I record it every day. I'll miss the guy."

"Well, I'm sure that by tomorrow they'll have another jerk to replace Vandervelt."

"He's not a jerk. He's right."

"Right-wing, maybe. He's wrong about everything else."

"Then I guess you wouldn't be interested in seeing his picture on this website with a big *X* drawn through it."

"What website is that, Jimmy?" Heller just barely knew what a website was. His secretary had to print out his email for him.

"It's called ACT NOW," Jimmy said. "Just a minute: I'll bring it up for you." He tapped the keys madly. "There you go."

Heller walked over and stood behind his son. There, on the monitor before him, were photographs of Senator Wallace and Van Vandervelt, both with big *X*s drawn through them.

"Just a sec, I'll zoom out for you. There you go."

Now Heller could see the whole page. There were at least twenty photographs, many of faces Heller knew or recognized from the news.

ACT NOW!!!

These men and women are all part of the vast right-wing conspiracy that is eating away at the heart of our democracy, with their constant attacks on civil

> liberties and any federal spending on programs that help people instead of the rich. It's time right-thinking people stood up to them and held them accountable for the destruction they have and are causing. Each of them is now a legitimate target for the wrath of any American with the guts to do the right thing. ACT NOW!!!

"Holy shit," the director of the FBI said.

"You told me not to use that word," Jimmy said.

15

HELLER WENT INTO the president's national security briefing with a confidence he had never before felt. He set his briefcase down beside his chair, sat back, and listened to the presentations of the chairman of the Joint Chiefs of Staff, the director of Central Intelligence, and the national security advisor.

"Jim?" the president said finally. "You're awfully quiet this morning. Do you have anything for us?"

"Yes, I do, Mr. President," Heller replied, setting his briefcase on his lap and opening it. He handed copies of the documents to the president and the others.

"What's this?" the president asked.

"It's a website run by the murderer of Senator Wallace and Van Vandervelt. As you can see, he's marked off those two, but there are a lot of other candidates whose photographs are displayed."

"Good God," Will Lee said. "You think he plans to kill everybody whose picture is here?"

"I think that we have to consider that a possibility," Heller replied.

"Can you trace this website back to its source?"

"I have a tech consultant working on that right now," Heller replied. He had told his son he could stay home from school that day.

"I'll get the NSA working on it, too," Kate said. "They've got more computer firepower than any of us."

"I don't think that will be necessary, Kate," Heller said. "We'll run this down."

"I want everybody who can help with this working on it," the president said, "and the NSA seems like a very good idea."

Heller flushed a little. The president was obviously covering his ass with his wife. "As you wish, Mr. President."

"Jim, I'm sure it has occurred to you that the existence of this website could benefit us."

"How do you mean, Mr. President?"

"Well, first of all, it gives us a possible opportunity to locate the killer. You got that, didn't you?"

"Yes, sir," Heller said, reddening even more.

"And second, it gives us a list of possible targets, if he should strike again. I mean, the speaker of the House is on this list, for God's sake!"

"Yes, sir, I understand that."

"Well, you're going to have to arrange some protection for these people, aren't you?"

"Protection?"

"Jim, the killer has given you a list of people he wants to kill. If you fail to protect them and more are killed, well, the public is going to want your head. Not to mention the Congress."

Heller gulped.

"I'll speak to the head of the Secret Service about getting you some help. I want the two of you to coordinate personal protection for everyone on this list."

"Yes, Mr. President. I'll speak to him this morning."

"And the next time you have new information about these killings, bring along that fellow you told me about—your deputy—what's his name?"

Heller had to think for a moment. "Kinney, sir?"

"Yes, Robert Kinney. I want to meet the man."

"Well, sir, he's pretty busy right now."

The president took off his reading glasses and massaged the bridge of his nose. "I'll try not to take up too much of his time, Jim."

"Yes, sir."

"Unless anyone else has something, we'll adjourn," the president said.

The group stood as one and walked toward the door.

"Oh, Jim," the president said, "I think we'd better keep the existence of this website quiet for the moment—at least until we have protection for these people in place."

Heller winced. "Ah, Mr. President, I'm afraid . . ." He stopped.

"Jim, have you already released this to the press?"

Heller whipped out his cell phone. "I'll cancel the press release," he said, and he kept walking, not waiting for the president's response.

• • •

BOB KINNEY LOOKED at the material his secretary had just handed him.

"I got it from the director's secretary," Helen said. "It's already gone out."

Kinney groaned. The phone on his desk rang, and Helen picked it up.

"Deputy Director Kinney's office," she said. She listened then pressed the hold button. "It's the director," she said, handing Kinney the phone.

"Yes?" Kinney said into the phone.

"Good morning, Bob," Heller said. He sounded as if he were on a cell phone.

"Good morning, Director."

"I've got some great news."

"I've just seen it. Did you really release this to the press?"

"I've put out word to cancel the release."

"Good."

"Now, Bob, I want you to call Ed Levy at the Secret Service and coordinate protection for all the people whose pictures are on that website."

"I'm sorry, sir, but my function on this case is to supervise the investigation, not to guard bodies. I believe you want to speak to personnel about that. Good morning, sir." He hung up.

Helen, who had been listening on an extension, hung up, too. "Are you trying to hurry along your retirement?" she asked Kinney.

"Helen, I don't much care if he fires me or not, and I've already told him that. Until he does, I'm going to run this case as I see fit, and I'm not going to be sidetracked by having to round up two hundred agents to act as bodyguards for"—he ran his finger down the rows of photographs—"conservative columnists and TV preachers."

"As you wish."

"He said he'd canceled the press release."

"He was too late. It had already been emailed to the whole media list."

"Where the hell did he come up with this website?" Kinney asked. "Who told him about it?"

"His fifteen-year-old son," Helen replied. "He's apparently a computer whiz."

Kinny began to laugh; he couldn't help himself. Helen laughed, too.

16

TED PARKED THE RV near a commuter bus stop in New Jersey and walked toward the waiting bus, swinging his umbrella. There wasn't a cloud in the sky.

He rode into Manhattan and got off at the Port Authority Bus Terminal. From there, he walked to the New York headquarters of CNN, near Penn Station. It was getting dark outside.

He checked out the lobby and noted the security guard; no good, he didn't want to be inside. He crossed the street and walked into a bar facing the CNN building. "Gimme a beer," he said, glancing at his watch. There was a tennis tournament on the TV over the bar, and nobody was watching it.

The bartender set the beer on the bar, and Ted put a twenty beside it. "Start me a tab," he said. "You mind if we put the TV on CNN? *Broadside* is on."

"Yeah, sure," the bartender said, switching channels and turning up the sound.

"I love this guy Brennan," Ted said. "He makes mincemeat of that liberal schmuck every night."

"Yeah, me, too," the bartender said.

Tim Brennan, a voluble right-winger, shared the platform each evening with Evan Turner, a bespectacled, bow-tied, tweed-jacketed example of the liberal breed.

"Tell me something, Tim," Turner was saying.

"I'd love to, Evan," Brennan replied. "There's so much you need to know."

"We've got the best fighter planes in the world, right?"

"Right, Evan. I'm surprised you knew that."

"And nobody is even trying to build a better one—not the Russians, not the Chinese, not anybody—right?"

"They couldn't even come close."

"Then maybe you can explain to me why we need a brand-new, twenty-first-century fighter plane to replace the terrific planes we already have—and at a cost of more than a hundred billion dollars."

"Sure, I can, Evan. We need that new plane so that we can keep our edge in the world of military aviation."

"But we already have that edge, and you've just admitted that it's not even threatened. Why can't we spend that hundred billion on a national health insurance initiative, on education, on cleaning up our environment."

"The usual littany of liberal sinkholes for cash, right? You think the Chinese are going to be impressed by national health insurance, or another round of tree hugging? Nothing impresses those people but hardware—military hardware—the sort of hardware that can send nuclear missiles right down their throats at the press of a button. That's what will keep the peace, and the new fighter is an integral part of that plan."

"That's telling him, Tim," Ted shouted, banging his hand on the bar. "Nuke the bastards!"

"Well, that's all we have time for tonight, folks," Brennan was saying. "Evan and I will see you tomorrow evening, same time." The theme music came up, and the two men began freeing themselves from their microphones.

Ted paid his bill, pocketed his change, and, swinging his umbrella, went outside, keeping an eye on the CNN entrance. He watched as Brennan and his cohost signed out of the building and left. They paused out front, shook hands, and departed in opposite directions, which seemed appropriate to Ted.

Ted crossed the street and fell in a dozen paces behind Brennan. He kept pace with the man until he was sure there were no guards watching him, then followed him into Penn Station, where Brennan headed for the New Jersey trains.

Ted caught up with him on an escalator, and as he walked past the man, he aimed the umbrella at his calf muscle and jabbed quickly.

"Ow!" Brennan yelled.

"Gosh, I'm awfully sorry, Mr. Brennan," Ted said. "The thing just got away from me."

"That hurt like hell," Brennan said, massaging his leg.

"I'm really sorry. The tip of the umbrella got caught in the escalator tread, and when I yanked it out, it hit you."

"It's okay," Brennan said. "Forget it."

"Great show tonight!" Ted said.

Brennan beamed. "Thanks."

"You take care now."

Brennan peeled off toward the trains, and Ted turned and found an up escalator. Half an hour later, he was on a bus back to New Jersey.

TIM BRENNAN let himself into his house and dumped his briefcase on the hall table. "Anybody home?" he yelled.

"Back here," his wife called.

He went into the kitchen and sat down at the little dining table in the corner. "Man, I'm beat," he said.

"That's unusual for you," his wife replied. "You usually get home full of piss and vinegar, ready to jump me."

"I think I'm coming down with some sort of bug, or something. I really feel rotten."

She set a plate of hot food before him. "Eat your dinner and go straight to bed," she said. "If you're not feeling better in the morning, I'll take you to the doctor."

Brennan nodded and began to eat. He had taken only a few bites when he suddenly vomited into his plate.

THE DOCTOR CAME through a swinging door and walked up to her. "Mrs. Brennan?"

"Yes." She stood up.

"Your husband seems to be suffering from some sort of bacterial infection. We haven't been able to identify it yet, so we're treating him with broad-spectrum antibiotics."

"Is he going to be all right?"

"I think so. We've given him something to help with the vomiting, and he's resting more comfortably now."

"May I see him?"

"I don't think you should, until we've found out exactly what's wrong with him, and I'd like to take a blood sample from you before you go home."

"You think he might be contagious?"

"I really don't know yet, but we're working on it."

"I'll be glad to give you a blood sample,"

she said. "Will you please tell Tim that I'll be back in the morning to see him?"

"Of course I will," the doctor said.

TED POINTED THE RV south on I-95 and headed for Virginia. He'd find an RV park along the way and get some sleep.

17

BOB KINNEY STOPPED at a pancake house for breakfast and opened his *Washington Post.* He was presented with a large photograph of the Arlington arson inspector accompanied by an interview about the facts surrounding the death of Van Vandervelt, including an extensive description of the bomb, some of which had to have come from the FBI people on the crime scene.

Kinney was an advocate of the Bureau being as open as possible with local law enforcement, but it seemed that every time they opened up, some local guy would jump in and either take credit for the investigation or reveal a great deal more than he should about it. Now the killer knew most of what the FBI knew about his technique of bomb building.

He finished his breakfast and went to the office. Helen was waiting for him with a notebook in her hand. “Have you been watching TV this morning?” she asked.

“No, I hate those shrieking tourists outside the morning shows.”

“Something has happened you may be interested in.”

“Not another murder of a right-winger.”

“A death, yes. Who knows if it’s murder?” She consulted her notebook. “This is what I gleaned on three channels: Tim Brennan, who is half the *Broadside* program on CNN, came home from work last night feeling ill, and in the middle of his dinner started throwing up. His wife got him to an emergency room where doctors found he had symptoms of a bacterial infection, which they were unable to identify.”

“Oh, my God,” Kinney half-moaned.

“What?”

“Go on.”

“He died at five o’clock this morning. That’s it.”

“Where did he die?”

“At a hospital in New Jersey.”

"Get me the head of pathology at that hospital."

Helen returned to her desk and, a moment later, buzzed him. "Dr. Mendelson on the line."

"Dr. Mendelson?"

"Yes?"

"This is Robert Kinney, deputy director for investigations at the FBI."

"Good morning, Mr. Kinney."

"Do you have the remains of Tim Brennan at your facility?"

"Yes, he's on ice in my morgue."

"Have you performed an autopsy yet?"

"No, I was about to go and attend to that myself."

"Please don't do that, Doctor, at least not yet. I want to send an FBI forensic pathologist and some special equipment up there to work with you on the postmortem."

"Why?"

"Do you have Brennan's medical record handy?"

"Right here. What would you like to know?"

"Cause of death."

Mendelson shuffled some papers. "Bacterial infection, unidentified."

"Doctor, the unidentified nature of the infection is a red flag for a possible biological or chemical assault."

"Assault?"

"Whatever Mr. Brennan had may have been induced."

"That's very disturbing, but it's not the first time we've had trouble identifying the cause of an infection, Mr. Kinney. What causes you to believe that Mr. Kinney may have suffered an assault?"

"There are other factors surrounding this death that tend to support such a conclusion. I can't go into it now, but until our pathologist arrives I strongly suggest that you quarantine your morgue and keep anyone involved in Mr. Brennan's treatment before his death under close observation for symptoms resembling his. I also suggest that you keep this as quiet as you can, under the circumstances, and that, in particular, you issue no statements to the press, except a statement announcing the time and supposed cause of death and say that an autopsy will be conducted in due course, but that's all."

"All right, Mr. Kinney," the doctor replied, sounding worried.

"I should be able to have my people with you by mid-afternoon. Please call me if you have any questions between now and then."

"Thank you, Mr. Kinney. I'll certainly look forward to seeing your people here."

Kinney hung up, then called the lab and gave instructions to assemble a team and get them to New Jersey, then he called the Trenton FBI office and instructed them to send an agent to interview Brennan's wife. "I want to know if Brennan told her about any sort of encounter with a stranger in the hours between the time he left his office and arrived home, especially any sort of physical contact. I'm thinking about a fan who may have shaken his hand, a panhandler, a drunk—anybody at all."

He hung up and called the New York City office and instructed them to send agents to interview anyone at CNN with whom Brennan had had contact during the hours between his arrival at and departure from CNN, with particular attention paid to any illness among them. "Tell your agents to remember that they're talking to newspeople and to take care not to alarm them. Just see if any of them called in sick today."

Helen came back into his office. "Have we got another victim?"

"I don't know," he replied, "but, given the circumstances, I hope not."

KINNEY REMAINED at his desk, waiting to hear from his pathologist. The call came shortly after seven o'clock.

"You want a summary, or all the details?" the doctor asked.

"Let's start with a summary."

"We conducted a full-blown antibiological field autopsy, complete with all the gear—sealed suits, the works. None of Brennan's blood work or tissue samples revealed any pathogen, biological or chemical. Everything came back normal. None of the people who came into contact with Brennan at the hospital have exhibited any symptoms of infection."

"Cause of death?"

"Complete collapse of the cardiopulmonary system, with no apparent underlying cause."

"Jesus."

"Exactly. I'm bringing blood and tissue

samples back to D.C. with me, and I'll run further tests and issue a report in a day or two."

"Did you find any sign of external injury?"

"He had a shaving cut, apparently inflicted yesterday sometime, and there was a small puncture mark on the left calf muscle, just below the knee. I examined his trousers at that location and found a tiny trace of xylocaine present."

"That's a local anesthetic, isn't it? The sort of thing you get at the dentist's?"

"Or in the emergency room, if you're, say, getting a cut stitched. You want my best guess?"

"Please."

"By some unknown means he was injected with a fluid containing an unknown pathogen and xylocaine. The anesthetic would relieve any pain from the puncture almost immediately, so Brennan would get over it quickly. I think the pathogen was chemical, rather than biological."

"So he was poisoned?"

"That's what it amounts to, but so far, there is absolutely no trace of the poison, not even on the clothing where I found the xylocaine. And that is very disturbing."

"An unanalyzable poison?"

"Yes. Such things do exist. A poison can be made by combining two common household cleaning agents in the right proportions. When ingested, it causes death within twenty-four hours, and it cannot be analyzed. Also, if some stranger injected the poison, it would have to have been done very quickly, so as not to arouse Brennan's suspicions, so the amount would have to have been very small, certainly much less than a cubic centimeter."

"There was a case like this in London back in the seventies, I think. A man was stabbed with a poisoned umbrella tip on the street."

"I'm familiar with that case, but Brennan died much more quickly than that victim, who, to the best of my recollection, took three days to expire."

"So he was killed by an injection of a tiny amount of an unanalyzable poison."

"That's my initial and unofficial diagnosis," the doctor replied. "And I need hardly point out that, if my diagnosis can be confirmed, we're likely looking at the involvement of a foreign intelligence service. The London killing was traced to the Romanian or the Bulgarian service, I believe. Cold War stuff."

"Get back to me as soon as you've confirmed something," Kinney said. "And thanks for calling." He hung up.

Helen came into the office. "So?"

"We've got another victim, and this is getting very, very strange."

18

KINNEY WAS ABOUT TO LEAVE his apartment when his cell phone rang. "Yes?"

"This is the director's secretary, Mr. Kinney," she said. "The director got your memo this morning about the Brennan death, and he would like you to accompany him to the White House this morning for the president's intelligence briefing."

"All right."

"The director's car will pick you up in fifteen minutes."

"Please tell the director that I'll drive my own car and meet him there, if he would be kind enough to notify White House security. I have an appointment that I'll have to drive to immediately following the briefing." This was a lie, but Kinney had no intention of being trapped in a car with the director for half the morning.

"I'll let the director know and notify White House security."

"Thank you."

KINNEY HAD BEEN to the White House before for meetings with presidential aides, but never with the president himself. He was passed through the main gate after showing his ID and being carefully compared to his photograph by the guard, then his car was parked for him, and an escort took him to a small waiting room. The director arrived presently, and the room filled up with the meeting's other participants.

After the others were called inside, Kinney waited until summoned. The director introduced him to the president, then, one by one, to the others.

"I understand we have another killing, Bob," the president said.

"I believe we do, Mr. President." He told the group about the circumstances of Brennan's death and the autopsy results.

"Now those results are preliminary, aren't they, Bob?" the director asked.

"Yes, sir, but I expect the final report to be the same."

"What do you make of this?" the president asked. "Are we dealing with a foreign intelligence agency?"

"I don't believe so, Mr. President."

"Then who?"

"I believe we're dealing with an individual who has knowledge of all sorts of technical skills—firearms, explosives, black chemistry. I've ordered that all the Bureau's retired or dismissed employees with such knowledge be investigated, and I want to extend that investigation to the retired employees of other agencies, too."

"Why retired employees, not current ones?"

"Because our killer seems to have the time to travel up and down the Eastern seaboard, murdering people. Apparently he's driving, and a current employee wouldn't be able to do that, unless he were on vacation, and that would call unwanted attention to him."

"What agencies are you talking about?" the president asked.

"FBI, CIA, ATF, DEA. Any with a tech services department."

Kate Rule Lee spoke up. "I'll have a list of such employees at the CIA printed out and messengered to you today, Bob."

"Thank you, ma'am."

The president sighed. "Bob, I'm afraid it's time to go public with your suspicions."

"Must I, Mr. President?"

"The press is already putting it together. Let's not wait until we're cornered. Anyway, going public might turn up some leads for you. We might get a phone call from a friend or relative with suspicions."

"I'll issue a press release this morning, Mr. President."

"Do that, but read it at a press conference. You dictate something to my secretary, and you can address the White House press corps at this morning's regular briefing."

"Yes, sir."

"Thanks, everybody, that's all." The president stood up, and everyone filed out of the room.

BOB KINNEY STOOD in the little auditorium and read his press release. "The FBI is investigating the murders of Senator Frederick Wallace, Mr. Van Vandervelt, and Mr.

Timothy Brennan, which we believe were committed by the same person."

There was a roar of questions from the reporters, which were shouted down by the White House press secretary.

Kinney continued. "We are concentrating our investigation, at the moment, on former government employees who may have acquired skills in the line of duty that are now being used to kill people."

"Questions?" the press secretary asked, and pointed at a reporter.

"Why do you think the murders are connected?"

"Because of the political connections among the victims and for other reasons I cannot go into."

The questions continued to come, and Kinney answered them as frankly as he could. Finally, the press secretary ended the questioning, and Kinney was escorted to an exit, where his car was waiting. He took off his jacket and hung it on the hook in the backseat, and it was only then he realized that he had sweated through his shirt. He was glad he didn't have to face the press every day.

• • •

WILL LEE CALLED his core aides into the Oval Office. "What do we know about Robert Kinney, the deputy director for investigations at the FBI?"

Kitty Conroy opened a file. "He's one of three or four people inside the Bureau on our list of candidates to replace Heller. All I have at the moment is a résumé, which is impressive."

"Find out more. He was just in here, and I liked him."

"What did you like about him?"

"No-nonsense, professional, has a certain gravitas."

"He did well at the press conference," somebody said.

"I didn't see that, but I could tell from his body language during the meeting that he doesn't think much of Heller, and that speaks well of him."

Kitty laughed.

"Of course, we couldn't give him the job until these right-wing murders are solved. He's in charge of the case."

"Is that what we're calling them? The right-wing murders?"

"Absolutely not," Will said. "Anyway, the press will come up with a name for them eventually."

Kitty crossed her legs, something she always did when she was about to bring up something important. "We're going to begin to get some political fallout from these killings pretty soon."

"What kind of fallout?" Will asked. "Is the right-wing going to start accusing me of ordering them murdered?"

"They already are, on some of the extreme websites," Kitty replied.

"You're kidding!"

"Of course, they hold you responsible for the kidnapping of the Lindbergh baby, too."

Everybody laughed.

"I'm not kidding. This is going to work its way up the food chain to Congress pretty soon, and we'd better be ready for it."

"Get somebody to ask a question about it at my press conference tomorrow," Will said.

"We won't have to plant anything. There'll be lots of questions."

"I suppose you're right," Will sighed.

19

THE POST OFFICE DELIVERED the mail to the Atlanta Federal Penitentiary at mid-morning, and the magazines and newspapers were hand-trucked to the library. A prisoner sorted them and put them into the racks, displacing the old issues.

Ed Rawls, who had a very good job in the library, got to the *Washington Post* first, as he always did, and his attention was drawn to the interview with the Arlington arson inspector, about the Van Vandervelt killing.

As Rawls read the piece, something began to sound very familiar. His mind traveled back to a murder that he himself had committed more than twenty years before, in Beirut. He remembered the bomb that had been specially designed and built for the purpose, the flat one with the squat switch, meant to go under a car seat, and he remembered who had designed and built it.

Rawls found a sheet of paper and an envelope and wrote a letter. He addressed it to a very special box number in the White House zip code and wrote PERSONAL AND CONFIDENTIAL on the envelope, though he had no idea if that would do any good.

He had not been this excited for a very long time.

The letter took two days to reach its destination, then it was X-rayed and sniffed by a machine designed to detect explosives. When the envelope was deemed to be safe it was routed to the first lady's office, where two secretaries opened every piece of mail and read it before deciding what the first lady should see. The secretary who received the envelope balked at opening it when she saw the PERSONAL AND CONFIDENTIAL note scrawled across the front. She handed the envelope to her older colleague.

"Should I open this? And what's that box number for the return address? It sounds familiar."

"The box number is the prisoners' return address for the Atlanta Federal Penitentiary," the older woman said. She held the envelope up to the light. "Seems to be just a piece of paper, and it's already been through security."

"Should I open it?" the younger woman persisted.

"It would probably be all right, but I'm not sure I would want to have opened it, if it turned out to be something really personal. Just put it in with the others and let the first lady deal with it."

"All right." The younger woman placed the envelope on a stack of other letters addressed to the box number and forgot about it.

KATE GOT HOME from Langley at a quarter to seven, and Will, who was already in his slippers in the family quarters, fixed her a drink and handed it to her. She accepted it, took a sip, and walked to the desk where her personal mail was placed every day. Riffling through the stack, the letter from Atlanta caught her eye; it was the first one she'd had for several months. She restacked the mail, leaving the envelope in the batch, and sat down next to her husband. "So, how was your day?"

"Pretty routine, except Kitty thinks the right-wingers are going to start blaming me for these murders."

"I didn't know you were that good a shot, or had the bomb-making skills," Kate said.

"You're probably a better candidate than I am," Will said. "You're certainly a better shot, and you have all that technical advice at the agency."

"You have a point, and I'm motivated, too. You know how I feel about those people. Who would you like me to take out next?"

Will thought about that. "How about Dr. Don Beverly Calhoun, in Atlanta," Will said. "He's featured prominently on the ACT NOW website. That son of a bitch has been annoying me since I ran against him for the Senate, and he's getting better at it."

"Will do," Kate said.

"And make it as painful as possible, please."

"Certainly."

"I hope to God nobody is bugging the family quarters," he said, and they both laughed.

The phone rang and Will picked it up.

It sounded like a long call, so Kate picked up her mail and went into her little study.

She ripped open the letter from Atlanta and read it.

> I believe I might be of use to you in figuring out who's doing those murders of right-wingers. I might even be able to name the killer, if the reward is attractive enough. You know I don't want money, but I do pine for the piney woods of Maine. Let me know if you'd like my help. Hope you are both well and happy.

Kate read the letter again then ran it through the shredder beside her desk. She didn't like hearing from Ed, and she wasn't going to bite, either. She went back into the living room, where Will was winding up his phone conversation.

He hung up. "What's for dinner?"

"You're asking *me*?" She laughed heartily.

"How about I grill us some steaks?"

"If you can get the staff out of the kitchen. And can your cholesterol level take it?"

"Walter Reed says I'm in great shape," Will replied. "And they won't be testing my cholesterol for another three months."

"Then what the hell," she said. "Let's have those steaks."

20

KATE ARRIVED AT CIA headquarters in Langley, Virginia, at 7:45 A.M. and was at her desk in the director's office by eight. Her secretary buzzed.

"Mr. Broward, from personnel, is here to see you," she said.

"Oh, yes, send him in."

Broward looked younger and more athletic than a personnel officer was supposed to look, and he carried a large cardboard box as if it were lighter than it really was. "Good morning, Director," he said.

"Just put them on the conference table in the next room," Kate replied, "and we'll go through them together." She followed him into the conference room.

"Yes, ma'am." He set the box down and took out a stack of file folders, some of them very thick. "There are eighteen printouts here, representing everyone who has left technical services during the past ten years, either retired, fired, or for any other reason. Is there anything in particular you're looking for?"

Kate pulled up a chair. "What's your first name?"

"Harold."

"It's like this, Harold: We're looking for someone with the technical skills and the motivation to have carried out the murders of Senator Wallace, Van Vandervelt, and Timothy Brennan. I'm sure you've read about them."

"Yes, ma'am."

"I'd like you to sit here and read these files and make notes on anything in any of them that might be relevant. Let me give you an example: Suppose you find in somebody's file that a man was given a hard time in one of the committees Senator Wallace served on. That's my idea of a motivation. Also, look for membership in any liberal-oriented groups—the American Civil Liberties Union, People for the American Way—any of those, plus subscriptions to publications like The Nation. Anything at all that would indicate a strong leaning to the left or an antipathy for the right. These files are going to go to the FBI, and I want to know what's in them before they leave the building."

"I understand, ma'am."

"When you're done, buzz me, and we'll talk about what you've found." She closed the door and left him to his work.

KATE WAS CONCLUDING a meeting just before lunch when her phone buzzed. "Yes?"

"It's Harold Broward, Director. I've finished."

"I'll be right with you, Harold." She concluded her business, then went into the conference room. Broward stood as she entered, and she waved him back into his seat. There were two stacks of files next to him and one thick folder before him. "Have you got something, Harold?" she asked.

"Maybe so, ma'am. At least, this guy meets the specifications pretty well."

"Tell me about him."

Broward consulted his notes. "His name is Edward Eugene Coulter. He retired two years ago at age sixty-five. He was an assistant director of technical services, having served in that department for thirty-nine years in a variety of capacities, gradually being promoted. He has expertise in firearms, explosives, drugs, document work, and almost anything else you could ask tech services for. He was a member of the ACLU, but that was his only political affiliation. He didn't subscribe to any publications, except *The New Yorker* and *Washingtonian*. He testified before the Senate Select Committee on Intelligence four years ago and was raked over the coals by Senator Wallace for his ACLU membership and for being associated with some documents that his department had prepared, which were later stolen and used in an operation against us in the Middle East."

"Now that's what I call a good fit," Kate said.

"Shall I send all this to the FBI?"

"Yes, but not yet. Call the office of Robert Kinney and tell his secretary that we're messengering the files over tomorrow. In the meantime, leave them here."

"Yes, ma'am."

Kate went back to her office and called the office of internal investigations. Fifteen minutes later, two officers stood before her desk. She handed them Coulter's file. "I want you to copy this, then conduct an immediate investigation of this man. Don't interview him, but I want to know how and where he lives his life; how much money he has; who, if anyone, he lives with; the organizations he belongs to; his hobbies; and anything else there is to know—and I want it all by nine o'clock tomorrow morning. Any questions?"

"Are we permitted to know the reason for this investigation?" one officer asked.

"He's a suspect in the right-wing murders you've been hearing about. By tomorrow afternoon, the FBI will be all over him, and if he's the killer, I want to know about it first."

"I understand," the man replied.

"Then get on it."

HELEN ENTERED Bob Kinney's office. "The CIA personnel office just called. They're sending over all the relevant files tomorrow morning."

"Good," Kinney replied. "Put a couple of people on them as soon as they arrive, and let's see if we can develop some suspects."

"There's something else," she said, laying a thick brown envelope on his desk.

"What's this?"

"When going through Senator Wallace's personal files, I found that more than two dozen cards had the president's name on them, going all the way back to when he was in college."

"Did you read them?"

"No, sir. I checked the early ones to see when they began and the later ones to see where they ended. There are notations dated as recently as a month ago."

"Thank you, Helen, I'll deal with these myself. When will you have your digest of the others prepared?"

"In a couple of days, I think."

"See that it contains no reference to the president."

"Yes, sir."

"Take a letter."

She picked up a pad and sat down. "Go ahead."

"To the President of the United States, for his eyes only: Sir, enclosed are index cards bearing your name from the personal files of Senator Frederick Wallace, the remainder of which are in my possession. To the best of my knowledge, no one except Senator Wallace has read them, certainly not I nor anyone else at the Bureau. The files bearing your name are not evidence in any case, and you need not return them to me. They may be disposed of as you wish, and no copies have been made. Sincerely, etc.

"Have the package hand-delivered to the president personally by an agent and have him sign for them. If he's busy, have the messenger wait until he can receive them. Let his secretary know to expect our agent."

"Yes, sir." She went to do her work and returned shortly with the letter for him to sign.

He signed it and sent the package on its way.

21

SPECIAL AGENT KERRY SMITH arrived at the White House and, after identifying himself twice and having his package X-rayed, he was admitted to the office of the secretary to the president.

Smith had been at the Washington headquarters of the Bureau for less than a month, after tours in Atlanta, Houston, and Seattle. He thought of himself as a supremely competent FBI agent, but being inside the White House rattled him. When he reached the office of Cora Parker, he was sweating.

"What's the matter with you?" she asked.

"It's hot in here."

She got up and walked over to the thermostat on the wall of her office. "It's sixty-eight degrees. Everybody else is wearing sweaters. Are you sick? I'm not having any viruses in the Oval Office."

"I'm not sick, I assure you."

She sat back down at her desk. "Is this your first time in the White House?"

"Yes, ma'am."

"That explains it."

"What?"

"The sweating. You've got the first-time-in-the-White-House sweats, that's all."

"Ma'am, I just want to get the president's signature on a receipt, and then I'm out of here."

"What have you got for him?"

"Didn't Agent Kinney's office call?"

"Yes, but they didn't say what was in the package." She held her hand out. "Let me have it."

"No, ma'am, it's for the president's eyes only."

"I'm not going to open it, I just want to feel it."

"Feel it?"

"That's what I said. Do your instructions say anything about somebody besides the president feeling it?"

"No, ma'am, but it's already been X-rayed and passed."

"Give it to me."

He handed her the package, but when she picked up a letter opener, he snatched it back.

"Boy, you nearly got a letter opener right through your hand."

"You can't open it, ma'am."

She burned a look right through him. "You sit down over there and wait until I can get to you."

He sat down, holding the package primly on his knees.

FORTY MINUTES LATER, a door beside Cora Parker's desk opened, and the president stepped through it. "Cora, will you please make some time for Senator Kennedy this afternoon, and let his office know when?"

Agent Smith leapt to his feet, attracting the president's attention.

Will Lee turned and looked at the young man. "Who's this?"

"Special Agent Kerry Smith of the FBI, sir. I have a package for you."

"Just give it to Ms. Parker," he replied and turned back toward the Oval Office.

"I'm sorry, sir, but Agent Kinney has

instructed me to deliver it to you, personally, and to no one else."

Will paused. "Let me explain how this works," he said. "One of these days, somebody is going to smuggle a bomb into the White House, and when they do, I'm determined that it's going to be Ms. Parker who opens it, not me."

Cora Parker stood up. "Mr. President, I quit," she said. "I'm not going to be a sniffer dog or a canary in a coal mine for anybody, not even the president of the United States."

"Well, in that case, Agent Smith," Will said, "you'd better give it to me. Ms. Parker is not cooperating."

Smith handed the package to the president and dug in his pocket for the receipt and a pen.

"Ms. Parker will sign for it," the president said. "That's not an exploding pen, is it?"

"No, sir," Agent Smith replied.

"How do I know that?" Cora demanded.

"Oh, all right, I'll sign for it," the president said. He scrawled his name on the receipt and handed it back to Smith. "Thank you, Agent Smith."

"Good morning, sir." He spun around and fled the office.

Will and Cora Parker burst out laughing.

"It's his first visit to the White House," she said.

"I figured," Will replied.

Will sat down in a comfortable chair and ripped open the package. He read Bob Kinney's letter, then he began to go through the index cards.

There, in a copperplate hand learned in a South Carolina schoolroom seventy-odd years ago, was a concise but surprisingly accurate history of his life, beginning with his dropping out of law school, at the behest of the dean, and spending a year in Ireland. His affair with a young schoolteacher named Concepta Lydon was mentioned—how the hell did Freddie find out about that? he wondered.

His affair with Kate was covered, too, much of it at a time when he had thought nobody knew about it. He felt his ears burning. He read quickly through the rest of the cards, finding nothing that caused him any great concern. Finally, he walked back into Cora's office and dropped the cards into her shredder.

"Well, what could that be?" she asked, reaching for the cards.

He slapped her wrist lightly. "It would only embarrass you," he said. He stayed until the remainder of the cards had fed into the shredder.

That night over dinner, Will told Kate about Freddie's files. "He knew all about us when we thought it was a secret," he said.

"How much did he know?"

"Pretty much everything."

She looked shocked. "Not what we did in bed."

"No, at least he didn't make notes about it. He outlined the whole business with Ed Rawls, too. You should have told me about it at the time."

"Come on, Will, aren't you glad I didn't? I mean, really?"

"Well, yes. At least I could have truthfully denied knowing about it."

"That can be important sometimes." She wasn't going to tell him about the most recent letter from Ed, either. "What did you do with the file?"

"I shredded it."

"Before I had a chance to read it?"

"There were things that didn't concern you in the file."

"Aha! Other women!"

"Well, yes, but long before I met you. It was all very innocent."

"Innocent?"

"Well, maybe not completely innocent. You would have approved."

"I doubt it," she said, kicking him under the table.

"Well, that's my best guess."

"We'll never know now, will we?"

Will beamed at her. "I guess not."

22

HELEN WALKED INTO Kinney's office and deposited a thick file on his desk. "Two agents and I went through all the files the CIA sent over, and this is the only one that we found interesting. I think you should read it."

"Have a seat," Kinney said, opening the file. He speed-read it, every page, then closed the file. "Send your two agents over to Judge Henry's chambers with the file, and tell them to get a search warrant for the home, vehicles, and any other property of Edward Eugene Coulter. I want it by lunchtime. In the meantime, assemble a search party and a tech team. We're going to do this right."

"Yes, sir," she said, then left his office.

Kinney took a deep breath. His hunch had

been right; their man was a federal retiree with a tech background, and before the day was over, they would have the son of a bitch in custody. He began thinking about retirement, but he hadn't gotten far when his phone buzzed.

"There's a Nancy Kimble on line one. Do you know her?"

"Yes, I'll talk to her." He pressed the button. "I was just thinking about you," he lied.

"That's a lie, but a nice one. I can see my way to get to D.C. for a few days. Are you receptive to that?"

"Receptive isn't a strong enough word. How soon?"

"Tomorrow?"

"We may have something to celebrate. I'll look forward to it." He gave her his address. "I'll leave a key for you at the front desk."

"Bye-bye." She hung up.

He liked it that she was brief on the phone. He hated phone conversations, except to exchange important information or to arrange meetings. His phone buzzed again, and he picked it up.

"It's the president," Helen said.

He nearly asked the president of what, but

he picked up the phone. "Good morning, Mr. President."

"Good morning, Bob. I want to thank you for your kindness in sending me that information yesterday."

"I was glad to do it, sir."

"There was nothing there I didn't already know, except how much the gentleman knew, and that was a surprise. It made interesting reading. How are you coming on the murder investigation?"

"We have a hot lead right now, Mr. President, a retired CIA employee with exactly the right background. I've already requested a search warrant."

"I'd appreciate a call when you know if it pans out," the president said.

"Of course, sir."

"Good morning to you, Bob." The president hung up.

It was the first call that Kinney had ever received from a president, and it left him a little breathless. Suddenly, he remembered that he had lied to the man. He had, after all, copied the files, and he made a mental note to shred the pages pertaining to the president when he returned home that night.

Kinney felt better than he had in months.

He had a suspect, his girl was on her way to D.C., and he had just taken a call from the president.

THE HOUSE WAS ON a pretty street in Arlington, Virginia, a comfortable, old-fashioned brick structure surrounded by other, similar houses. It was on a half-acre lot with a three-car garage, which set it apart from its neighbors, and one garage door was half again as big as the others. "Look at that door," Kinney said as they made their pass. "He has an RV. We were right about that. I hope you didn't talk to any of his neighbors."

"No, sir," Smith replied "We've stayed away from the house. Besides the RV he has two cars—an Audi Six and one of the newer VW Bugs. He owns four handguns, all licensed."

"You and I will make the first approach. We'll radio when we've secured Mr. Coulter. I don't want to arrive with a SWAT team, especially since he's armed. Let's try not to alarm him."

"Yes, sir. You want me to park now?"

"Go around the block once more. I want to

see the house from the back, if it's possible."

"It's not, but we've got half a dozen agents ready to go in through the back door."

"Keep them calm," he said to the team in the backseat of his car.

"Yes, sir," an agent replied. He spoke into a handheld radio. "Everybody relax. The deputy director and Smith are going in first. They'll call us when the house is secure." The radio crackled with terse responses.

They were coming around the block again. "Just pull right into the driveway," Kinney said. "We'll get out of the car real casual-like, then go slowly to the front door and ring the bell like citizens."

"Yes, sir." Smith swung the sedan into the driveway and stopped.

"You two stay here and be inconspicuous," Kinney said to the two men in the backseat. "Let's go, Smith." He got out of the car and stretched as if he'd driven a long way, looked around the neighborhood, then slowly made his way to the house and up the front steps. The doorbell was a friendly chime, but it wasn't answered immediately. Kinney looked at Smith. "Are they home?"

"The first team in the neighborhood talked to the mailman, who says they're always home in the mornings."

The front door opened. A small woman in her sixties stood there. "Yes?"

"Good morning," Kinney said, smiling. "Are you Mrs. Coulter?"

"Yes, I am."

"My name is Robert Kinney. I'm from the FBI. May I see your husband, please?" He didn't flash a badge, didn't want it to seem too official.

"Of course. Please come in. He's in the den, having his lunch."

Kinney followed her across the living room toward another door. He could hear the sound of a TV set—CNN.

"Now?" Smith asked quietly.

"Not yet," Kinney replied.

They emerged into a room lined with books, with a large projection TV in one corner. Across the room a man sat in a recliner, his feet up, a tray in his lap.

"Ted, this is Mr. Kinney, from the FBI," Mrs. Coulter said. "He wants to talk to you."

Coulter looked up. He looked younger than his sixty-seven years, with black hair and an unlined face. "Morning," he said. "Forgive me if I don't get up."

"That's quite all right, Mr. Coulter," Kinney said, producing his badge. "I'm Bob Kinney, this is Special Agent Kerry Smith."

"How do you do?" Coulter said. "Betty, will you get my thing for me?" He held out his tray and she took it away and went toward the kitchen.

Kinney nodded at Smith to follow her. "Give Mrs. Coulter a hand, will you, Kerry."

"What's this about, Agent Kinney?" Coulter asked.

Kinney reached into an inside pocket and produced the legal document. "Mr. Coulter, I have a search warrant for your home, your property, and your vehicles." He handed it to Coulter, who opened it and began reading.

Kinney waited for him to finish. "Do you understand the warrant?"

"Yes, I do," Coulter replied, "though I confess I'm baffled. Why do you want to search my place?"

"I'm afraid I can't go into that right now, Mr. Coulter, but we'll be as quick and efficient as we can, and I'd appreciate your cooperation."

Coulter waved a hand. "Help yourself," he said.

At that moment, Smith returned followed by Mrs. Coulter. She was carrying a familiar object, and she set it down next to Mr. Coulter's recliner.

Kinney nearly flinched. The object was a walker. Coulter moved forward in his chair and grasped the aluminum framework, then hoisted himself painfully to his feet.

"You'll have to forgive my husband," Mrs. Coulter said. "He had a pretty bad stroke late last year, and he still has trouble getting around."

Kinney watched Coulter move, and it was obvious that his right side had not yet completely recovered from paralysis. He waved Smith over. "Go outside and use the radio. I want only four agents inside, no weapons displayed," he whispered. "It looks like we're in the wrong place."

"This won't take long," he said to Coulter.

"Take your time," Coulter replied. "This sort of makes my day."

23

KINNEY DIDN'T LIKE MAKING the phone call, but he did. The president couldn't take the call but returned it half an hour later.

"Tell me the news, Bob," Will Lee said.

"Mr. President, I'm sorry, but our man was the wrong man."

"I'm sorry to hear it."

"He looked perfect, but the man had a stroke last year and, in spite of a lot of therapy, he still has to use a walker, and his right side is partially paralyzed. He's right-handed, too."

"You checked with his doctors?"

"Yes, we went over his medical records and talked with his physiotherapist. Our search of the house turned up absolutely nothing except four handguns, all registered and legal."

"Well, keep at it, Bob. It's only a matter of time before this man kills again."

"I know, sir, and we'll give the case everything we've got."

The president hung up.

Kinney was discovering that he did not like disappointing presidents.

He called a meeting of his team, and when they were assembled, he spoke. "Let's go through the whole thing again, every detail of every murder. There's bound to be something we've missed."

The team discussed every murder at length, and when they had finished, they had come up with nothing new.

"Have we found any other suspects at any other federal agency?" Kinney asked.

"No, sir," the man in charge replied. "Coulter was perfect, but he's obviously not our guy."

Kinney thought for a moment. "Suppose he faked the stroke and is lying to his therapist about his paralysis? It's elaborate, but it's an excellent way of diverting suspicion from himself."

An agent spoke up. "I spoke to his neurologist, who treated him for the acute effects of the stroke, and the man says there's no way he could fake what he went through. Coulter nearly died. His physiotherapist says he's worked extremely hard but has recovered very slowly. Faking is not an option."

"I want a team on Coulter at all times. If he shows the slightest sign of not being paralyzed, we'll be on top of it. See if we can get a wiretap warrant, too. I want us to listen to his phone conversations."

One of the senior men spoke up. "Bob, this is a real stretch. The only benefit I can see in it is if, rather *when* there's another murder, if we could establish Coulter's whereabouts at the time, we could prove he's not involved."

"Do it," Kinney said.

KATHARINE RULE LEE sat at the head of her conference table and looked at the people around her. "Do you agree with the FBI's conclusions about Coulter?" No one spoke. "Anybody?"

Finally, an officer spoke up. "Reluctantly, yes. God knows it would have been easy if

Coulter had been the man, but he's clearly not. He's just not physically capable of doing what this killer has done."

"Could he have done these murders, using an accomplice?" Kate asked.

"Possibly," the man replied, "but I have to consider it very unlikely. Certainly, Coulter has the expertise to tell somebody how to build the bomb and use the poison, and lots of people are good shots, but we can't find anyone in Coulter's background who would be a candidate. We've gone through all of his periodic personnel reviews and polygraph tests. We've looked at all his known associates and at his personal politics, which are pretty much nonexistent. The man's not even registered to vote. Before his stroke, he and his wife had no interests more boisterous than bingo at their church and a regular bridge game. They're dull as dishwater."

"Certainly, his employee evaluations back that up," Kate said, fingering his file. "I've never read anything duller. When he was still on active duty, the man actually recorded the daily soap operas, so he could watch them at weekends."

"There's no intellect at work there," somebody said.

"Is everyone satisfied that there's no current or former employee of the Agency who comes even close to fitting the profile for this killer?"

There was a murmur of assent from the group.

"All right, then: I can tell the president that the man is not from our ranks." She stood up. "Thanks, everybody."

BACK AT HER DESK, Kate called Will. He came on the line immediately.

"What's up?"

"I just wanted you to know that our people here have reviewed the Coulter file and every other possible suspect employed by the Agency, both now and in the past, and that none of our people fit the FBI profile of the right-wing killer."

"You feel certain of that?"

"As certain as we can be. We've given it our best shot, and there's just nobody. Apart from Coulter, we don't even have anyone to interview."

"Thanks for letting me know," Will said.

"I'll see you this evening. You going to be on time for dinner?"

"I should be, if nothing comes up."

"See you then." The president hung up, and the first lady went back to work.

24

Dr. Don Beverly Calhoun wrapped up his Sunday morning sermon as he often did, casting aspersions on the patriotism of the president of the United States and the Democrats in Congress, and in his wrap-up prayer he gave thanks for the guardians of the American faith on the right wing of his own party. The service was carried on one hundred and twenty-one television cable and satellite systems around the country.

As the choir intoned a protracted amen, Calhoun stepped down from his pulpit and walked quickly up the aisle toward the rear of his huge church, his eyes downcast as if in walking prayer, so as to greet his congregation one by one as they left the church—or, at least, those members of the congregation who wished to delay their Sunday dinners for an hour or so in order to have their flesh pressed by the reverend.

Calhoun took up his station at the end of a funnel created by a series of brass stands and velvet ropes, and volunteers helped herd the crowd into the increasingly small space. A volunteer stood on each side of the reverend, the better to assist individuals in not stopping to chat, since their spiritual leader's time was more valuable than theirs.

The first handshakers were those who occupied the rearmost pews in the great tabernacle, and most noticeable among them to the reverend was a creature who nearly turned his stomach. He was of medium height, but of great girth, wearing a loud necktie with matching suspenders and no coat. He sported a waxed mustache, the ends of which pointed heavenward, and the worst toupee the reverend had ever encountered—a reddish brown that contrasted sharply with the gray, nearly white fringe of the man's own hair, which flopped over huge ears. He had protruding front teeth and wore heavy, black eyeglasses with extremely thick lenses.

He reached for the reverend's hand with

both of his, grabbing it in a viselike grip that made the preacher's eyes water.

"Yes, yes, Reverend," the man said, "you preached the truth!"

And then he was gone, whisked down the front steps by volunteers, leaving the reverend to nurse his crunched hand. The man walked with a pronounced waddle, as befitted someone of his girth.

The reverend looked down at his hand, and to his astonishment, found that it was bleeding from a tiny wound. He whipped a handkerchief from his pocket and dabbed at it, then faced the coming throng. So many more hands to shake, and his hand had been nearly disabled. "The miserable son of a bitch!" the reverend muttered under his breath, startling the little old lady who was next in line.

Ted waddled through the huge parking lot and, near its outermost fringe, boarded the RV, where he stripped off his clothes, the padding, the teeth, the mustache, the ears, glasses, and two wigs. Shortly, he was on his way north on Peachtree Road, toward the highway around the perimeter of Atlanta and the interstate north.

• • •

KINNEY WAS SLEEPING soundly in his own bed, with Nancy Kimble's naked body intertwined with his own, when the phone rang. He reached for it automatically. "Kinney," he mumbled.

"It's Kerry Smith, Mr. Kinney," the younger man said. "I've got the duty this morning, and we've had a call from the trauma center at Piedmont Hospital, in Atlanta. They've got a patient presenting with similar symptoms to those of Timothy Brennan's, last week."

"Who is it?" Kinney asked, knowing it wasn't going to be anyone anonymous.

"Dr. Don Beverly Calhoun, the television evangelist. He had just gotten home from his Sunday morning service when he became ill, and his wife called an ambulance. The hospital wants to know if there's any treatment for what killed Brennan."

"Give me the name of the doctor in charge and his phone number."

Smith dictated the information.

"I'll call you back," Kinney said. He disentangled himself from Nancy, swung his feet onto the floor, opened a bedside drawer and reached for a thick address book. He dialed a very long telephone number and waited while it rang.

"Carpenter," a woman's voice said.

"It's Bob Kinney at the FBI, in Washington," he said. "We met when you were over with your boss a few months ago."

"Of course. How are you, Bob?"

"Terrible. You remember, some years back, you had an incident in London where a Bulgarian dissident was poisoned by somebody from that country's intelligence service, stabbed with a sharp umbrella tip?"

"Yes, I remember that incident."

"I seem to recall that your people were working on some sort of antidote to whatever the Bulgarians used."

"Yes, we had a medical team on that for several months."

"Were they successful?"

"They think so, but we've never had another case on which to try it."

"I may have one for you now. Do you have a pencil and paper handy?"

"Yes."

"This is the number of the physician in charge of the case, at Piedmont Hospital in Atlanta. Please contact the relevant person on your end and have him or her communicate directly with the doctor." He read out the name and number, plus his own number. "Will you let me know how this comes out?"

"I'll make some calls and get back to you as quickly as I can," Carpenter said, then hung up.

Kinney hung up the phone and sat on the edge of the bed, shivering in the air-conditioning. He called Smith back. "We may have some medical help from the British intelligence services," he said. "They'll call me back. Now tell me everything you know."

"Not much, I'm afraid. Dr. Calhoun complained of a bone-crushing handshake from one of his congregation, standing on the front steps of his church after the service, and he found himself with a small, bleeding wound on his hand."

"Have you been in touch with the agent in charge of the Atlanta office?"

"I've paged him, and I'm waiting for his call now."

"Get him and his people on this, and find me some witnesses to this event. There must have been a lot of people around. Isn't this preacher on television?"

"Yes, the service was televised nationally."

"Find out if he was still on television when this guy shook his hand. We may have a shot at a picture of the guy, or at least a description from a witness. There had to be a bunch of witnesses around."

"I'm on it," Smith said, and hung up.

Kinney crawled back into bed and gathered up Nancy in his arms.

"You're freezing," she said, rubbing the back of his neck.

"You heard?"

"Sort of."

"Looks like we've got another murder on our hands, or at least an attempt." He sat up. "Excuse me a minute." He grabbed a robe, went to his computer, and logged onto the Internet, then to the ACT NOW website.

Sure enough, a big *X* had been drawn through the photograph of Dr. Don Beverly Calhoun. The phone rang, and he picked it up. "Kinney."

"It's Carpenter. I got hold of our lead medical man on the golf course. He's calling your doctor in Atlanta. Apparently, they came up with a possible antidote, and he's going to have somebody fax it to the Atlanta doctor. It can be formulated in the hospital pharmacy.

It's the fastest way to get the man treated, and, apparently, time is of the essence."

"Thank you, Carpenter," Kinney said. "I'll let you know if this works." He hung up and dialed the White House, but the president was unavailable. "Tell him Robert Kinney called, and there's been another attempted murder. The victim is Dr. Don Beverly Calhoun. He's being treated at an Atlanta hospital. This is my number, if he needs to reach me."

WILL PUT DOWN the phone at Camp David and turned to Kate. "Now I feel terrible," he said.

"Why?"

"You remember that I sort of wished that Dr. Calhoun would be the next victim?"

"Yes."

"He is."

25

DR. DON BEVERLY CALHOUN looked at his wife through swollen eyes. "Where is that fucking doctor?" he demanded.

"Donald, watch your mouth," his wife replied primly.

"Where is he?"

"He had to take a phone call from somebody who might be able to help," she said.

The reverend looked at the clock on the wall. "That was an hour and a half ago."

"The prayer circle is outside," she said. "I want to bring them in here and get them praying for you."

"Tell them to pray out there," the reverend replied testily. "Tell them the Lord can hear them, wherever they're praying from."

"You're clearly not yourself," she said. "It

must be the fever. I'm going to bring them in here now, so you compose yourself."

The reverend tried to object, but she was already out the door. He felt another wave of fever and thrashed in the bed, but his wrists had been restrained. "Goddammit!" he screamed. "Get that doctor in here!" He looked toward the door to find a group of men and women, shocked looks on their faces, filing into the room.

"Reverend, we're here to pray for you," a woman said.

"Get the hell out of here!" the reverend shouted, and they fled.

His wife marched back into the room and slapped him sharply across the face. "You get ahold of yourself!" she screamed at him.

Taken aback, the reverend shut up, just in time for the doctor's arrival.

"We've had some help from Britain," the doctor said, holding up a syringe. "Are you willing to try it?"

"I'm not going to be a guinea pig for anybody!" the reverend shouted.

"He's delirious," his wife said. "Give it to him. I'll sign the consent form."

A nurse supplied the form, and Mrs. Calhoun signed it.

"I won't take it!" the reverend yelled.

"Oh shut up!" his wife said. "Doctor, give it to him."

The reverend tried to writhe away as the doctor stepped forward, but the man simply jabbed the syringe into his IV and stepped back.

"How long will it take to work?" Mrs. Calhoun asked.

"I don't know," the doctor said. "I don't know if it will work at all. Apparently, Dr. Calhoun is the only human being ever to receive it."

"I'm a goddamned guinea pig!" Dr. Don screamed, tears rolling down his cheeks.

KINNEY SAT at his kitchen table eating a chicken Caesar salad that Nancy had prepared. Both were wearing only terrycloth robes, which Kinney had purchased for the occasion.

"Let's go back to bed," Kinney said.

"You are awful," she replied. "Eat your lunch."

"I can't help it."

"Where are you getting all this sexual energy?"

"I've been saving it up for about four years," he said.

She stroked his cheek. "Poor baby."

He pushed back his chair, swept her into his arms, and marched back into the bedroom.

"We'll starve," she said, kissing him.

"It's worth it." He ripped off both their robes and took her. They were both in climax when the phone began to ring. Kinney answered on the tenth ring. "Yeah?" he panted.

"It's Smith," Kerry said. "Are you all right? You sound out of breath."

"I just got in from jogging. What's up?"

"Calhoun is responding to the treatment the Brits sent," Smith said. "His temperature is down nearly to normal, and he's taking solid food."

"Good news. What did we get from the TV cameras, anything?"

"No, the handshaking on the front steps is not televised. However, there was a security camera working. The tape is on its way here."

"You get out to Peachtree DeKalb Airport and charter an airplane. I want to look at it with you."

"Yes, sir, I'll be in Washington just as soon as I can."

"Call me when you know your ETA, and I'll meet you in my office."

"Will do." Smith hung up.

Kinney collapsed into Nancy's arms. "We may have caught a break," he said.

"Oh, good," she replied. "Are you ready to fuck me again?"

"Mercy," he cried. "Mercy!"

She dissolved in laughter. "Well, I'm glad to know you can be worn out."

"Give me a few minutes," he replied.

"Oh, God."

KINNEY WATCHED as a TV and a VCR on a stand were rolled into his office and plugged in. "Have you seen this?" he asked Smith.

"No, sir. I left for the airport the minute the tape was in my hands." He switched on the TV and shoved the cassette into the machine. An image, in black and white, appeared, sharp and clear. A series of poles and velvet ropes were being set up on the church steps. The shot was from above, at a nice angle.

"Thank God Calhoun's people are using

high-resolution equipment," Kinney said. "I was afraid we'd get something like a convenience-store image."

"Here comes Calhoun," Smith said, "and here comes the crowd."

"Where are the marshals?"

"Calhoun declined federal help, said he'd provide his own security. A lot of good it did him."

The man was sixth or seventh in line, waiting patiently to move forward.

"Jesus, what kind of clown is that?" Kinney asked.

"A clown in a clown suit," Smith replied. "He can't be for real."

"Get our video people on this and see if they can get an image of him without all the disguise." Kinney watched as the man stepped up to Dr. Don and grabbed his hand. Calhoun's face reflected shock and pain, and the man was hustled away by attendants. "Well, at least we have a clear image of a man wearing a disguise," Kinney said. "Did our Atlanta people interview any witnesses?"

"Yes. The people behind the guy in line saw him, but from behind. We've managed to get one person who saw him in the parking lot."

"Anybody see him get into a vehicle?"

"No, but there was an RV in the line of cars waiting to get out of the lot. There are always RVs there on a Sunday," Smith said. "People come from all over to hear the reverend preach."

"So we have nothing specific—a plate, a brand of RV?"

"No, I'm afraid not. Something occurs to me, though."

"What?"

"Our man is running out of ways to kill. He's repeated himself, now."

"Thank God he didn't use a bomb. The carnage at the church would have been horrific."

"Yes, it would have."

"Get our video people and an artist on that image right away," Kinney said. "Call people at home and get them in here. I want to know what he looks like without the getup."

26

JEB STUART CALHOUN of South Carolina, newly that state's senior senator, rose in the well of the Senate to address his colleagues.

"Mr. President," he intoned, bowing slightly toward the senator who was presiding that day, "we have now reached a new low in the meanness of politics. The left in this country is now stooping, almost weekly, to actual political assassination!"

A dozen senators were on their feet, shouting "No!" and "Shame!" above a general uproar, as the presiding senator banged his gavel for order. Nearly ten minutes passed before quiet was restored.

"And," Calhoun went on, "responsibility for these acts must be laid squarely at the feet of the president of the United States!"

This time the uproar was so loud and the epithets hurled so abusive, that the chair was unable to restore order. After all else had failed, he declared the Senate in adjournment, banged his gavel, and walked out of the chamber. Capitol guards were called in to protect Senator Calhoun and walk him back to his office, while other senators threw newspapers and other trash at him.

WILL AND KATE watched the scene together on the evening news. "I don't believe it," Will said. "I knew it was coming, but I still don't believe it."

"I think it might actually help," Kate said.

"How?"

"Calhoun has disgraced himself by uttering those words, and that will make it more difficult for others to utter them. By the way, did you know that he and Dr. Don are first cousins?"

"No, but I can't say I'm surprised."

"Their daddies are brothers. That kind of insanity must run in the family."

"Dr. Don is recovering nicely after the injection of the British antidote," Will said glumly. "But Kinney reports that the security camera tape from Atlanta wasn't much help in identifying the suspect."

"He has hairy wrists," Kate said.

"What?"

"The suspect has thick, gray hair on his wrists, unless he was wearing a wrist wig, too. That was the only part of his body, except for his neck, that was of any help to the FBI. I read the report this afternoon."

"His neck and his wrists?"

"He was wearing two wigs, a false mustache, maybe false ears, and heavy, horn-rimmed glasses. It's surprising how the glasses helped conceal his face. They made it difficult to tell much about his nose, which is normally a major ID point. They could tell from the size of his neck and wrists that he wasn't anywhere near as heavy as he had made himself look with the padding, so they put his weight at between one-fifty and one-eighty."

"Such a big range?"

"His neck and wrists may be larger than natural from exercise, but then again, maybe not. Oh, his height is about six feet. They got that by comparing him to Dr. Don, who is also six feet. That's if our guy wasn't wearing lifts in his shoes, which he may well have been."

"I don't believe it. They got the guy on high-resolution videotape and all they can figure is his neck, his wrists, and his weight within thirty pounds?"

"And that's just a guess. This guy is very smart, Will, and he's not going to be easy to catch. I feel sorry for Kinney, because the whole thing rests on his shoulders, and he's got almost nothing to work with. I think the profile he's drawn up is good, but since he was unable to find a current or recent employee of federal law enforcement or intelligence who matches it, he's at a dead end."

"He's still got this guy in Silver Spring—what's his name?"

"Coulter. Coulter died this afternoon."

"What?"

"He had a second stroke, died before the ambulance could get there. He was getting out of his car, with his wife's help, when he collapsed. The two FBI agents who were watching his house called an ambulance and tried to help, but it was no use."

"So now we have no suspects at all?"

"I'm afraid that's the case."

"Poor Kinney. And I had such hopes for him."

Bob Kinney, drained of sexual energy, had kissed Nancy Kimble goodbye and put her in her car for the drive back to South Carolina. Now he was at his desk, staring straight ahead, when Agent Kerry Smith knocked and entered.

"Good morning, sir."

"Hmmm?"

"Sir, are you all right?"

"Just tired, Kerry."

"You can't let this get you down, Mr. Kinney. We're going to get something on this guy soon, and when we do, he'll be toast."

"You know Coulter's dead?"

"Yes, sir. I told you, remember?"

"Oh, yes." Kinney made an effort to bring himself fully alert. "What have we failed to look at, Kerry? What have we failed to do?"

"I think we've looked at and done everything anyone could reasonably expect us to do, in the circumstances, sir."

"There are two things wrong with your statement, Kerry: One, we are not expected to act reasonably, only effectively; two, nobody cares what the circumstances are, they just want results."

"That's unfair, sir. We have to work within the constraints of the evidence."

"No we don't. A prosecutor has to work within the constraints of the evidence; investigators have to be brilliant, even when there is no evidence."

"Well, we have some, sir."

"Oh, yes? Tell me."

"He has hairy wrists and a strong neck."

"That's not going to look very good on a wanted poster. We can't even put this guy on our list of top ten criminals, since we don't have a name or a description. How do you organize a nationwide search for someone with hairy wrists and a strong neck?"

"Well, not nationwide, sir, just the Eastern seaboard, from Atlanta to New York. I-95, basically."

"So we put out an APB to the state troopers along the route, telling them to look out for a suspect with hairy wrists and a strong neck, driving an RV?"

"Well, we're not exactly sure about the RV, are we?"

"All right, Kerry, put out a bulletin to all the state police units that patrol I-95. Anytime they stop an RV, they're to pay particular attention to the wrists and neck of the driver and report any similarities to our description at once. And for Christ's sake, don't put this out to the press. It'll make us sound like idiots."

"Yes, sir."

"And what's wrong with our computer people? Why haven't they tracked down the ACT NOW website?"

"It's not as easy as it seems, sir. The guy keeps changing things, so that we have to contact it through different servers."

"I have no idea what that means."

"It's as if we went to search a house for him and he'd moved to another house."

"Oh."

"They're still working on it, though. We might get lucky."

27

KATE HAD BEEN AT HER DESK in Langley for half the morning when the mail arrived. She had a personal mailbox at CIA headquarters, just as she did at the White House, but mail rarely arrived that way. This morning, though, there was one letter, and she recognized it immediately.

Kate,

How long does this have to go on? How many people have to die before you will address the issue at hand? I can help you take this guy out of circulation within a very short time, if only you will help me. I'm old, I'm ill, and I don't want to spend my last days in this joint.

You ask, how could a man in prison help to catch a rampaging murderer on the outside? The answer is, I once knew him, and I recognize his technique. I want to be a good citizen, but I want to die free, too. Help me help you.

Kate slid the letter and its envelope into the shredder, which, after shredding, reduced the paper to ashes. First of all, she didn't believe Ed Rawls; second, she was still extremely angry with him because of his betrayal of the Agency. He had been her mentor for all of her early career, and a close, personal friend.

She thought about it some more, and decided that she did believe Ed. But if Ed knew this guy, it would have been through work. She might even have known him, too. Still, they had run all the records of former employees of the technical services department and had come up with nothing. She buzzed her secretary. "Please call Harold Broward in personnel and ask him to come up here soonest."

Broward appeared within minutes. "Yes, ma'am?"

"Harold, I want you to do another personnel search—same time parameters, but I want you to expand it from technical services to the whole of operations. Some of our agents have had the training it would take to pull off these murders, and I want to isolate all possible candidates."

"Yes, ma'am."

"How long do you need?"

"We're talking about more files, but I'll try to have something for you by the end of the day."

"Bring all the files to me, just like last time, and we'll go through them together."

"Yes, ma'am." Broward went back to his office, and Kate called Bob Kinney.

"Good morning," he said.

"Morning. It's occurred to me that some of our operational people have the training it would take to pull off these murders, so I'm expanding our search to other areas of the Agency."

"Excellent idea," Kinney replied. "I'll look forward to the results."

"I suggest you do the same at the FBI and at the other agencies you've been looking at."

"I'll issue the instructions immediately, Ms. Rule, and I appreciate your suggesting this."

Kate hung up and tried to think about something else.

KINNEY WAS ANNOYED that he had not thought of this; it was simple enough. He called Kerry Smith in and issued the instructions.

"I'll get on it, sir, and a man in computer operations has some information for you. Shall I send him up?"

"Right away, please."

THE MAN LOOKED LIKE no more than a boy. He had an awful haircut and a scraggly beard. The kid could not be an agent; he would never have made it through Quantico, Kinney thought. "What have you got for me? And skip the gobbledygook, because I won't understand it."

"Okay . . ." the kid began.

Kinney hated people who started sentences with "Okay . . ."

"Okay . . . this guy is very smart. He changes his setup daily, sometimes more often, which makes it harder for us to trace him back to his home server. But I've got it, now."

"Let's have it."

"Have you ever heard of Sealand?"

"No. Sounds like a contradiction in terms."

"It's an island in the North Sea, off the coast of England."

"What does this have to do with our suspect?"

"As I understand it, we don't have a suspect, exactly, but let me finish."

Kinney sighed.

"A few years ago a group of—I don't know—anarchists, radicals, whatever . . ."

Kinney hated the use of "whatever."

". . . landed on this island, claimed it for themselves, and proclaimed it the Republic of Sealand. They waited for the Brits to come get them, so they could get on TV, but they didn't bother, and they haven't bothered since. So these people stayed on the island, and to support themselves, they set up an Internet support and cell phone service, offering confidential Internet access to individuals who didn't want to be traced. It's sort of like the electronic equivalent of a

Swiss bank. Our guy's website is based there."

"Can you hack into it and find out who he is?"

"Well . . . not yet is the best answer I can give you. It involves more than hacking into his website. That doesn't contain his identity. It involves breaking into the Sealand company records for the information, and they have very good and constantly updated security software in place."

"And, I suppose, he could be registered under a false name."

"Possible, but not likely."

"Oh? Why would he use his own name when he could use an alias?"

"Because the Sealand people are punctilious about checking out their subscribers. They don't want to be liable for, say, protecting a pedophile or, as in our case, a murderer."

"But by concealing his identity, they are protecting him."

"Of course, but the way they see it, as long as he's registered under a real name, they're not protecting him."

"That doesn't make any sense at all."

"I didn't say these people were logical,

though they've been smart enough to succeed at what they're doing."

"Can we get a court order through the British?"

"Since they consider themselves a separate nation, they would ignore a court order, and it would require a good-sized police or military operation on the part of the Brits to enforce it. The Brits regard Sealand as something less than a flea on a dog, and, since the island isn't much more than a rock in the sea, with no harbor, it has no strategic or tactical significance for them. There's a case on record of Interpol's trying to track down one of their subscribers, and they hit a stone wall with the Brits."

"So what you're saying is, that if we want the name and address of this murderer, we're going to have to launch a military invasion of Sealand?"

"That's about the size of it. And although the Brits obviously care nothing about Sealand, they might take umbrage if a foreign nation invaded what is, after all, British soil."

"An international incident," Kinney muttered.

"Exactly."

"How does one communicate with these people?"

"They started their own cellular phone company some time back, and they're plugged into all the usual networks. You can call or fax them—I can get the numbers—or you can email them."

"All right, give my secretary the fax number, and thanks for your help."

"You bet," the kid said, then left.

Kinney dictated a letter to the Sealand Company requesting the name and address of the operator of the website, and gave his reasons.

"Fax it," he said. "Let's see what happens."

28

KATE CLOSED THE LAST of the stack of files and looked at Broward. "It's surprising how mundane are the lives of people who used to be spies," she said. "We've got a man running a filling station in Arlington. Another is an innkeeper in Lynchburg. Still another is working for the NRA."

"And not a single one of the twenty-odd people who are candidates fit the profile," Broward said, "or would seem to have the time, the politics, or the inclination to be the killer."

"Send them over to Kinney at the FBI and let him make that determination for himself," Kate said. "He's not going to take our word for it."

• • •

Bob Kinney closed the last of the files and handed it on to be passed around the table. "Has anybody seen anything in these files that he thinks would be worth investigating?"

His question was greeted with silence.

"I didn't think so," Kinney said glumly. "Anything of promise from any other agency?"

Smith spoke up. "The retired employees of the other agencies we're canvassing are much less likely to have the kind of comprehensive training in multiple skills that the CIA employees have. All the other agencies, including the Bureau, rely on departmental units to supply the skills in things like explosives, and nearly all their attention is devoted to prevention, rather than action. The Agency is the only one that trains its employees to shoot, explode, and poison."

"What about Alcohol, Tobacco and Firearms?"

"Again, their emphasis is the defensive. The CIA operations department is the only offensive agency in government, outside the military, and we've checked with every special ops unit in every branch and checked out maybe a dozen likely candidates. We haven't come up with a shred of evidence that could connect any of them to these crimes."

"We're adjourned," Kinney said, standing up. He went back to his office where his secretary was waiting with a sheet of paper.

"Here's your answer from Sealand," she said, handing him the paper.

It was his own letter, upon which someone had scrawled in large, block capitals, "GO FUCK YOURSELF."

"I guess that's clear enough," Kinney said.

"Have you read this morning's *Post*?" she asked, handing him the paper.

"No."

"Upper right-hand corner."

BRITISH PRIME MINISTER ARRIVES IN D.C.

"He's coming in this afternoon," she said.

Kinney read the piece. "Call the president's secretary and request an appointment soonest."

THE PRESIDENT BLINKED. "You're not really suggesting we send in the marines, are you?"

"No, sir, I'm not. I'm suggesting you raise

the issue with the prime minister while he's here."

"You mean ask him to send in the Royal Marines?"

"I'm not sure what to ask of him, Mr. President. All I know is that these ridiculous people on this little rock in the North Sea might have the information we need to arrest the man who's been doing these killings. Maybe there's something he can do to help us get it." He handed the president a copy of his letter to the Sealand Company with their scrawled reply. "They have not been cooperative."

The president looked at the letter. "I guess not. Have your people tried hacking into their computers?"

"Yes, sir, repeatedly. Their security has, so far, been impenetrable."

The president laughed. "Maybe we should hire them to work on White House security. Somebody got in last week and read some of my email."

"The Bureau is working on that, sir."

"All right, Bob, if I have an opportunity, I'll bring this up with the PM, but don't expect much."

"Thank you, sir, that's all I ask."

• • •

It was late, and the two men sat alone in the residence, their black ties undone, sipping brandy. Will thought that John Ridgeway, the prime minister of Great Britain, was a little worse for the wear. Must be the jet lag, he thought.

"John, I suppose you're acquainted with this island off your coast called Sealand?"

Ridgeway laughed. "It wasn't called anything until those people made camp there. Do you know they helicoptered in Portacabins?"

"What?"

"Prefabricated buildings. They choppered in a cement mixer and poured pads, then they sent in these buildings and put them together."

"They must have financing, then."

"I suppose. My people estimated they spent three, maybe four hundred thousand quid. We thought that at the first sign of cold weather they'd pack it in, but it's been three years now, and they seem to be thriving."

"Have you given any thought to ousting them?"

"Well, yes, but the consensus among the cabinet and the military is that it's hardly worth the effort. Plus, we'd be fighting them in court for years, spending a lot of the people's money. Why does this interest you, Will?"

"Well, we have a little situation with Sealand, and I thought I might mention it and see if you have any ideas." He went through the problem.

"Yes, of course I've read about these murders, and it's awful—even if the killer is eliminating your enemies."

"A senator actually accused *me* the other day."

"Good God! Was he serious?"

"He was preaching to the converted, as we say, getting in a dig to appeal to his right-wing constituency."

"So this is becoming a real problem for you?"

"No one really believes that I have anything to do with the murders, but the fact is we have a serial killer on the loose, and the FBI and the relevant local law enforcement haven't been able to track him down. He's very intelligent and has left us without any traceable evidence."

"I see. And you'd like me to ask my people to get this information for you?"

"If you can see a way to do it without causing an uproar in your press or otherwise compromising your personal position."

"Gosh, I just don't know," Ridgeway sighed. "Let me talk to some people and see if anybody has a suggestion."

"I'd appreciate that, John. I wouldn't bring it up if I thought we had any other option—at least, at the moment. I mean, eventually, the man will make a mistake and we'll catch him, but how many more murders is he going to commit before that happens?"

"Quite."

WILL CLIMBED INTO BED, his bones aching.

"Was Ridgeway willing to help?" Kate asked.

"He says he's going to talk to his people."

"That sounds like a no."

"Probably. When he gets home, he can drop me a little note saying that he can't help. I suppose it's easier than looking me in the eye."

Kate almost told him about the latest letter from Ed Rawls, but she thought better of it. Maybe the Brits would surprise them.

29

ED RAWLS WAS WORKING at his desk in the library when his mail was delivered by a trusty pushing a metal cart. He picked up the stack—three magazines and a couple of envelopes—and set it next to the computer where he was working. He had intended to look through the stack later, but he recognized his own prison-issue envelope in the pile.

He picked it up and looked at it. NO LONGER AT THIS ADDRESS, NO FORWARDING ADDRESS, the stamp said. "Shit," Rawls said aloud, attracting a frown from the librarian, a fifty-ish schoolmarm type who Rawls had been screwing on a sofa in her office for two years, twice a week, like clockwork. "Sorry, Imelda," he said.

"You must learn to control your language,

Ed," she replied, then went back to her filing.

Rawls finished his work, read the other letter, which was a fund-raising appeal from a Republican candidate, who hadn't figured out yet that his box number address was the Atlanta Federal Penitentiary. He threw that away, ripped the returned letter to shreds and put the pieces in his pocket, then he went back into the stacks as if he were looking for something.

He found the volume, *Songbirds of North America,* a book that had never been checked out of the library, and opened it. He had cut out the pages enough to allow him to hide a cell phone in the book. The charger was hidden elsewhere in the library. He switched on the phone and dialed a number.

"Yes," a man's voice said.

"You know who this is," Rawls replied. It wasn't a question.

"Yes. What can I do for you?"

"I want to find a guy we used to know at work," Rawls said. He spoke the name. "Remember him?"

"Yes. I don't see how I can help."

"Do I have to remind you that you would

be in my company at this very moment, had I chosen to—"

"All right," the man said, cutting him off. "Do you have his last address?"

"Sixty-nine Riverview Drive, Arlington. Mail is being returned from that address. They're not forwarding."

"You have any clue where he might be?"

"He's traveling, I think, but he's got to have a base somewhere."

"Does he have any family?"

"He had a wife. I don't know if she's still alive."

"Kids?"

"I don't think so."

"You're a big help."

"I do what I can."

"How will I get in touch with you?"

"Email me, but be circumspect." Rawls gave him a Hotmail address.

"Give me a couple of days," the man replied.

"Thanks for your help," Rawls said, and hung up. He replaced the phone in the book and went back to his computer. He logged on to the Internet and checked his email. There was one from Hotbooks.

"Dear Fast Eddie," she wrote. "I'm still wet

from your last email. I printed it out and took it to bed with me last night, and I still can't get it out of my mind." She described what she had done to herself while reading it, then what she would have done to him, if he had been there. "Are you sure there isn't some way we can get together soon?"

Rawls wrote back that he'd love to, but the demands of work kept him constantly on the road. "I'm in Kansas City right now, putting out a fire, then I have to go to Witchita, then to L.A. Believe me, I'd rather be with you. We'll work it out soon." He would, too, just as soon as he had a fix on this guy, as soon as he was a free man again. Rawls finished his workday and went to the rec room to wait for dinner. There had been a time when he had been uncomfortable in the company of large numbers of prisoners, but he had grown accustomed. Anyway, when prisoners were gathered in the yard or the common room, they tended, like everybody else in the world, to gather in groups that had something in common—murder, rape, gang activity—and Rawls nearly always sat with the stockbrokers, accountants, bankers, and other con men who, in their past lives, had worn suits to work. Today, however, he took a seat with a tall, skinny man who sat alone at one of the steel tables.

"Hello, Nickolai," he said. "I hear you wanted to talk." Rawls had known the man professionally, when they were working opposite sides of the street in Scandinavia. Nickolai had posed as a chauffeur for the KGB at the USSR embassy in Stockholm, and later, in Washington, until CIA people had caught him working in their embassy without a diplomatic passport. His lengthy interrogation had been a disappointment, and now they kept him on ice in Atlanta for a time when they might want to exchange him for an American agent. But time had overtaken Nickolai; the USSR was defunct, and it was extremely unlikely that he would ever be exchanged.

"Hello, Ed," Nickolai replied. He sounded less mournful than usual. "I wish you to send a message to your people at Langley."

"What sort of message?"

"I have something to offer them in exchange for . . . exchange."

"Yeah? And what would that be?"

Nickolai's thin mouth twitched into something resembling a smile. "I cannot tell you that, of course. Not until we have established contact."

"And what makes you think they would want to hear from me?" Rawls asked. "I'm no more popular at Langley than you are."

"Ah, but you have friends, right, Ed? People whose friendship is stronger than . . . what you were punished for."

"Maybe, but what's in it for me?"

Nickolai looked serious, now. "I may be able to get myself sent home and you released from this place."

Rawls laughed heartily. "Nickolai, don't you understand that 'home' isn't there anymore? Everything has changed. The KGB, or whatever they call it now, is run by people your children's age. Everybody you knew there is dead or pensioned off." He waved an arm. "This is your home now."

"Ed, I can make my way in the new Russia. Don't worry about that. But aren't you interested in getting out of here before you die?"

"Well, sure, Nickolai, but you're going to have to convince me that what you've got is important enough to get us both out before I'm willing to contact anybody at all. Now tell me about it."

"And what's to keep you from acting for yourself and forgetting all about me?"

"Well, I guess you're just going to have to trust me, Nickolai. After all, who else in here could do what you want?"

Nickolai sighed. "Ed, do you give me your word that you will not act just for yourself, that I go, too?"

"Yeah, sure I do. Now tell me what you've got. We've been talking too long already."

Nickolai placed his hands on the table and interlocked his fingers. "Tell them that I can give them this fellow who's killing your reactionaries everywhere."

Rawls blinked and looked shocked, because he was. "And how the hell can you do that?" he asked.

"Because I know his name."

"And how the hell do you know his name?"

"In my former profession I had reason to know this man's work," Nickolai said.

"You're not making any sense, Nickolai," Rawls said. He was alarmed, and he had to get this out of the man.

"Ed, just as your people tried to know as much as possible about our people, so did we try to know as much as possible about your people."

"Are you saying that this guy was a Company man?"

"Precisely."

"Did I know him?"

"No, you would have been in very different jobs."

"How do you know for certain that the name you have is the guy they want?"

Nickolai shrugged. "I know, that's all. When they check out the name, they will have their man. If he's not the man, then they have lost nothing. They will not owe me—or you—until they have arrested him."

"What's the man's name?" Rawls asked. "They'll want to know that right away."

"Of course they will, Ed, but that will have to come directly from me to them."

"And how will you do that?"

"I'm sure you could arrange a telephone call. I will give this information directly to Ms. Katharine Rule."

"You think the director is going to call you on the phone?"

"I suppose that depends on how badly they want this person. Tell them to act quickly, before he kills somebody else important."

"I'll see what I can do," Rawls said. "In the meantime, don't you mention this to anybody else, you hear?"

"I will deal only with you, Ed, unless I become convinced that you can't help. Then I'll have to use other means."

The dinner bell rang and both men got up and joined the crowd heading toward the mess hall. Rawls was frightened and angry. Unless he played this right, Nickolai could screw up his chances for a pardon.

30

THE CABINET MEETING WAS breaking up at Number 10 Downing Street, and people were filing out, putting on their coats against the driving rain outside. Ridgeway's private secretary came and stood close to him. "General Sir Ewan Southby-Tailyour and the lady from military intelligence are waiting," he said.

"Show them in as soon as everyone is out the front door," Ridgeway instructed. "No, better put them in my private study now, and I'll join them in a moment."

"Yes, Prime Minister," the man replied.

Ridgeway packed some papers into a dispatch box and gave them to an assistant, then he dictated replies to some letters. He dismissed his staff for the day and went through the bookcase/door and into his study. The two people waiting came quickly to their feet.

"Sir Ewan," he said, extending his hand.

"Prime Minister." General Sir Ewan Southby-Tailyour was a handsome man with thick, white hair, wearing a beautifully cut uniform. He was the senior commander of the Royal Marines, and a former commando himself.

"Good afternoon, Carpenter," he said to the woman.

Although he knew her name was Felicity Devonshire, the intelligence people preferred sobriquets. She was an elegant, handsome woman in her late thirties, dressed in a tweed suit designed to de-emphasize her sexuality, which Ridgeway thought was a failure.

"Good afternoon, Prime Minister," she said warmly.

"Please sit down," he said. "I believe the sun is well over the yardarm. Please let me get you something to drink."

"A dry sherry, please," Carpenter said.

"A small whisky," Southby-Tailyour replied.

Ridgeway went to the concealed liquor cabinet and made the drinks, asking with his eyebrows how much water the general wanted in his Scotch. Then he mixed himself a large bourbon with ice. The president of the United States had given him a case of Knob Creek, and he kept it in an unlabeled decanter, so that no one would know he was drinking American whiskey.

He handed the drinks around, then sat down and took a long pull on his drink. "Thank you for coming," he said. "I hope I haven't pulled you away from something terribly important."

The two people made demurring noises.

"There's something I'd like you to look into and make a recommendation on— Good God, do you two know each other? I didn't introduce you."

"We met on a previous occasion," Carpenter said.

"Oh, good. Well, what this is about is Sealand."

Carpenter seemed to stifle a smile, while Sir Ewan just looked interested.

"You both know about it?"

They nodded.

"Now I know it isn't terribly important to us in any sort of strategic or even tactical sense—"

"Might make a nice bombing practice range," Sir Ewan said.

". . . but I've had a query about it from the American president."

"Why on earth would he be interested in Sealand?" Carpenter asked.

"You know, I expect, that these Sealand people are offering Internet and cell phone services from the island."

Both nodded.

"I expect you've heard, too, that there have been a series of murders of important conservative political figures in the U.S.?"

They nodded again.

"Well, there seems to be a connection. The fellow who's committing these murders is running a personal website on one of Sealand's servers, and President Lee and his security people would very much like to know who registered this site—his name and address, if possible, and anything else that might help them run him to ground."

"Well," Sir Ewan said, smiling, "I think my people would enjoy putting on a little show to gather this information."

"And I think I'd enjoy going along," Carpenter said.

"We don't want this all over the papers, if

we can help it," Ridgeway said. "Can we help it?"

"Perhaps not," Carpenter replied, "unless we can get in and out without causing a ruckus."

"Could your chaps do that, Ewan?"

"I should think it's highly likely, if I choose my people well. But still, if the people on the island twig, and they want it known, well . . ."

"So there's a risk of it becoming public?"

"A not-unreasonable risk," Southby-Tailyour replied.

"If it should break, I would not like to see your names mentioned," Ridgeway said.

"Thank you, sir," Carpenter replied. "I should think we could guarantee you that that will not happen."

"Quite," the general said.

"Well then, get back to me with something soon?" The PM stood up, and so did his guests. "Carpenter, could you stay for a moment?" he asked.

"Of course, Prime Minister," she replied.

He waved her back to her chair and waited until the door had closed behind Sir Ewan. "Well, Felicity, how are things going at your firm?" he asked.

"We're making the adjustment," she said. "I suppose we would adjust more quickly with the question of the appointment resolved."

"Ah, yes," Ridgeway said. "Sir Edward's replacement." Sir Edward Fieldstone, the head of British Intelligence, had been murdered in the men's room of the Four Seasons restaurant in New York some weeks before, while Carpenter had sat at dinner in the dining room with the director of the FBI. "I'm working on that."

"I'm sure you are, sir."

"You know, Felicity, were you a few years older, your name would be on the short list to succeed Sir Edward."

She appeared surprised. "Well, that's very flattering, Prime Minister."

"I believe I could successfully appoint a woman," he said, "perhaps even a beautiful woman." He waited for the compliment to sink in. "But not a beautiful *young* woman."

"How nice to be referred to as young," Carpenter replied, smiling, "and just when I was beginning to feel old."

"Your conduct in the operation in New York was much appreciated, and I think no one assigns any responsibility to you for the death of Sir Edward. Fortunately, we have been able to blame the FBI for that one."

"Quite."

"And of course, we are all very relieved to have that woman, La Biche, out of the picture. I must say, it took courage to do what you did."

"It was necessary," she replied, gazing into her drink.

"You are quite a remarkable woman, Felicity," he said. "If I thought there were the slightest chance of success, I'd be inviting you for a quiet dinner for two this evening. My wife is at Chequers for a few days."

"You are kind, Prime Minister, but our positions make that impossible."

"Of course they do," he replied, chuckling to cover his embarrassment at being rejected. "Well, back to our original subject. What do you think are the chances of pulling off this Sealand thing without making the papers?"

"Well, there is always the Official Secrets Act," she said, referring to the act of Parliament that made it possible to hide almost anything from the public. "But, of course, that doesn't apply to the European media, and these days . . ."

"Quite, quite."

"I think there are three possibilities for an outcome," she said.

"And they are?"

"One, we go in, find what we want, and get out without being discovered. I think this is the least likely, but it could happen."

"Yes, that would be desirable."

"Two, we go in, and they discover that someone has been there, but they don't know who. I think we have a better chance of that."

"And three?"

"We go in, are discovered, and the Sealand people blab to the press. I think that, for planning purposes, we should think of that as the likely outcome."

"Mmmm," the prime minister said, non-committally.

"I think in that case, we should take some pains for them not to know who we are, to make them think that our party is there for commercial purposes. I can do some work on that."

"I *like* that," Ridgeway said. He stood up. "Well, get back to me when you and Sir Ewan have a plan."

She stood up and set down her drink.

"Thank you, Prime Minister. We'll try to be quick."

"More important to be thorough," he said. He watched her exit the room, regretting that he had not been more persuasive.

31

KATE ARRIVED AT HER OFFICE in Langley at her usual time. She had a regular weekly briefing scheduled from her deputy director for intelligence, who ran the Agency's analysts, and her deputy director for operations, who ran its spies.

They appeared in her office on schedule, Morton Koppel, the DDI, and Hugh English, the DDO, and she listened to their reports and discussed many items at length. Their deputies and assistants took notes as did the deputy director for central intelligence, her number two, Creighton Adams.

Two hours later, when the briefing was concluded, Kate dismissed everyone but her DDI, DDO, and DDCI. She offered them a short break, and after everyone had been to the john and poured another cup of coffee, she plunged ahead.

"There's something I want to discuss with you," she said. "This is entirely informal: no notes are being taken and no recordings made. I simply want your opinion on something."

Everybody looked interested.

"Ed Rawls is ill," she said. "He's been in prison for sixteen years, and he had heart surgery last summer. His doctor has told me that his prognosis is guarded, at best, and that he could, in fact, die at any time." She paused.

Nobody said anything, but Hugh English, the DDO, looked annoyed.

"Ed did a despicable thing," she said, "and I, for one, will never forgive him for it, but I'm considering a recommendation to the president that his sentence be commuted to time served, on compassionate grounds. He was sentenced to life without parole, so parole is not an option. I want to hear the views of each of you on the subject." She turned to her DDCI. "Creighton?"

"How quietly could this be done?" he asked. "And what would the reaction of Congress be? Would such a commutation reflect badly on the Agency?" Creighton Adams was the most cautious of men and the most highly attuned to political considerations.

"It would have to be made public, of course, and I'm sure the Post and the Times would spend a day recapping Ed's crime and trial. As for the Congress, pardons and commutations are the president's prerogative, and he would have to take any heat generated. There would be less heat, of course, if the Agency's top management acquiesced."

Adams nodded. "I'm not opposed, in principle. I'd like to think a bit more about the consequences."

Kate turned to her DDI. "Mort?"

"I didn't know Rawls as well as the rest of you, so there's no personal consideration involved. Ordinarily, I'd want him to die in prison, but . . ." He shrugged. "If he gets out I hope to God I won't bump into him at cocktail parties in Virginia and D.C."

"Yes," Adams said, "that would be awkward."

"Ed still owns a house on an island in Maine, Islesboro. He says he wants to go there to die. It's a long way from Washington."

"You've spoken with Ed?" Adams asked.

She shook her head. "No. He's written to me a couple of times." She looked at her DDO, who was staring into his coffee cup. "Hugh?"

English raised his head and looked at her. "If there were a way to have him tortured, I'd vote for that. I will never, ever acquiesce in having him pardoned."

"That's pretty vociferous, Hugh," Koppel said. "What are your reasons?"

Kate was glad he had asked, because she didn't want to.

"Well, let's see," English said, and began ticking things off on his fingers. "He's betrayed his country and this agency, and he did it for money. He's humiliated all of us. And he's directly responsible for the deaths of two of our best people in the Stockholm embassy, and they were my friends. Is that enough?"

"Just to set the record straight," Adams interjected, "he was blackmailed by the Soviets. It was sex, not money, that was his downfall, and as bad as that was, I knew Ed well, and I don't think he would have ever knowingly done anything that would have caused the deaths of Lewis and Barbara Moore. They were his friends, too, and Ed had a gift for friendship."

"You're in denial, Creighton," English said. "You're unable to see the facts clearly."

Koppel spoke up, and there was an edge in his voice. "Nobody is ever able to see the facts as clearly as you do, Hugh."

English stood up. "That's it for me. You asked for my opinion, Kate, and I've given it to you. Now, if you'll excuse me . . ." He walked out of the room and closed the door behind him.

"I suppose I should have expected that," Kate said.

"*I* didn't expect it," Adams replied. "I've never heard Hugh mention Ed's name in any context whatever. Kate, will you go to the president with the support of three of the four of us?"

"Three out of four ain't bad," Koppel said.

"I don't know," she said. "I think it would be easier for the president if he could say that the management of the Agency unanimously supported him."

"He can still say that a majority—a large

majority of management supports him," Adams said.

"Then you're on board, Creighton?"

"On reflection, I am."

"Mort?"

"Count me in."

"Thank you both. We'll see where this leads."

She watched them leave and reflected that even though she couldn't bring Hugh English on board, at least he had had the effect of strengthening the resolve of Koppel and Adams.

Her secretary buzzed. "Ms. Rule, do you have anything on your calendar for dinner the day after tomorrow? There's something at the British embassy, and we haven't responded."

Kate looked at her calendar. "Yes, we have the new Russian president for dinner that night," she said.

"I'll send regrets, then."

Kate regretted it, too. She liked the British crowd and enjoyed their dinners. Still, she'd have an opportunity to get to know Georgi Majorov. He was ex-KGB, and that made him very interesting to her.

32

CARPENTER GATHERED WITH the small group of Royal Marines in a sterile conference room at a training establishment far down the Thames Estuary. They were all dressed in jeans or foul-weather gear and with a variety of headgear—baseball caps, woolen watch caps, and navy blue yachting caps with yacht club insignia. They looked like the crew of a world-class racing yacht—young, fit, and eager—as long as one didn't know how quickly and quietly they could kill.

General Sir Ewan Southby-Tailyour stood at the foot of the conference table, manipulating transparencies on a projector. His first was taken from an admiralty nautical chart. "Now, you see here the position of the island in relation to the coast and the Thames Estuary," he said. "We'll have about a six-hour sail with the wind giving us a nice close reach, and in bright sunshine for most of the afternoon. The met office tells us conditions will deteriorate rapidly after sunset: the wind will back to the southwest and increase to around force seven, giving us a cross-swell and a very dark night, which should suit our purposes admirably." He switched to a satellite photograph in which Sealand filled the entire frame.

"Now you see the landing, just here." He pointed on the transparency with a pencil. "It's certainly not what one would call a harbor, but it has some shelter from the southwesterlies, so we shouldn't have much more than a light chop inside the point. There's a dock, here.

"Now the buildings: There are six Portocabins, all identical from the outside, and I am indebted to Carpenter and her people for supplying us with some intelligence about the interiors. The southernmost is sleeping quarters and bathrooms; the next up the line is a mess hall and lounge for the inhabitants. These accommodations should be quite comfortable for them, since the island has a standing population of eight to ten. Provisions and mail are brought over from an East Anglian port twice a week, but never at night, which suits us.

"The third building in line is the computer installation and some offices, and the fourth houses the cellular telephone equipment and offices. The other two are purely for utility—storage, tools, et cetera. It is the third building, here, that interests us, but we will place guards on buildings one, two, and four as well, so that our workers are not disturbed.

"Carpenter's intelligence tells us that there is one man each on duty in the computer and telephone buildings, so they should be easy to deal with. Sergeant Simpson, please show us how we will deal with them."

A thick-set man in his early thirties stood up and placed one end of a yard-long tube in his mouth, pointing it at a dartboard at the other end of the room. His cheeks puffed out, there was a *whfft!* noise and a dart struck the board at dead center. Carpenter was impressed.

"Very good," Sir Ewan said, walking to the board and extracting the dart. He held it up for the group to see. "Since our orders are not to damage any of the inhabitants, this will be our means of subduing any who require subduing. It is, in fact, a syringe, as well as a dart, and it will hold up to two cc's of whatever we care to put into it. In this case, Carpenter's people have supplied a liquid which they call 'Sleepytime Down South,' or just 'Sleepytime,' for short.

"The injection of this fluid causes nearly immediate unconsciousness for a period of two to four hours, depending on how much is administered, but the really sweet thing about this drug is that, when the subject awakes, he has no memory of what occurred up to an hour before he received the dose. He will believe that he simply fell asleep."

Sir Ewan held up a shorter tube. "This is a compressed-air version of the sergeant's blowpipe; each of you will carry one and two doses of the drug. Two of our team will carry sawn-off shotguns with beanbag loads that are the equivalent of a strong punch. In the event that it becomes necessary to use these, the preferred target is the abdomen. You are not to aim at the heads of these people because of the risk of breaking their necks.

"I must stress most strongly that no team member is to carry any other weapon, not a knife or even a truncheon, and should you have to counteract violence, you will use only those means prescribed and *you will employ restraint.* It is not our task to cause the death or significant injury of anyone. I know that goes against your training, but there it is.

"Your task is to land on the island unseen, enter building three unheard, let Carpenter and her bloke do their work undetected, clean up after yourselves, and depart the island unremembered.

"Because a higher authority has ordered me not to land on the island, I will stand offshore with the yacht, with one crew to aid me, and will receive the dinghy on its return to the yacht."

He looked at his wristwatch. "You will board the yacht in forty minutes, and we will sail in forty-five. At no time will more than three hands appear on deck in daylight, and only when I need more than one. The rest of the time you can all sit below with your filthy magazines and drink Bovril and cocoa, which you are all very good at." There was a low chuckle from the group. "Any questions?"

There were none.

"Good. Take your seasick pills now, if you

need them, and assemble on the dock in thirty-five minutes. Dismissed."

The group filed out, leaving Southby-Tailyour, Carpenter, and a young man from Carpenter's firm called Roofer, who would do any required computer work.

"They seem like a good lot," Carpenter said.

Sir Ewan sat down beside her. "They're razor-sharp, all of them," he said. "The crème de la crème." He looked at the computer technician. "You ever been aboard a yacht, young fellow?"

"No, sir," the man said.

Sir Ewan placed two small pills on the table. "Take these now," he said, pushing a carafe and a glass toward him.

"What are they?" he asked.

"The pink one is phenergen, a child's antihistamine, and the white one is ephedrine, a slight upper. Twenty-five milligrams of each prevents seasickness in nearly everyone. The Americans worked this out for their astronauts, to prevent motion sickness in space."

"I don't think I'll need them," Roofer said.

"Shut up and take them," Carpenter said softly.

He did. “Is there a bathroom nearby?” he asked.

“Next door,” Sir Ewan said, jerking a thumb.

Roofer left.

“You ready for this?” Sir Ewan asked.

Carpenter smiled. “Oh, yes. It’s been a while since I’ve been on this sort of jaunt. I’ve missed it.”

“My boys are disappointed that they won’t get to throttle or knife anybody,” Sir Ewan said.

“Poor babies.”

“Quite,” Sir Ewan replied.

33

KATE WATCHED WILL as he tied his black bow tie in one smooth, continuous motion. It always came out perfectly.

"I always meant to ask you: Where did you learn to do that?" she asked.

"Cary Grant movie," he replied, slipping into his waistcoat.

"You're kidding."

"I am not. I think it was *Indiscreet,* but I'm not sure. I finally got it right on about the two-hundredth attempt."

"And how old were you when you did this?"

"Forty," he replied.

She pinched him sharply on his ass.

"All right, nineteen." He got into his dinner jacket, turned around, and slipped his arms around her waist. "Now tell me, how is it that you got ready before I did? This has never happened before."

"I had a head start," she said. "When you were on the phone with the British PM."

"Oh, yes."

"What did he want?"

"I'm not sure I should share that with the director of Central Intelligence. Or are you asking as the first lady?"

"Whatever will get you to cough it up."

"Well, somewhat to my astonishment, he's sending in the Royal Marines at Sealand. It's one of those outrageously flamboyant Brit military operations: The commander of the service is sailing a bunch of men over to the island in his yacht, and they're taking a rubber dinghy ashore in the dead of night."

"If somebody gets hurt, this could boomerang," she said. "I wish you'd asked me. We could have come up with something."

"Better to let the Brits do it. It's on their soil, more or less, and they have the Official Secrets Act to cover their asses."

"I wish we had that," she said.

"No you don't, and don't you ever let anybody hear you say so. We're for an open society and sunshine on government, remember?"

"Oh, yeah, I forgot. You be sure and preach those virtues to Georgi Majorov at dinner."

"Absolutely. You ready?"

"Don't I look ready?"

AFTER THEY HAD seen off the last of their dinner guests, the two presidents and their first ladies repaired to the family quarters of the White House for coffee and brandy. Not that the Russian president needed a brandy, Kate reflected. He had drunk at least half a bottle of vodka at dinner, not bothering with the wine.

Ignoring his very pretty wife, Majorov took Kate's arm and steered her toward a sofa. Will saw this and led Tatyana Majorov to the opposite sofa.

Kate and Majorov practically fell onto the sofa, laughing, while Kate managed to put another six inches of space between them. She didn't want him getting grabby. When the steward had served the coffee and brandy and departed, Majorov raised his glass to Kate and polished off the vintage cognac in a gulp.

"So," he said, in heavily accented but otherwise very serviceable English, "you are CIA."

"I am CIA," she agreed.

"I am KGB, you know. Pardon, I *was* KGB."

"I know. Did you like the work?"

"I liked the travel," he said. "Paris, Stockholm, Vienna. I had all the good posts. Nobody likes to live in the USSR."

"When were you in Stockholm?" she asked.

He gave her a sly look. "I know what you are thinking." He chuckled.

"What am I thinking?" Kate asked.

"You are thinking, 'Is this the Russian agent who turned my friend Rawls?' "

Kate took a quick breath. That was exactly what she had been thinking. "You know about Rawls?"

"I know *all* about Rawls," he said. "Yes, I am the spy who turned him."

"Blackmailed him," Kate corrected.

"Blackmail? So what? I turned him, doesn't matter how." He reached for the brandy decanter and poured himself a double. He hadn't touched the coffee.

"How, exactly, did you do that?"

"Easy," Majorov replied. "What you call 'Badger Game.' "

"And what is that?" she asked, knowing full well what the Badger Game was.

"You get your mark a girl. Rawls loved girls, the younger and prettier, the better."

"Go on."

"Then you photograph your mark and the girl in odd positions. Then you show your mark the photographs and offer him alternatives: Would he like to go home to Langley in disgrace, have wife take everything in divorce? Or would he prefer maybe to share a little bit information from time to time, maybe put some money in his pocket, maybe even continue to see the girl? Easy choice, eh?"

"Rawls made the stupid choice," she said.

"Maybe, from your point of view. Not from my point of view."

Kate looked him in the eye and shot the question. "Did Rawls give you Lewis Moore and his wife?" She watched his eyebrows go up.

"Ah," Majorov said slyly, "this is state secret."

"The state doesn't exist anymore, how could it be a state secret? Who cares?"

Majorov shrugged. "You have the point," he said. "USSR is no more. All my good work all those years for nothing."

"You fought the good fight," Kate said. "Now tell me, did Rawls give you the Moores?"

Majorov shook his head gravely. "No. Rawls didn't give."

"Then how did your people know they would be where they were?"

A wicked grin spread over Majorov's face. "Because I know everything the Moores do," he said.

Kate looked at him closely. "You had them watched constantly?"

Majorov tapped his ear. "I had them *listened* constantly," he said.

Kate gulped. "In the embassy?"

"In their house," he said. "For two years, almost, we hear everything—sex, fight, yelling, love—everything."

"And that's how you knew they'd be there?"

"Absolutely."

"Not from Rawls?"

"Rawls never give me any American agent. Couple Hungarians, a Pole or two, no Americans."

"Why did you kill the Moores?"

"Because they wished to kill me. Lewis got off two shots first."

"They weren't supposed to be armed."

Majorov shrugged. "'Supposed' means nothing. They both had pistols."

"Rawls wasn't there?"

"No Rawls."

Kate sat back on the sofa with a big sigh.

"This is surprise?" Majorov asked.

"This is surprise," Kate replied.

34

CARPENTER LEANED BACK in the navigator's seat and sipped her Bovril. She had been sitting in the saloon of the forty-five-foot yacht, next to the Royal Marine sergeant with the blowpipe, but he had been too attentive, so she had moved to the navigation station, which she preferred anyway, since it held the charts, the radar repeater, and the chart plotter that combined all the inputs onto one screen, including the Global Positioning System readout.

On the display the yacht was a little boat-shaped wedge, and Sealand was just appearing on the edge of the twenty-mile range screen. There were other dots here and there—fishing boats and buoys, the odd merchant ship or foreign naval vessel. It was a little after 11 P.M., and the GPS gave their time en route to Sealand as 3.2 hours. They were averaging about six knots.

She polished off the Bovril, then poured a mug of steaming tea and added a large dollop of brandy to it. She slid back the hatch and stood on the companionway ladder. "Permission to come on deck?" she asked.

"Permission granted," Sir Ewan called back. He gave the wheel a slight turn to take a wave, then got back on course.

Carpenter climbed the ladder, stepped into the cockpit, and closed the hatch behind her. She handed Sir Ewan the tea.

"Many thanks," he said, sipping from the mug. "Ah, that's a fine recipe."

"Like me to take her for a while?" Carpenter asked.

"Good idea," he said, stepping aside and letting her take the wheel. "I need to concentrate on this tea." He gave her the course.

"We're three point two hours out," she said.

"That should put you ashore at the right moment, I should think."

A dark form slithered from the foredeck into the cockpit. "All made fast, sir," the marine said.

"Good man. Go below and get something hot in you."

The man went below and closed the hatch.

Carpenter let the yacht settle onto her course, then looked ahead, waiting to acquire some night vision after the shaft of light from the hatch. She could see the navigation lights of a large merchantman a couple of miles off their port bow, a ship that had already crossed their course and that was of no further danger to them. She couldn't see anything else nearby.

The night was pitch black, and all she could see around them was the foam from the short seas, illuminated by the nav lights. The North Sea was shallow and made short, steep waves. The anemometer was showing thirty to thirty-five knots, and the seas were a good five feet, making for an uncomfortable ride below. She was glad Roofer had taken the seasick pills; she didn't want him lying useless in a bunk.

"She's a nice boat," Carpenter said. "The coal stove below is a good thing for a night like this."

"Makes for a snug passage," he replied.

"You said it had been a while since you'd done a job like this. What was the last one?"

"It was hardly like this. I had, with two others, to break into a building in the middle of the Arabian desert and photograph the unmanned radar installation inside. The installation turned out *not* to be unmanned, and we had a bit of a tussle, had to kill a man, and one of ours took a bullet in the foot during the struggle. It was a long walk back to our Land Rover, taking turns carrying him."

"Odd business for a woman," he said.

"Well, you've got women in the Royal Marines these days, though I don't see any on this little jaunt."

"We've got some very good women. Pure accident that none came along. Best, ah, person for the job, and all that."

Whatever you say, she thought. "Just out of curiosity, who ordered you not to go ashore tonight?"

"My wife," he said. "Well, not really, it was more like the PM, who obviously thinks I'm too old for this sort of thing. He was happy for me to use my own yacht, though. If something should go wrong, he won't lose a vessel, or have it identified as belonging to the government."

"You're going ashore anyway, aren't you?" she asked.

Sir Ewan grinned. "I thought about it, but if anything should go wrong, my presence would greatly increase the embarrassment level for the government. I suppose I'll stay aboard and let you and the men have all the fun."

A large wave slid under them with a hiss as it passed.

Sir Ewan seemed to doze, with the mug held in both hands, so Carpenter stopped talking. She glanced at her watch. Three hours to go.

BOB KINNEY SAT at his desk while various members of his team came and went.

"What time are they going ashore?" Kerry Smith asked.

"Dead of night," Kinney replied. "I don't have an hour."

"Dead of night is pretty soon," Kinney said. "They're five hours ahead of us."

"I know."

"I wish I were with them." Smith sighed.

"God, I don't. There's half a gale in the North Sea tonight, which makes it good for the operation, but I wouldn't want to be out there in a small boat."

"You must be getting old, Bob," Smith said, the first time he had ever been so familiar with his superior.

Kinney looked at him sharply, then nodded. "Too old for that," he said. "Not too old to kick your ass."

Smith held up his hands in surrender. "No argument there, boss."

"That's better," Kinney said.

"I still can't believe that we're going to crack this thing because the president went to the prime minister, and the prime minister sent in the marines. Does this sort of thing happen often?"

"Not often, but it happens."

"I wish we were following this thing by satellite," the young agent said.

"It's a dark and stormy night. We'll know soon enough, just relax."

"You're not relaxed," Smith said.

"Oh, shut up, Kerry. Go get me some coffee and one of those awful doughnuts."

Smith got up and left the office.

• • •

WILL ENTERED the situation room, and everyone present stood. "Be seated, please." He looked around the room at the collection of military and National Security Council faces. "Any word about anything?"

General Moore spoke up. "They're due to go ashore any time now. Nobody knows how long this is going to take, but they'll have to be off the island well before dawn."

"Well, unless you people actually want to stay up and wait for news, I suggest you leave a skeleton crew here and get some sleep. That's what I'm going to do, and I don't want to know what happened until I wake up in the morning. If they get a name and address, fax it directly to Kinney at the FBI. Good night."

They stood again as he left the room.

Will got on the elevator, yawning.

35

THEY WERE LESS THAN a mile from the island before Carpenter saw it, briefly illuminated by a flash of lightning. Sealand was a low, black collection of rocks, with no vegetation visible in the lightning flashes.

Sir Ewan opened the hatch and shouted, "Four men on deck to inflate the dinghy!"

The lights below were extinguished; four men clambered into the cockpit and began unrolling the rubber boat, which had been lashed to the stern pulpit.

"And switch off those nav lights!" Sir Ewan called down. "I want a man at the nav station to warn me of any vessel that comes within two miles of us!"

"Aye, aye, sir!" someone called back.

Sir Ewan turned and directed the men with the dinghy. "Plug the tube in right there," he said, pointing to a port in the side of the cockpit. The tube was plugged in, a switch filled, and the electric pump began quickly inflating the rubber boat.

Carpenter hung back on the opposite side of the cockpit and watched the sixteen-foot pile of rubber become a boat.

"Team on deck," Sir Ewan shouted down the hatch, and two other dark shapes joined them. The dinghy was slipped over the side, and, while two men held the bow and stern close to the yacht, the others began jumping into it, timing the boat's rise with the waves. They were hove to with the storm jib aback, and the yacht's wind shadow made a fairly calm area to leeward.

Carpenter looked down into the heaving dinghy and launched herself toward it, putting her faith in the Royal Marines' desire to manhandle a woman. She was caught and lowered into the boat with only a minimum of groping. Four men began paddling toward the island.

At first there seemed no place to land, but as they progressed, a shallow bay opened behind a point of land, and when they were a couple of hundred yards out, a flash from the sky illuminated a short jetty.

"Thank God for the lightning," the sergeant said. "Otherwise we'd have to use our torches and probably get spotted."

"We were told there wouldn't be sentries," Carpenter said.

"Don't believe everything you're told," the sergeant replied. "Just be ready to handle it."

They came up on the leeward side of the jetty, and two marines jumped out and made the dingy fast. From that point, no one issued orders; everyone did as he had been instructed.

While the men fanned out to their assigned positions, Carpenter and Roofer followed the sergeant toward the only light. It began to rain heavily, and the light seemed to blink on and off as they approached, finally becoming steady as the outline of a portable building became visible.

Carpenter hunched up her slicker and pulled its hood tight around her head, for shelter and better visibility. She and the sergeant ran to a window and looked inside. Through the rain-spotted glass they could see the dimensions of a large room, lit by a single lamp on a desk. A single figure, a young woman, sat at the desk.

"Looks good," Carpenter said.

"Not yet," the sergeant replied. "Check the other windows."

They ran around to the other side of the building and found another window lit. Inside, a large lump of a man was slumped over a desk, apparently asleep, illuminated by a single lamp and the glow from a computer screen.

"Double trouble," the sergeant said. "I can only use the blowpipe on one at a time, and they're in different rooms."

"I've got my compressed air pipe," Carpenter said. "I'll take one."

The sergeant thought for a moment. "I'll take the guy, you take the woman. We'll go in as quietly as we can and try to sneak up on them."

Carpenter shook her head. "The woman is in profile to the door. As soon as we go in, she's bound to see us. And as soon as we open the door, she'll hear the weather outside. Let me go in first and close the door behind me. Give me five seconds, or until I'm well past the office door. I'll take care of her, then you can do the man."

The sergeant shrugged. "Why not?"

Roofer spoke up. "What do you want me to do?"

"Stay outside. Don't come in until I call you," the sergeant said.

Roofer nodded.

They walked back to the door. "Ready?" Carpenter asked rhetorically, then opened the door, walked in and closed the door behind her.

The woman at the desk looked up as Carpenter entered. "What?" she said.

"God, it's filthy out there," Carpenter said, shucking off her slicker and hanging it on a hook by the door. She pulled off her watch cap and shook her hair free, then she started toward the woman at the desk, a hand in her pocket.

"Who are you?" the woman asked. "You weren't on the boat this afternoon."

Carpenter approached the desk, smiling. "They made a special run for me. I'm doing the software updates."

"What fucking software updates?" the woman asked. "We download the software updates."

Carpenter heard the door open and close behind her.

"Who's that?" the woman asked.

Carpenter's hand closed on the cylinder in her pocket and she brought it out. "It's a new kind of disk drive," she said, walking around the desk behind the woman, as if to look over her shoulder at the computer monitor.

"I don't get this," the woman said, as Carpenter held the cylinder near her neck and fired it. There was a small hiss, the woman slapped at her neck, and then she seemed to dissolve into a heap.

Carpenter stretched her out on the floor and glanced toward the door in time to see a large mass hurtle out of the office and collide with the sergeant. The blowpipe flew from his hand and bounced off the wall, out of his reach.

The man was very big, bearded, and bellowing. "And who the fuck are you, my man?" he yelled, sitting on the sergeant, a hand at his throat.

Carpenter began running toward them, aware that she had fired her only dart, and as she did, the outside door opened and Roofer stepped inside. Quickly, before Carpenter could get there, he held out his cylinder before him and fired it in the general direction of the big man's head.

"Ow!" the man yelled, clawing at his face. He ripped the dart out and tossed it away.

"Oh, shit," Carpenter muttered to herself. "The blowpipe, Roofer!" she called out, as she picked up a heavy bookend from a table and threw it at the big man's head. It caught him high on the skull and knocked him off the sergeant, but he immediately began to get to his feet.

Carpenter threw the other bookend at him, striking him in the chest. Roofer tackled the man from behind and, for his trouble, was shucked off like a shawl.

Carpenter, out of weapons, pointed a finger at the man. "Listen to me, you stupid son of a bitch!" she yelled.

"Huh?" the man said, turning toward her.

"Do you know who I am?"

"No, I don't," he said, not noticing the sergeant's movement.

"Well, you'd bloody well better get on the phone and find out, hadn't you?"

The man looked at her, baffled. "The phone? Who am I supposed to call?"

The sergeant blew his dart from three feet, and Carpenter and Roofer simultaneously threw themselves onto the man.

"Just hold him!" the sergeant yelled, grabbing an arm.

Roofer grabbed the other arm and the man shook him like a puppy.

"Listen to me!" Carpenter shouted, inches from his face. "Listen to me!"

The man looked at her, ready to say something, then his knees gave way, and he fell forward, like a long sack of potatoes.

Carpenter stepped out of his way. "Nighty-night," she said. "Roofer, get on the computer."

The sergeant was on his hands and knees, searching for something.

"What are you looking for?" Carpenter asked.

"The other dart," the sergeant said. "Help me. We're going to need it."

Carpenter began looking, too, and a moment later, the sergeant found it. He went to the big man, who was not quite unconscious, and stuck it into his neck.

"I don't know how long this is going to last on someone of his size," the sergeant said, "so tell your man to hurry."

Carpenter looked over her shoulder. Roofer was at the computer, typing rapidly.

36

CARPENTER WRUNG THE MOP into the pail and turned to the sergeant. "Do you think you could *do* something around here? We've got to clean up."

The sergeant reluctantly took a dry mop from the broom closet and began going over the area Carpenter had wet-mopped.

"Thank you," she said. She turned to Roofer, who had been working at the computer for half an hour. "What about it?" she asked.

"It's a tough one," he said. "These people know what they're doing. Do you think there might be some paper files with this information?"

"Perhaps you didn't notice, but there are no filing cabinets in this building."

"Oh." He began typing again.

Carpenter checked the time. "It's going to start getting light in less than an hour, and we don't know what time the watch changes."

"Pressure won't help," Roofer said. "Kindly shut up and let me work."

Carpenter resisted the temptation to ream out the junior officer. He was right, after all.

The sergeant sat down at a table and pulled out a pack of cigarettes.

"Don't do that," she said. "Have you noticed that there are no ashtrays in the building? If they're all nonsmokers, they'll smell the smoke."

The sergeant sighed and put away the cigarettes.

"Go and check on the big one," she said.

The sergeant got up and went into the office, then came out again. "Sleeping like a baby," he said. "I put him in the same position he was in when we arrived. When he wakes up, he'll think he had a bad dream."

"He'd better not wake up," Carpenter muttered. She was looking at the door to the outside when the knob started to turn.

She waved at the sergeant to get his attention, then pointed at the door. The sergeant tiptoed toward it and took up a position to one side.

The door opened, to reveal one of their own men. “When are you going to be done?” he asked. “It’s going to start getting light soon.”

“Shut up and get back to your post,” the sergeant said. “We’ll be done when we’re done.”

Carpenter walked over to Roofer and stood looking over his shoulder.

“If you want to help,” the young man said, “wake up those people and torture them until they give you a password.”

Carpenter picked up the woman’s purse and dug out her wallet. “Try Susan,” she said.

Roofer typed. “No good.”

“Try Anne, with an *e*.”

“No good.”

Carpenter found a National Health card and read off the number. “If that doesn’t work, try the last four digits.”

Roofer typed. “Well, I’ll be damned,” he said. “I’m in.”

“Good, now find the client list, and let’s get on with it.”

“What’s the website’s name again?”

"ACT NOW."

"Right."

Carpenter replaced the wallet and put the purse back where she had found it.

From inside the adjoining office came a loud moan. Carpenter ran to the door and looked inside. The big man was trying to lift his head. It fell back onto the desk with a thud.

She ran back to Roofer. "We've got to get out of here."

"I'm doing a search," he said. "It's a slow computer."

The sergeant stood and picked up one of the bookends Carpenter had used. "I'll put him to sleep," he said.

"No," Carpenter replied. "He's not awake yet. Just watch him."

Roofer typed a few keystrokes. "Got it!" he shouted.

Carpenter ran to the desk and looked over his shoulder. "Print it out, and quickly!"

Roofer hit the print button and collected a sheet of paper from the machine.

Carpenter snatched it from him, folded it, and put it into the hip pocket of her jeans. "Put the computer back the way you found it," she said, grabbing the young woman under the arms and heaving her toward the desk.

"Done," Roofer said, standing up and helping Carpenter with the woman.

They put her in her chair, folded her arms on the desk, and laid her head on her arms.

The sergeant clapped his hands, and they both turned and looked at him. He pointed to the office. The big man was waking up.

Carpenter ran over, took the bookend from him and put it back in its place. She got into her slicker and led the way out the door.

It was still raining, but not as hard, and a dull light was penetrating the heavy clouds. They ran toward the jetty, collecting the others as they went, and soon they were in the dinghy headed toward the point.

The sergeant produced a handheld radio. "Mother, this is baby," he said.

"Go ahead, baby," the general's voice came back.

"I've begun my journey."

"I'll switch on the masthead light."

As they cleared the point a wave struck the dinghy, and Carpenter slipped off her seat into the bottom and about two inches of water. She clawed her way back, then felt in her hip pocket for the sheet of paper. It was wet. She pulled it out, stuck it under her slicker and her shirt, next to a breast. It was cold and clammy, but it soon absorbed her body warmth.

A moment later, the sergeant pointed to a light in the distance. "There!" he shouted. "Make for the light."

Five long minutes later, they were alongside the heaving yacht, and men were pulling Carpenter on deck.

"Shall we sink the dinghy?" the sergeant asked.

"No," Sir Ewan called back. "It might wash ashore. Get it aboard and suck it out."

The men heaved the large dinghy aboard, connected it to the pump, and hit the reverse switch. The dinghy began to collapse.

Carpenter went below, found her small duffel and retrieved the satellite phone. She slid back the hatch, pulled the spray hood over her head, and tapped in a number.

"Yes?" a voice said almost immediately.

"It's Aunt Rose," she said. "Your cousin lives in Arlington, Virginia. Do you want me to read you the name and address?"

"No," the voice said. "Bring it ashore and fax it. How was your journey?"

"Piece of cake," she said.

"Good Auntie," he replied, then broke the connection.

Carpenter went below and made herself a mug of tea, adding a lot of brandy.

37

Bob Kinney jerked awake. He had a terrible pain in his neck, where it rested on the arm of the sofa, which was too short for his body. "What?" he said.

"The White House Situation Room is on the phone," his secretary repeated.

Kinney leapt off the sofa and grabbed the phone. "Bob Kinney."

"Agent Kinney, you're getting a fax any minute, now. It goes to the president first."

"Was the mission a success?"

"Completely, as I understand it."

"Who is the guy?"

"I haven't seen the name. It will be in the fax. I did hear that it's an Arlington address."

"Thanks." Kinney hung up. Kerry Smith had appeared at the door.

"Wake up the team," Kinney said. "The

Brits got the name, and they're faxing it to us momentarily."

"Who is he?"

"I don't have it yet, but he has an Arlington address, and we're going to roll the minute we've got the name."

"Great!" Smith replied, then went to start waking people.

Kinney stuck his head out the door. "Assemble everybody in the garage!" he yelled after Smith's disappearing back. Smith waved and turned a corner.

Kinney went back to his secretary's desk and stared at the fax machine. "Come on," he said under his breath.

"You know that talking to it doesn't work," she said. "Go sit down, and I'll bring it to you the moment it arrives."

The fax machine rang.

Kinney went and stood over it, willing it to print faster.

The machine made the requisite noises, then slowly spat out a sheet of paper. Kinney snatched it from the machine and read it aloud. "Edward E. Coulter, Riverview Road, Arlington." He furrowed his brow. "Why does that sound familiar?"

"What was it again?" his secretary asked.

"Edward E. Coulter."

"Edward Eugene Coulter?"

The name came like a spear through the heart. "Our CIA retiree? The one we talked to?"

"The one who's dead," she said helpfully. The phone rang, and she picked it up. "Yes, Mr. President, he's right here." She handed him the phone.

"Bob Kinney," he said, feeling sick to his stomach.

"Bob, they faxed me this name," the president said. "Edward E. Coulter. Isn't that the retired CIA guy, the one who died?"

"Yes, sir, it is."

"What do you make of this?"

"We'll be interviewing his widow again first thing this morning," Kinney replied. "I'll have to get back to you, sir."

"Please do," the president said. "At your earliest convenience." He hung up.

"Call the garage and tell the team to stand down," Kinney said to his secretary. "Tell Kerry to pick up a tape recorder and be prepared to leave the building at eight A.M." Kinney went back into his office and stretched out on the sofa again. If he were alone, he would cry, he reflected. Instead, he was going to get some sleep.

AT 8:25 A.M., Kinney and Smith pulled up in front of the Coulter residence, just in time to see Mrs. Coulter step onto the front porch in a bathrobe and pick up her newspaper. She watched as they got out of the car and walked up her driveway.

"Agent Kinney, isn't it?" she said, looking puzzled.

"Yes, ma'am," he replied. "And Agent Smith. May we come inside and talk with you?"

"Of course. I was just putting on some coffee."

They went inside and waited impatiently while Mrs. Coulter moved around her kitchen and finally came out with a coffeepot and some small pastries. "I bake them myself," she said. "There's nobody to eat them since Ed died, but I bake them anyway." She poured them all some coffee and sat down.

"Please accept my condolences," he said.

"Thank you, that's very kind."

"Mrs. Coulter," Kinney said, "I want to tell you why we're here."

"Does it still have something to do with the sniper?" she asked. The papers still referred to him as the sniper, even though he'd killed only once in that manner.

"Yes, it does. Let me tell you why we interviewed your husband. One of our theories about the case is that the killer, because he had expertise in several ways of killing, might have been a retired employee of a government agency that trained him."

"So that's why you talked to Ed?"

"Yes, ma'am."

"Well, Ed knew about firearms," she said, "and that was it. He was just a glorified gunsmith. He wasn't even a very good shot."

"Yes, ma'am, and that was why we eliminated him from our list of suspects." Some list; Coulter had been the only name on it. "That and the state of his health."

"Good point," she said. "He could hardly have roamed the country, killing people, while using a walker."

"Yes, ma'am. The reason we're here now is, we've traced the name of the operator of an Internet website called ACT NOW, where the killer posted pictures of his victims and, perhaps, his intended victims."

"And who is he?"

"I'm afraid the name was Edward E. Coulter."

Mrs. Coulter laughed. "Well, I'm afraid the only thing Ed ever did with a computer was word processing and check writing. He didn't even do email, nor do I."

"What we now think is, that since the killer used your husband's name and address to register the website, he might be someone Ed knew at work—a colleague or a friend."

She nodded. "It's possible, I suppose."

"Can you think of anyone like that? Probably someone who's retired?"

"Well, this neighborhood is full of retired CIA folks," she said. "We knew a lot of them."

"Could you give us a list of their names and addresses?" Kinney asked.

"Just a minute," she said. She got up and went into her husband's study. A moment later she returned with several sheets of paper and a pen. She sat down and began making checkmarks on the paper. "This is our Christmas card list," she said. "I'm checking off the CIA people and putting two checks by the retired ones."

"Thank you, Mrs. Coulter. Is there anyone on the list to whom your husband was particularly close?"

"Well, sure, there was Teddy Fay."

"Is he on the list?"

She handed it to him. "Yes, and it's in alphabetical order. Teddy and Ed worked in the same department, Technical Services, they call it. Ed called it the Devil's Workshop."

"And is Mr. Fay retired?" Kinney found the name on the list.

"I don't know. He stopped coming around after Ed had his stroke. I'm not sure why. Ed wouldn't talk about it."

"And this address, Riverview Circle, where is that?"

"Just around the corner." She pointed. "You take two lefts, and it's the second—no, the third—house on the right."

Kinney and Smith stood up. "Do you know what Mr. Fay did in Technical Services?"

"Teddy? He was a jack of all trades. Teddy could do anything, fix anything, Ed always said."

Kinney's pulse quickened. "Do you know anything about Mr. Fay's politics?"

"Oh, Teddy's as left-wing as they come," she replied. "He and Ed used to argue about it all the time. Ed was a rock-ribbed conservative."

"Thank you, Mrs. Coulter, and thank you for the coffee, too," Kinney said.

The two agents were running before they were halfway down the driveway.

38

KERRY REACHED FOR THE RADIO. "I'll call for backup."

"Not yet," Kinney said. "I want to look at the house first, see what we need." He turned into Riverview Circle and looked at the third house. A man who appeared to be around sixty was mowing the lawn.

"There's our man," Kerry said.

"We're going to talk to him now," Kinney said.

"Without backup?"

"He's armed with a lawn mower. I think we can handle that. You be ready, if he does anything funny or tries to run." Kinney slowed as he approached the house, then he stopped and pressed the button to lower the passenger-side window. "Excuse me," he said. The man seemed not to hear over the lawn mower. *"Excuse me!"*

The man shut down the engine and walked over to the car. "Morning, can I help you?"

"Yes, we're looking for Riverview Drive," Kinney said. "Can you direct us?"

"Yeah, sure. Turn around and make two rights. That's Riverview Drive."

"Got it. Say, this is a real nice place you've got here, looks real well kept."

"Oh, I don't live here. I work for the real estate company."

"Real estate company?"

The man walked over to the mailbox and picked up the sign he had uprooted in order to cut the grass. FOR SALE, the sign read. "River Realty, Janice Hooks." And a phone number. "The house is empty," the man said. "I just cut the grass for the real estate company."

The two agents got out of the car, and Kinney walked around to the other side and flashed his ID. "We're FBI," he said. "Could I see some ID?"

"Sure." The man dug in a pocket and came out with a wallet and a driver's license.

Kinney looked at it and compared the face

to the photo. "Thanks, Mr. Warren. Do you know the man who lives here?"

"No, he was already gone when I started cutting the grass."

"How long ago was that?"

"About a month. This is the fourth time I've been."

Kerry pulled his boss aside. "I'll get a search warrant and a team out here."

"No, wait," Kinney replied. "I don't think we have probable cause, but there's another way." He walked back to the real estate sign and called the realtor, then he came back. "Ms. Hooks is on her way over here. Mr. Warren, you can go back to your work. Again, I apologize for slowing you down."

"Let's take a look," Kinney said, and led the way up the lawn toward the house. It was brick, modest in scale, in good repair. He stepped through some shrubs and looked through the window into the empty living room. "Kerry, get a criminalist out here now, and tell him to bring some help."

Kerry got on the phone.

"And get my secretary to dig into those personnel files the CIA sent over and dig out Fay's records. Ask the Agency for a photograph, if there isn't one in his files." Kinney circumnavigated the house, looking into every window. Empty rooms stared back at him. As he came back to the front of the house, a Cadillac pulled into the driveway, and a woman got out.

"Agent Kinney?" she asked.

"That's right, Ms. Hooks," he replied, shaking her hand. "This is Agent Kerry Smith."

"What can I do for you?" she asked.

"I'd like for my people to go into the house and collect some evidence."

"Has a crime been committed here?" she asked, looking puzzled.

"I don't know yet. That's what I want to find out."

"Don't you need a search warrant for that?"

"I can get a search warrant, but it will take several hours, and another crime might be committed while I'm doing it. On the other hand, you have the authority to let us into the house."

"I don't know," she said. "Mr. Fay might sue me."

"That's very unlikely, Ms. Hooks. It would be a great help to us if you could let us in now. This is extremely important."

She put a hand to her mouth. “Oh, God, it’s that sniper guy who’s killing all those people, isn’t it?”

“I can’t comment on our investigation, Ms. Hooks, and please don’t tell anyone that, particularly anyone from the media. It could greatly impede our investigation.”

The woman dug into her handbag and came up with a key. “Here,” she said, “go to it. I want you to get the bastard. I listened to Van Vandervelt every single day.”

“Thank you, Ms. Hooks. Again, please don’t mention this to anyone.”

“Is there anything else I can do to help?”

“Did you ever meet Mr. Fay?”

“Just once, when I came to look at the house.”

“Can you describe him for me?”

“Just average-looking, I guess. Gray hair, fairly slim, not as tall as you, maybe five ten or so?”

“Do you know where Mr. Fay is?”

“No, he said he was going to see the world. He had a big auction here, sold all his household goods, his car, and his RV. Said he was burning his bridges. His wife died a couple of years ago, I think.”

"What were your instructions if you found a buyer?"

"I have a power of attorney to accept a suitable offer and close the sale."

"And what are you to do with the proceeds of the sale?"

"Well, that was kind of strange. I'm to run an ad in the *International Herald Tribune,* saying, 'T.F.—Sale complete, instructions, please.' And then I would get a phone call or a fax with instructions for wiring the money."

"And you haven't sold the house, yet?"

"I've had one lowball offer that I turned down, since it didn't meet Mr. Fay's minimum price."

"Ms. Hooks, I'd like you to run the ad, please, and I'd like you to phone me the moment you get the wiring instructions." He handed her a card.

"And what do I tell him when the money doesn't arrive?"

"If we get that far, tell him the seller failed to close, and you're back to square one. See if you can get him to tell you where he is. If he won't, then tell him the power of attorney he signed—how long ago did he sign it?"

"A few weeks."

"Tell him it expires in sixty days from signing by law, and you'll have to send him a new one, if you're going to continue to market the house. Get an address or a fax number for that purpose."

"All right. I'll go back to the office and place the ad."

They shook hands, and she got into her car and left.

"That was very good," Kerry said.

"Let's hope it works. And when the team arrives, put their vehicle in the garage. Let's keep the place looking as normal as possible. Go tell the lawn guy to do his job and keep his mouth shut."

"Okay." Kerry walked down the lawn toward the curb.

Kinney walked back to the front door and waited for his team. He was determined not to get too excited about this. But his heart wouldn't stop beating faster.

39

KATHARINE RULE LEE looked up to see her deputy director for operations standing in her doorway. "Good morning, Hugh," she said. "Thanks for coming." She waved him to the sofa and went to meet him there.

"What's up, boss?" he asked. This was meant to be ironic; Hugh English had never gotten over the fact that an independent commission had recommended Kate over him for the director's job.

"I had a conversation last night with President Majorov that I think you might like to know about."

"Something new for the Majorov file? I'm always happy to have something new on him."

"It's not just about Majorov. It's about Ed

Rawls, too. You'll need to add this to his file, as well."

"Okay."

"You may remember that Majorov was the KGB station head in Stockholm when Rawls was there, so he would have been running Rawls."

"I remember, but that's not necessarily true. He may have appointed somebody else to run Rawls."

"He confirmed to me that he, personally, ran Rawls."

English's face became expressionless. "So he would have ordered the hit on Lewis and Barbara Moore."

"That's a reasonable conclusion, but Majorov denies it."

"I'll bet he does."

"Given the kind of conversation we were having, which was well-oiled on his part, he had no real reason to deny it."

"Rawls set up Lewis and Barbara," English said. "It's the only way it could have happened."

"No, there was another way. Majorov says he had a bug in the Moores' apartment."

"I don't believe it," English said. "Staff apartments are swept on a regular basis."

"I want to know if this is true," Kate said. "First, get in touch with our Stockholm station and find out if a bug was ever detected in that apartment. If one was never found, then it's still there."

"Our people would have found it."

"You remember the brouhaha when we learned that the Soviets were bugging the new American embassy in Moscow, while it was being built?"

"Of course."

"I think that shows us that the Soviets had some bugs that were very difficult, if not impossible, to detect."

"I suppose so."

"If there's no record of a bug being found in the Moores' apartment, then I want the place taken apart, and I mean right down to ripping off the drywall and the plumbing. Move whoever is in the apartment now out and into a new place, and do this thing right."

"I think this is a monumental waste of time, Kate."

"If that's so, it won't be the first time."

"I don't really have the budget for that sort of thing, and officially, those apartments belong to the State Department."

"Charge it to a renovation of the apartment, which is what we're going to have to do when the search is over. If you have any trouble with State, let me know, and I'll deal with it. One more thing, Hugh. Majorov says that when they were confronted, the Moores drew weapons and started firing, and that it was self-defense on the part of his people. I want to know what weapons the Moores had drawn from the station's arsenal and if they were ever recovered."

English looked at her for a moment. "You're determined to get Rawls pardoned, aren't you?"

"No, I'm not. I'm determined to know the truth about this. There's more going on here than you know about, Hugh."

English looked incredulous. "More than *I* know about? More than the fucking DDI for Operations knows about?"

"Not all the information we possess arises from your operations, Hugh. Stuff comes in from outside all the time, you know that."

"Well, if there's something you know, why don't I know it?"

"Because it's not time, yet. If we find a bug in that apartment, you'll know everything soon. You'll have to be content with that for the moment."

"Right," English said, getting to his feet and heading for the door.

"And, Hugh?"

He stopped and turned. "Yeah?"

"I want work to start on that apartment today."

English looked at his watch. "It's four-thirty in Stockholm now. It'll have to wait until tomorrow."

"I want the occupants out tonight—put them in a hotel, if necessary. I want a crew in there at eight o'clock tomorrow morning, and I want them to work 'round the clock until they're done. Clear?"

"Clear, Madame Director," English said. He turned and stalked out of her office.

Kate swallowed her anger and went back to her desk. She was getting tired of swallowing her anger where Hugh English was concerned. Sooner or later, he was going to have to go. At his level, there was no sideways move for him; he either had to be promoted or fired, and the only job he could be promoted to was hers. She'd wait until Will was reelected, when there wouldn't be as much political fallout.

40

Bob Kinney stood on the doorstep of the house, wearing booties, latex gloves, and a hairnet. He hated wearing the hairnet, but it had to be done, if the scene was going to be preserved and protected from contamination.

"You ready?" the criminalist asked.

"Jack, this is the most important scene you've ever worked. The president has taken an interest, and I want everything done right, by the book."

"That's the only way I know how," Jack replied. He nodded to his three assistants. "This is a full-scene sweep," he said. "That means everything, and with maximum caution. Let's go." He turned the key, opened the front door, and stepped inside. "Uh-oh," he said, looking around.

"What's the matter?" Kinney asked from the doorway.

"Man, this is clean, and I mean *clean*."

FOUR HOURS LATER, Kinney, who was sitting in a chair on the front porch, looked up to see Jack coming out of the house, stripping off his latex gloves. Kinney stood up. "You're not done, are you?"

"Let me tell you about this house, Agent Kinney," Jack said. "This house has been cleaned by a professional crew, maybe two or three professional crews, then it's been wiped down by a pro."

"You mean you found *nothing*?"

"No, I found the fingerprints of eight people on the doorknobs, on the refrigerator, and on the bathroom medicine cabinet—all the places you'd expect to find the prints of people who are considering buying a house. I'll run them all, but I'm telling you now there is not a fingerprint, not a hair, not a ball of fluff in this house that can be used to trace your man. I've never seen anything like it."

Kinney sighed. "All right, if you say so. Can I go in now?"

"Yep, but wear the gear, if you want the scene preserved."

Kinney got dressed again and pulled on the latex gloves. He walked through the front door and stood in the middle of the living room. Everything shone with cleanliness—the hardwood floors, the trim, the kitchen beyond. Only a thin layer of dust revealed the footprints of the crime scene team, and only the black fingerprint dust here and there marred the pristine cleanliness.

He walked around the house, into the bedrooms, bathrooms, and closets, encountering yet more of the obsessive cleanliness. He opened a door, flipped on a light switch, and walked down the stairs into the cellar, which was larger than he had expected, and, of course, spotlessly clean. Every corner was brightly lit by the dozen fluorescent ceiling fixtures. He looked around with some envy. This had been one hell of a workshop, one he would have been thrilled to own himself. The worktables were fixed to the walls, and the walls of the large room were lined with pegboard, which had the outlines of tens of dozens of tools meticulously painted on them. It was possible to tell from the outlines the extent of the equipment in the shop, and it was breathtaking. Teddy Fay could fix anything, Mrs. Coulter had said. Well, he certainly had owned the tools required to fix anything or, for that matter, to build anything.

"This is our guy," Kinney said aloud to himself.

"I don't doubt it," Kerry Smith said from the stairs. "You ever seen anything this clean?"

"No, and neither has anybody else."

"Quite a workshop he had, too," Smith said, looking around.

"What have you got?" Kinney asked.

"You're not going to like it," the young agent replied.

"Tell me anyway."

"There was no file on Teddy Kay among those that the CIA sent over."

"That's not possible, unless the Agency is holding out on us."

"I've spent the last two hours on the phone with a guy in personnel over there, Harold Broward, and he swears that the Agency has no record of *anybody* named Fay ever having worked there."

The two men stood silently, while Kinney tried to work this out.

"Not that Teddy Fay never worked there," Kinney said finally, "but that they have no *record* of his ever having worked there?"

"That's what Broward said."

Kinney walked over to a wall and pointed at a receptacle. "That's for a fast Internet connection," he said. "Let's suppose that our Teddy was as good at computers as he was at everything else."

"Okay, I'll buy that."

"Is it possible that, while doing his job, he could have obtained the passwords necessary to erase all record of himself from the CIA's computers?"

"Well," said Smith, "let's say that if he knew what he was doing and had the time, it's not *im*possible."

"Did you run a credit report?"

"I ran all three major reporting agencies. He lived in this house for thirty years, had one employer for all that time, a CIA front business, which, according to Broward, has no record of him, either. He paid off his mortgage ten years ago, had one bank account, one brokerage account, and three credit cards, all canceled by his executor upon his death."

"His death?"

"That's what the credit reports said. Same for his bank account, driver's license, and Social Security account. Officially, Teddy Fay no longer exists."

"Who was his executor?"

"The law firm of Schwartz and Schwartz, which doesn't exist, either. The proceeds of his estate were placed in the nonexistent firm's trust account, which was closed shortly after the funds were wire-transferred to a Cayman Islands bank, a little over a month ago."

"In short, Teddy Fay took a deep breath and disappeared up his own ass."

"That's about the size of it," Smith agreed. "And if he indeed worked at Technical Services at the CIA, then he had all the tools at hand to create a new identity—or multiple identities—for himself before he retired and disappeared."

"You know what this says to me?" Kinney asked.

"What?"

"He intends to get away with it."

"With all these killings? You think he expects to just walk away?"

"That's exactly what I think. He's not some fanatic who wants to kill a lot of people, then commit suicide by police. He's completely rational, if not exactly sane. He's a planner—methodical and meticulous—and he expects to walk. Otherwise why would he have cashed in and vanished?"

"This is scary," Smith said.

"It's worse than that. It's depressing. Here's what I want you to do: I want you to go and see Mrs. Coulter again, then assemble all the people on her Christmas card list who knew Fay at the Agency. Put them in my conference room. If we don't have access to any official record of Fay, then we'll have to rely on people who knew him."

"Will do."

"Get them there this afternoon, if at all possible, and send transport for anybody who needs a ride." He took out his cell phone. "Now I've got to call the president."

41

KATE GOT BACK to the family quarters at the White House a little after seven. Will was sitting in the living room watching CNN. She headed for the bar.

"Not so fast," Will said, switching off the TV. "You're still on duty."

"I am? Until when?"

"Until I tell you some things. Have a seat."

Kate sat down next to him on the sofa and kissed him.

"No kissing the commander-in-chief," Will said.

"All right," she replied, folding her hands in her lap. "No sexual harassment until the workday is over. Get to it. I want a drink."

"Kinney at the FBI called this afternoon. He thinks they've found the killer. Well, not found him, exactly, but identified him."

"Who is he?"

"It's bad news."

Kate's face fell. "Not one of mine."

"Yes, but fortunately, he retired before you took charge."

"Who is he?"

"His name is Theodore Fay."

"Doesn't ring a bell with me."

"He was in Technical Services, so as an analyst, you probably wouldn't have had contact with him."

But Ed Rawls might have, she thought. As much as she hated learning that the killer was ex-CIA, she was relieved that she wasn't going to have to deal with Rawls to find out who he was. "Is the evidence against him strong?"

"Well, that's the problem. There isn't any evidence just yet."

"Then how do we know Fay is the guy?"

"First, he has all the qualifications—the skills to make the bombs and poisons. That's apparently what he did at the Agency. Second, he's faked his death, cashed in everything he owns, except his house, which hasn't sold yet, and sent the proceeds out of the country. It seems likely that he would have created one or more new identities for himself before he left the Agency."

"But how is the FBI going to connect him directly to the killings?"

"I don't know. Maybe their lab will find something in one of the crime scenes that will connect him. Or a witness will turn up, somebody who can put him at a scene."

"And what do you want me to do?"

"This evening—right now, in fact—Kinney is assembling some retired Agency people who knew Fay. He wanted to do it earlier, but none of them would talk to the FBI without Agency approval. I want you to call Kinney's office, speak to the group on speakerphone, and tell them to cooperate fully." He handed her a sheet of paper. "This is a list of their names."

"Okay, I can do that right away."

"Then I want you to let the FBI talk to anybody in Technical Services who can help them catch Fay."

"Where?"

"At the Agency, where they work."

"You want me to let FBI agents into Technical Services? My people down there would rather meet with Osama bin Laden and his boys and show them around the shop."

"Kate, this is not about interservice rivalry, this is about catching a murderer who is an embarrassment to the CIA and to this administration. Tomorrow morning at ten o'clock, two FBI agents are going to present themselves at Langley, and I want them to talk directly to anybody they need to talk to who can help them find him."

"They don't have to see the labs and the shops, do they?"

"They are to see anybody and anything that will help them."

"That's it?"

"That's it until they need something else. And there will be something else. When they catch this guy there'll be a trial, and an appropriate person in Technical Services is going to have to testify about how he made the Vandervelt bomb and the Calhoun poison and about any other skills or devices he has employed to murder people, and when that happens, I don't want any crap from the Agency about revealing its secrets."

"You're really a barrel of fun, you know that?"

"You're talking to your commander-in-chief. Watch it."

"Yes, sir."

"That's better. Now, are we perfectly clear on what you have to do?"

"Yes, sir."

"Then go do it, and then you can have a drink."

Kate went meekly to the phone and made the calls. When she came back, there was a gleaming vodka martini waiting for her on the coffee table.

"Hey, sweetheart," he said, kissing her.

"Hey, Will," she said. "How was your day?"

"I've had worse," he said, touching his glass to hers.

42

KINNEY WATCHED THE FACES of the five men and women sitting around his conference table as they listened to Katharine Rule Lee instruct them on cooperating with the FBI. He understood that these people had spent their working lives not talking about their work, their coworkers, or their employer, and he was hoping to see the bland defiance in their faces dissolve into something more amenable. It did not happen.

Mrs. Lee finished her instructions. "Does anybody have any questions?" she asked.

A man spoke up. "How do we know you're who the FBI says you are?"

Mrs. Lee's voice came back. "Call the White House switchboard and ask for me. Use the code name Huntress."

The man nodded. He was handed a

phone, and he did as Mrs. Lee instructed. When she answered, he thanked her and hung up. "All right," he said, "I'm on board."

"Anybody else have a problem?" Kinney asked.

Everyone shook his head.

"Now, let me tell you why we're here. We have reason to believe that a former coworker of yours, Theodore G. Fay, known as Teddy, is the person who has murdered three prominent Americans over the past few weeks." He paused to let this sink in, and there was shock on some of the faces.

"Why do you think Teddy Fay would do that?" someone asked.

"His political views were antithetical to those of the people he murdered. He possesses the skills used to murder them. He has faked his death, moved his assets out of the country, and has disappeared."

"That doesn't sound like hard evidence," someone else said.

"It's convincing circumstantial evidence," Kinney replied. "Starting there, we expect to develop more material information, but we need your help. Teddy Fay has destroyed all the CIA's records of his employment, so we have no fingerprints, no photograph, and no other evidence that would help us find him."

"Smart," a woman said.

"He is not a stupid man," Kinney replied. "What I want from you is a description that we can use to make a drawing of him, and—"

A man spoke up. "Give me a drawing pad, and I'll do one for you."

Kinney motioned to the FBI artist who was sitting against the wall, and the man provided the materials.

"While you're doing that, do any one of you have one or more photographs of Fay? Something taken at a reunion or a party?"

They all shook their heads.

"Do any of you have knowledge of Fay owning or having access to a second home? A cabin in the mountains, a house on Chesapeake Bay, anything like that?"

They all shook their heads.

"Wait," one of them said. "He used to keep a boat at a yacht club in Annapolis. I had a conversation with him about it once."

Kinney motioned Kerry Smith forward. "Would you please go with Agent Smith and tell him everything you know about it?"

The two men left.

"Do any of you have any other information

of any kind that might help us locate Fay? Anybody with knowledge of family members or friends inside or outside the Agency that he might feel safe with or try to contact?"

A woman spoke up. "Teddy's wife died several years ago. She was all he had. They were childless, and I'm pretty sure Teddy was an only child. He didn't like her parents, so if they are still alive, he wouldn't go to them."

"Did any one of you ever take a vacation with Fay? A weekend sailing or hunting trip, anything like that?"

No one spoke.

"All right, I'd like the personal impressions of Fay of each of you in turn. May we start with you?"

He pointed to a woman.

"Brilliantly inventive, technically accomplished in many skills, very self-contained, tightly wound."

She sat back and folded her arms.

"Did you ever work with him on assignments?"

"Many times."

"Did any other personal characteristics stand out?"

She shook her head.

A man spoke up. "I worked with Teddy, oh, maybe a dozen times," he said. "What Jean says is true. I also felt that he was an angry man, though I never knew about what."

Another man spoke. "I'll second that. He didn't encourage knowing him. He always brought his lunch and ate it in the garden in warm weather and at his desk when it was cold. I don't ever recall seeing him in the cafeteria, let alone lunching with anybody."

"He was knowledgeable about investments," another man said. "I was talking to someone about putting some money into a mutual fund on one occasion. Teddy overheard me and named three other funds he said were better, and he was right."

"Did you have any idea of the extent of his own holdings?"

"No, he would never have talked about that."

A woman spoke up. "You have to understand that Teddy wasn't exactly an oddball in Tech Services. There were lots of people who would have seemed odd in other surroundings. Lots of us were freaks, techies, nerds, and bookworms."

There was a chorus of agreement from the group.

"Does anyone have any inkling of where he might have gone when he disappeared?"

There was a moment's silence, then a man spoke up. "You have to understand the work we did. Apart from the weapons—the bombs, the exploding fountain pens, the exotic firearms—what we did was to invisibly alter perceptions. We manufactured personalities, created documents, constructed legends—all the things that would make an agent or friend seem to be something other than what he was—and verifiably so. Teddy not only had access to all those techniques and equipment, he invented much of it. If he chose to disappear, then he would have done so in such a way that you could not find him. You would never think of looking for him where he went, and neither would I or anyone else here."

Another murmur of agreement.

Another man spoke up. "You've got just one chance of finding him," he said.

Kinney turned to face him. "Tell me."

"If Teddy turns himself in."

Kinney was still thinking about that when the artist shoved his drawing pad across the table to him. Kinney looked at it and saw a bland face with a slight smile, one that seemed nearly featureless. He turned the pad around and showed it to the group. "Is that Teddy Fay?"

There was a chorus of assents.

"Thank you all for coming," Kinney said. "My secretary will give each of you my card, and should you think of anything else pertinent or, especially, if you should hear from Mr. Fay, please call me at once, day or night."

He watched them file from the room, then looked again into the face of Teddy Fay—enigmatic to a fault.

43

KINNEY AND SMITH DROVE out to MacLean, Virginia, the following morning and presented their ID to a guard at the main gate of the Central Intelligence Agency. They were admitted, parked in a visitors' spot, and walked into the main lobby, which was familiar to Kinney, with its memorial wall of dead agents, from various movies and magazine photographs. A middle-aged woman in a business suit was waiting for them.

"Agents Kinney and Smith?"

"That's right," Kinney replied. "Is it so obvious?"

"Yes, it is," she said without smiling. "Would you please follow me?" She led them into an elevator, then inserted a plastic card into a slot and pressed an unnumbered button. The elevator seemed not to move for several moments, but then the door opened and they stepped into a hallway.

Kinney was not sure if they had gone up or down. He followed the woman, who had not mentioned her name, down a long hallway and into a conference room, where she asked them to wait. A few moments later a gray-haired man, apparently in his fifties, came into the room while struggling into his suit jacket.

"Agents Kinney and Smith?"

They rose and shook hands.

"Call me Gil," the man said. He waved them to seats. "I've been instructed by the director to cooperate with your investigation, so I will answer any of your questions that seem relevant. I understand you want to know about Theodore Fay?"

"That's correct," Kinney replied. "We want to know everything you can tell us about him."

"Of course, I wanted to print out his employment record for you, but as you're now no doubt aware, it has been removed from our computer files, and there is, apparently, no hard copy."

"Yes, we know about that. What can you

tell us about the nature of his employment here?"

"I understand you already have the personal recollections of some of our people who are retired."

"That's correct."

"They would have known Teddy as well or better than I, so I'll tell you what I know about what he did here until his retirement."

"Thank you, that would be very helpful."

"I must ask you to treat everything I tell you as secret and not to share this information with anyone not directly connected to your investigation. I would also prefer it if you would not make written notes of our conversation or include them in any reports circulated to your own people or others."

"We understand your need for secrecy," Kinney replied, "and we'll do everything we can to keep your confidence."

"Thank you. First, let me give you an overview of the kinds of things we do here. Our Department of Technical Services is divided into, roughly, four segments: weapons, both offensive and defensive, including firearms and various others; chemical, again both offensive and defensive, including explosives and poisons;

communications, including radios and computers; and documents, including manufacture of same, as well as analysis of found materials. Our capabilities in all these areas are far beyond those of any police department in the world, and very probably, well beyond those of your own FBI labs."

"In which areas did Teddy Fay work?" Kinney asked.

"All of them," Gil replied, "at one time or another. Teddy came to work here at a time when the department was less segmented that it now is. He had degrees in mechanical engineering and chemistry from MIT and a growing reputation as an inventor. He already held a number of patents that continued to produce income for many years. He was an amateur gunsmith, and in his youth, an amateur actor, and he started here working on firearms and disguises.

"When personal computers became available, Teddy bought one at Radio Shack and taught himself programming. He wrote some software products that, updated for the newer operating systems, are still in use here. Computers remained an obsession with him, but then, Teddy was obsessed with nearly everything. He was the ideal employee—completely dedicated to his work and, apparently, nothing else. We could have kept him in a cage and thrown him meat once in a while, and he wouldn't have noticed. He'd have just shown up for work every morning with a new idea. I hated to lose him."

"What was he doing in, say, the last two years of his employment?" Kinney asked.

"He was a key supervisor. Let's say we were planning to insert an agent into a foreign country: Teddy would draw up a plan which would include documentation and backup, weapons, disguises, clothing, transportation, and communications, plus anything else the agent might need. Then Teddy would supervise the obtaining or creation of all the things the agent needed. His skills were such that he could fill the shoes of anyone who worked for him, if necessary. If his passport artist was down with the flu, Teddy could create a passport from scratch, or figure out where to steal a blank one."

Kinney interrupted. "You said documentation and backup. What did you mean by backup?"

"Let's say that our agent was detained while crossing a border. The local police would do everything possible to check out his background and his legend, so every document, every word he said, every part of his legend, had to be verifiable. Teddy was an absolute genius at that. I'll give you an example, though I can't be too specific. Some years ago, Teddy broke into the computer systems of an Eastern European country and downloaded thousands of passport records. From that he learned how to create a passport file for an individual that was indistinguishable from the genuine article, then upload it into their system. So, if an agent's passport was checked against the central files, there he was, making his passport unassailable."

"You said he could create documents from scratch?"

"Yes, if he had to, and if he had a sample to work from. Something our agents are always looking for is blank documents from other governments—expense reports, criminal records, employment applications, anything a government uses, and especially passports. If we couldn't get the real thing, then Teddy could make the paper, the watermarks, the holograms, the seals and stamps, and anything else that went into the manufacture of the original. It was time-consuming, but it saved many lives."

"We know that Teddy has faked his death, and we're sure he's out there somewhere in America with one or more fake identities. Based on what you do here, what would one of those identities consist of, and how would it be backed up?"

"It would consist of everything in your wallet—credit cards, driver's license, club and museum memberships, insurance cards, the works. And it would all be real. Let's say he got stopped for speeding, and the cop ran his driver's license and car registration. It would come back as genuine, and the address of record would be real, if somebody went and knocked on a door. Suppose he was questioned by the police when suspected of a crime. He would have college and high school transcripts inserted into the correct computers, and his fingerprints would not turn up any previous arrests. If he were employed, the employer would be real. He would have a credit record going back an appropriate number of years—he could even walk into a bank and borrow money. It would all be airtight, and there wouldn't be any leaks."

"Wouldn't he need help from other people to make it airtight?"

"Not necessarily. Most background checking is done by requesting records, which are computerized. Let's say his legend includes working for a large insurance company. The cops would call to verify his employment, and a clerk would enter his name into a computer and pull up his employment record. It would all be there for the clerk to read to the police, or he could even email them a copy. He would only need help if the police tried to telephone his supervisor and actually speak to someone who knows him. We would cover that for an agent, but Teddy might find it difficult, working alone."

"So what do we look for? How can we pierce this legend, if we find him?"

"Odds are, you can't. He will have constructed it in such a way as to make it completely plausible and verifiable. He could tell you his life story, and when you checked it out, it would all be, well, 'true.' "

"Do you have a record of his fingerprints?"

"No, I checked. It's gone, along with everything else about Teddy."

Kinney had a thought. "Could you check something for me?"

"If I can."

"Teddy retired, so he's on a pension, right?"

"Right."

"Will you check with your accounting department and see if his pension is being paid, and if so, to what bank? And what address they have for Fay?"

"Give me a few minutes," Gil said. He left the room, and a woman brought coffee and cookies for them.

TEN MINUTES LATER, Gil returned. "He didn't delete his pay records. His pension is being paid into an account at the First National Bank of Arlington, and his address is the one on Riverview Circle where he lived for many years." He laid a sheet of paper on the table containing all the information. "What else can I do for you?"

Kinney stood up. "I think that will do it. May I call you, if I think of anything else?"

"Sure. My extension is ten-ten." He offered his hand. "Good luck on finding Teddy. You're going to need it."

• • •

DRIVING BACK to the Bureau, both agents were silent for a long time. Finally, Kerry Smith spoke up. "What do you think he's doing?"

"Doing?" Kinney asked.

"He's not finished," Smith said, "but after the first spate of murders, he hasn't killed anybody for a while."

"You're right, he's not through," Kinney replied. "He's planning. He's just getting ready to move again, in his own time."

"Well, we've got a guard on everyone pictured on his website. We can't do more than that."

"We can anticipate him," Kinney said.

"How?"

"We've got to get inside his head, to figure out who the most likely target would be. If you were Teddy, who would you go after?"

Smith was quiet for a while. "Somebody high up," he said finally.

"The president?"

"No, the president's politics aren't the kind that Teddy hates."

"Speaker of the House?"

"That would be my bet. He has all the

qualifications for getting hit by Teddy—right-wing, in-your-face politics—"

"That seems to be Teddy's only criterion."

"That and being well known."

"Let's get back to the office and make a new list."

44

TED EXITED I-95 and made his way to Manassas Regional Airport, south of Washington, D.C. He inserted his security card to open the gate, then drove to the west side of the field, past some T-hangars, to a larger hangar behind them. He drove around back and punched a garage-door opener; the large bifold door opened, and the lights came on. Ted drove the RV inside and used the remote to close the door again. A large fan heater came on immediately, to compensate for the heat lost through the open door.

Ted maneuvered the RV into its assigned space, then got out and connected the power cable and the flexible drain leading to the septic system. He was home. He went into the RV and gazed at himself in the bathroom mirror. A very different Ted Fay stared back at him, one with a head of thick, gray hair and a walrus mustache. He peeled off the mustache, then the toupee and washed them both, leaving them on a form to dry. Then he went "outside" into the hangar.

The hangar held the RV and his car—a five-year-old Mercedes E320, which wasn't really a 320, because he had modified it, installing an AMG Mercedes engine of five and a half liters and upgrading the suspension and tires. What he had now was a bland-looking family sedan that was capable of zero to sixty miles an hour in under five seconds, and he had replaced the speed-limiting chip with one that allowed a top speed in excess of a hundred and eighty miles an hour. Ted loved cars, and he loved this one best of all.

The final fixture in the hangar was a glassed-in office with a toilet and shower. Inside that were a desk and chair, a sofa, a comfortable recliner, and a large rear-projection television set. Ted loved TV, too. On the desk was a very powerful computer that he had assembled himself, modeled after the units used in Tech Services at the CIA, and incorporating their stolen chip, with a twenty-one-inch flat-screen monitor. With it he could access almost any government system, from the Pentagon to the CIA. Occupying an adjoining area was his workshop, which he had disassembled at his home and reassembled in the hangar.

Ted logged onto the ACT NOW website and gazed at the photographs displayed there, lingering over Efton, the speaker of the House. Efton was a tempting target, but in some ways Ted thought him a good man to have in the job, since the way he conducted himself often engendered great opposition among moderates. He eliminated the speaker from consideration.

He needed a more important, more pivotal figure. He went to another website where he had stored more photos and biographical information on other public figures, and he came to the Supreme Court. He quickly eliminated four of the nine justices, then lingered for a moment over a fifth, the one who was often a swing vote, finally eliminating her. He was left with four justices, including the chief justice, whom Ted had disliked for years. He was very old, now, and rumor was he would be leaving the Court soon, leaving President Lee to appoint his successor. No point in creating a fuss by dealing with him, so he eliminated the chief justice from consideration.

Now he was left with three justices, each of whom qualified politically. Each slavishly followed the chief justice's lead on important cases, and the elimination of any of them would be good for the country, Ted figured. One, however, stood out. Thomas Graydon was the newest appointee to the Court, a man who had managed, during his confirmation hearings, to convince enough Democrats that his views were moderate to get him confirmed. Once on the Court, though, he had revealed himself as a hard-line right-winger, infuriating the senators he had fooled during the hearings. He often addressed conservative groups, making inflammatory speeches backing far right-wing legal positions. He was the youngest member of the Court, only forty-nine years of age, and he could very well be there for thirty years or more, tossing legal hand grenades at the Bill of Rights.

Here was a man who had earned Ted's attention. His elimination would allow the moderate president to make perhaps the most important appointment of his presidency, after the chief justice, should the old man die or yield his seat. The Democrats held a one-vote majority in the Senate, and Lee could get his appointees confirmed without too much trouble.

Ted eliminated the other justices, leaving only Thomas Graydon. Now he had to decide how to accomplish this death. He thought it should be done more subtly than the others, in fact so subtly that the FBI might think that Ted had not been responsible. An "accidental" death would certainly be preferable.

He scrolled through newspaper and magazine articles about Justice Graydon that he had collected during his confirmation hearings and the three years that Graydon had sat on the Court, and he was struck by a photograph of the man getting out of his car at the Capitol during the hearings. The car was a black, American-made SUV, and he found another shot of Graydon in the car, taken on a fishing trip, this shot more recent, which meant that he probably still owned the car. He would do a drive-by and see if it was parked at the Graydon home.

Then Ted hacked into the computer systems of the manufacturer of the car and went into the design department's files.

After a few minutes, he came up with the design for the main chip in the car's computer system, the one that directed everything from its fuel management to its antilock braking system. He printed out the design and went carefully over it, seeing opportunity.

Next, he went to the manufacturer's parts distribution center, entered the part number of the chip and got a list of dealers who had it in stock. The part was not one that was often replaced, so few dealers had it, only one of them east of the Mississippi, in Baltimore, which would do nicely.

He went back to the RV and made himself some dinner, then relaxed in front of the TV for the evening. His mind was preoccupied with the computer chip, however, and how he could modify it to suit his purposes.

Tomorrow morning he would check Justice Graydon's house for the presence of the vehicle, and if he still owned it, then Ted would need to make a trip to Baltimore.

This would take time and effort, but it would be worth it; after Graydon, he would make his exit from the scene. A very nice little island cottage waited for him, and he looked forward to a quiet life, after he had made his mark on American political history.

Then the evening news came on, and Ted was surprised to find a very good drawing of himself staring out of the screen. He hadn't thought the FBI were so close, and he settled in to watch their performance.

"Now we take you to the press office at the White House, where Assistant Director Robert Kinney of the FBI is holding a press conference."

Bob Kinney's face filled the screen, and Ted studied it carefully.

45

KINNEY TOOK A DEEP BREATH and leaned into the microphone. "Ladies and gentlemen, we have a suspect in the three murders and one attempted murder that have captured so much attention in past weeks." He pressed a button, and the drawing of Teddy Fay filled the monitors in the room. "His name is Theodore Fay, and he is a retired employee of the Central Intelligence Agency. Mr. Fay worked in the Technical Services division of the Agency for more than thirty years, where he acquired the skills that he employed in these crimes. Mr. Fay is sixty-seven years of age, five feet eleven inches tall, a hundred and eighty pounds, and physically fit. He has gray hair and is balding and has green eyes. Although he has gone to some lengths to fake his own death and move his assets out of the country, we believe Mr. Fay is living somewhere within fifty miles of Washington, D.C. He may drive a recreational vehicle. We expect that, due to the nature of his work at the CIA, he has established one or more identities, complete with driver's licenses, credit cards, and other forms of identification, including valid U.S. passports, and that he may also employ various disguises.

"We ask the cooperation of the media and the public in finding Mr. Fay, and to that end, we have established a toll-free hotline where sightings may be reported." He flashed the number on the screen. "I am authorized by the president to say that a reward of one million dollars, tax-free, is being offered for information leading to the arrest of Theodore Fay. We regard Mr. Fay as armed and dangerous and I urge members of the public not to approach him, but to call the hotline number or local law enforcement. Now, I will take questions." He pointed at a woman in the first row.

"Mr. Kinney, what does the FBI believe is Mr. Fay's motive for these killings?"

"We believe that Mr. Fay is unhappy with the present political situation in the United

States and that he is seeking to redress it by removing certain figures from the scene."

"Is Mr. Fay a communist?" someone shouted.

"That is extremely unlikely," Kinney replied. "We believe that he simply holds political views to the left of the mainstream. Obviously, he is very angry."

"Is Theodore Fay insane?" a reporter asked.

"Our profilers think that is unlikely, at least in the legal sense of the term, but clearly he is not behaving like a normal person. Normal people do not employ violence and murder to redress grievances."

"Mr. Kinney, when Mr. Fay is caught, where will he be tried?"

"Obviously, law enforcement agencies in Virginia and Maryland are helping in the search for Mr. Fay, but when he is arrested he will be charged in a federal court with the murder of Senator Wallace. Murder of a U.S. government official is a federal crime and carries the death penalty."

"Mr. Kinney," a reporter called out, "does the FBI have any physical evidence against Mr. Fay?"

Kinney felt his ears redden. "I can't comment on the evidence at this time," he replied. "Thank you, ladies and gentlemen," he said, then walked off the platform.

TED MUTED the TV during the commercial and thought about the last question. Kinney had looked a little embarrassed, he thought, and well he should. Ted had left no evidence anywhere to be found, except for tiny pieces of the Vandervelt bomb, which would be of little use to the FBI lab. It was clear that the Feds were desperate now. They had identified him, but he had expected that would happen; all they had was that drawing.

The FBI's special toll-free number would now be swamped with reports of sightings, but the man they were looking for just wasn't there anymore.

IN HIS CELL at the Atlanta Federal Penitentiary, Ed Rawls switched off his TV set in disgust, if not despair. He began composing a new message to Kate Lee, one that he believed would lend a new urgency to any thoughts she might have of a presidential pardon. There was something new to look forward to, as well—the prospect of a one-million-dollar reward, which would sweeten his golden years considerably.

BOB KINNEY DROVE back to the Hoover Building and went up to his office. In a conference room across the hall, four agents were manning the phones, and, predictably, calls were already streaming in. Kerry Smith stood, waiting to speak with plausible callers.

"Anything promising?" Kinney asked Smith.

"One that sounds genuine, if not promising."

"What do you mean?"

"A trucker saw someone he swears was Fay at a rest stop on I-95."

"Did he ID a vehicle?"

"He said there were a couple of RVs at the rest stop, but he saw Fay sitting at a picnic table, eating a sandwich."

"You're right, it's genuine, but not promising. 'Useless' might be a better word."

Kinney pulled up a chair and picked up a phone, listening to each of the four lines in turn. Finally, he hung up. "Remember," he said to Smith, "if we get anything from this, it will probably be only one phone call, so don't miss it or underrate it when it comes in." He left the building and went home.

46

KATE ARRIVED AT HER OFFICE and presided over a scheduled meeting, then she checked her email. There was one from Ed Rawls. Her first impulse was to delete it without reading it, but she couldn't get past her curiosity.

"My Dear Kate," it read, "Congratulations to somebody on ferreting out Teddy Fay's name. The FBI has outshone itself, for once; they have the right man. Or rather, they don't have him, do they? I can tell you where to find our Teddy—at one of two locations—and all I ask is my freedom and, of course, the reward the FBI has posted, to keep me in my old age. Come on, girl—let's get this done before somebody really important gets waxed."

Kate deleted the email and sat at her

desk, staring at the Helen Frankenthaler painting hanging on the wall opposite, soaking it in. Finally, she pressed the intercom button.

"Yes, ma'am?"

"Please ask Morton Koppel, Hugh English, and Creighton Adams to come and see me right away. It's urgent."

"Yes, ma'am."

THE THREE MEN were in her office in five minutes.

"Something up?" Adams asked.

"Yes, Creighton," she said. "We talked about this before, but now we have to talk about it again, and very seriously. It's about Ed Rawls."

Hugh English tossed a pencil onto the conference table in disgust, while Koppel and Adams sat quietly, waiting.

"Hugh, what do we hear from Stockholm?" she asked.

English shrugged. "All right, there were four bugs in the apartment."

Koppel spoke up. "What apartment?"

"Let me bring you up to date," Kate said. "After dinner, when he was here, Majorov, who was KGB station head in Stockholm at the time of Rawls's arrest, told me that Ed was not involved in the killings of Lewis and Barbara Moore, that he didn't set them up. The Soviets learned of their activities from a bug in the Moores' apartment—or rather, as Hugh tells us, four bugs. I asked Hugh to have the apartment torn apart, and they were found."

"This still doesn't make Ed Rawls anything other than a traitor," English said petulantly.

"It makes him less than a man who would betray two people who worked for him in Stockholm, costing them their lives. Can we agree on that?"

English shrugged.

"Hugh, does this new information mitigate at all your determination not to see Rawls let out of prison?"

"No," English said, "it doesn't. I want him to rot there until he dies."

Neither of the other two men looked at English.

"Mort, Creighton, are you still of a mind to see Rawls out of prison?"

"I have no objection," Adams said.

"Neither do I, given his age and health problems," Koppel said.

"All right. Hugh, I have other information for your consideration."

"Sure, I'll listen," English replied, making an attempt to sound reasonable.

"I've had several communications from Ed regarding the identity of the man who killed Wallace and Vandervelt and Brennan, and tried to kill Calhoun. He told me that he knew the identity of the murderer."

"Well, now we all know, don't we?" English said. "Anybody with a television set knows."

"The problem is, we don't know how to find him," Kate said. "Given the skills that he acquired at this Agency over the years, he could remain free for the rest of his life, killing at will, and he might never be caught. Rawls says he knows where Theodore Fay can be found."

English sat up. "How the hell could he know that?" he demanded.

"I don't know. Certainly, it's possible that the two worked together on some assignment in the past, and it's possible that Fay told Ed something that might be of use in finding him."

"So Rawls is trying to trade this information for a presidential pardon?" English asked.

"Yes, he is. Does this at all change your views on letting him out?"

English said nothing, but seemed to be grinding his teeth.

"Hugh, we're talking about two rogue Agency people—one who betrayed us and has served a long time in prison, and another who has betrayed us and is at large, killing prominent Americans."

"Does the president know about this?" English asked.

"No. I learned about it only a few minutes ago, in an email from Rawls."

"He has your email address?"

"I don't know how he got it, but I've had the same address for a long time. It wouldn't be all that hard to figure out."

"What do you want me to do, Kate?" English asked.

"I want to go to the president and recommend a commutation of Ed's sentence, if that's possible, or a pardon, if it is not, based on Ed's information leading to the arrest of Fay."

English looked at Adams. "Creighton, you worked with Fay, didn't you?"

"Several times, over the years," Adams replied.

"Do you think he could be this murderer?"

"Yes, I do," Adams replied. "And if he isn't, we'll know after he's found, and no harm done."

"Except his reputation and ours are smeared all over the media."

"That's already done. Nothing we can do about it. What about you, Hugh? You knew Teddy, could he be the killer?"

English's shoulders sagged. "Yes, I suppose he could. All right, Kate, you've got me in a box. I'll sign off on a commutation or a pardon or whatever. But I don't like it."

"You're not in a box, Hugh, at least not one of my construction. You can dissent from this recommendation, and I'll go to the president with Creighton's and Mort's backing and tell him of your objections."

English raised his hands in submission. "No, no, I'll go along quietly."

"Fine," Kate said. "I'll compose a memo to the president and my secretary will bring it around for your signatures."

"Why don't you just call him?" English asked. "You've got the number."

"I want this done properly and on the

record," Kate said. "And I want the president to have it in writing from us for his own protection."

"I didn't know this was about covering your husband's ass, Kate," English said.

"I would do the same for any president," Kate said, "and Hugh, if you ever speak that way to me again I'll fire you in the same instant."

"I apologize," English said, unapologetically.

The three men left, and Kate sat down at her computer to compose the letter. She had not wanted to do this, but she was the one in a box.

47

TED DROVE AT A MODERATE PACE past Justice Graydon's house near Rock Creek Park, ignoring the security van parked across the street. The black SUV was parked in his driveway, and Ted noted the license plate number. That was easy; now the hard part. He headed for Baltimore.

THE PARTS MANAGER stared at the number on the sheet of paper Ted had handed him. "Gee, I don't think we've got this in stock; we wouldn't ordinarily keep one, unless we had ordered it as a replacement for somebody's wrecked car."

"The manufacturer's customer hotline says you've got it," Ted said.

The manager went to a computer terminal

and typed in the part number. "That's what it says here, too. Let me go check."

Ted sat down and picked up an old magazine. He had to be patient; he didn't want to create any clear memories of him in the parts manager's mind.

Ten minutes later, the man returned, holding up a plastic envelope. "Got it," he said. "How do you want to pay?"

"I'll give you cash," Ted said, relieved. He paid for the computer chip, then drove back to his hangar at Manassas Regional Airport. He put the chip under a strong magnifier and compared what he saw to the design he had downloaded from the manufacturer's computer. Shortly, he had what he was looking for—the location of the microchips that controlled the SUV's automatic stability program and antilock brakes. This feature had finally filtered down from the high-end sedans to SUVs, and what it did was automatically apply the brakes to individual wheels in critical situations such as a skid, helping the car correct its path. He also removed the chip's restriction on acceleration and top speed, which had been designed for fuel economy.

Ted spent most of the rest of the day

adapting a chip reader, connecting it to his computer, and testing it. Finally, with the chip displayed on his large computer screen, he reprogrammed the stability program to do the exact reverse of what it had been designed to do. It was now, effectively, an instability program.

Now he had to get the chip into Thomas Graydon's car, which, with the security detail watching him, was not going to be easy. He read through his clippings file on Justice Graydon again and found something he thought might be useful: Graydon kept a cabin in a fairly steep and remote area of the Maryland mountains, not all that far from Camp David.

Ted picked up the phone and got the number for the Supreme Court, then dialed it and asked for Justice Graydon.

"Justice Graydon's chambers," a young woman's voice said.

"This is Tim Johnson in the Attorney General's office," he said. "The general has a friend of the family, a recent graduate of Yale Law School, who would like to interview for a clerk's position. She's coming to Washington for the day later this week, and the general wondered if Justice Graydon could possibly see her on Friday afternoon?"

"I'm afraid Justice Graydon won't be in on Friday afternoon," the young woman said. "He goes to his country place most weekends. Could she possibly come in on Friday morning?"

"I'm afraid not," Ted said. "Let me call you back to arrange this when I know more about her schedule. Thanks very much." He hung up.

By noon on Friday, Ted was in the Mercedes, parked not far from the garage exit at the Supreme Court building. It was nearly three o'clock before the black SUV emerged, followed by the gray security van. Ted started the engine and followed, keeping one or two cars between himself and the security van. The Friday afternoon exit from Washington was building, and the traffic was helpful to him in keeping the two vehicles in sight.

Graydon returned to his home to pick up some luggage and his wife, and with a security agent at the wheel, the car drove away from the house a little after four. A light rain was beginning to fall, and Ted switched on his wipers and lights.

He followed the entourage to the beltway, then to the interstate north, and forty-five minutes out of Washington, he watched as the SUV and the security van pulled off the highway into a rest stop with a restaurant and a service station. The SUV had to park some distance from the restaurant, because of the lack of free parking spaces, and Justice Graydon, his wife, and his bodyguard all got out and walked a hundred yards to the restaurant. The security van followed and parked at the curb outside. It was facing away from the parking lot, which suited Ted's purposes.

He parked the Mercedes near the SUV, got out, and looked around. He waited until a couple nearby had left their car and the area, then he quickly walked to the SUV, took a slim-jim tool from under his jacket, and unlocked the door. He popped the hood, and, after another quick look around, raised the hood and, with a small screwdriver, removed the cover from the central computer box, extracted the central processing chip, and replaced it with his modified version. Seconds later, he was back in the Mercedes and on his way back to the hangar, where he had much work to do.

WHEN THEY RETURNED to the SUV, the agent pointed the remote control at the car and pressed the unlock button. The horn beeped, and the parking lights flashed. It did not occur to him that the car might already be unlocked.

TEDDY WAS BACK in the hangar by early evening, and he began packing things into the RV and the Mercedes. With only a short break for dinner, he worked until past midnight, cleaning up after himself. Finally, he maneuvered the Mercedes behind the RV and hooked up the towbar. He fell into bed after 1 A.M. A good night's sleep and he would be on his way.

48

WILL READ THE LETTER from his wife once more, then he pressed a button on his intercom. "See if you can get Mrs. Lee," he said. "She's probably on her way home by now."

"Yes, Mr. President," the secretary said.

Shortly, Kate came on the line. "Hi, I've just left Langley."

"I got your fax," Will said. "Are these people really on board for this?"

"Koppel and Adams are. Hugh English was reluctant, but with the new information that came in, he folded."

"What new information?"

"Our acquaintance in Atlanta says he can be helpful in locating Mr. Fay."

"Can anyone hear you?" Will asked.

"No, I'm in the backseat, and the partition is up."

"How the hell can he be helpful with that?"

"He has been in touch with me, saying he knew who the killer was, and he wanted a pardon in return for the information. Then, when we finally got Fay's name and description, he emailed me this morning and said he knows where to find him. What we're recommending is the promise of a pardon if his information is good."

"I hate tradeoffs like this," Will said.

"I know you do, but what choice do we have? If someone else is killed because we didn't act on this, the consequences could be very bad for you."

"Not to mention the victim and his family."

"Exactly. Oh, Rawls wants the FBI reward, too."

"I suppose, if his information is good, he'd be entitled to it."

"Yes. I suggest you announce the pardon at Christmastime, when you do the annual list of pardons. Never mind that he'd already be free by then. I think you can justify the delay in announcing."

"All right, I'll have an answer for you by the time you get home."

"See you soon." She hung up.

Will read the recommendation again. He didn't like this at all. Rawls had been Kate's mentor at the CIA, and this was going to look too cozy, as if she were doing a favor for an old friend. He went into his small study and locked the letter from Kate and her colleagues in his personal safe, then he called his secretary in and dictated a letter.

"Get ahold of Deputy Director Kinney at the FBI and ask him to come to the White House immediately. Tell him he's going to have to fly to Atlanta tonight and to make the travel arrangements."

He read over the letter, then he signed it and sealed it in a White House envelope.

Bob Kinney was sitting at a table in a Georgetown restaurant, gazing into Nancy Kimble's eyes. "God, I'm glad you're back," he said.

"So am I."

They clinked glasses, and as they did, his cell phone rang.

"Dammit, I forgot to turn it off," he said, glancing at the instrument. He flipped it open. "Kinney." He listened for a moment. "Atlanta? Why?" His shoulders sagged. "I'll be there inside half an hour." He closed the phone.

"What is it?"

"I have to go to the White House, then to Atlanta on some mission or other for the president. I'm awfully sorry."

"It can't be helped," she said. "I'll be here when you get back."

"You have your key to the apartment?"

"Yes, you go ahead. I can walk home."

He stood up, kissed her, and ran for a taxi. On the way to the White House, he called the duty officer in the Hoover Building. "This is Deputy Director Kinney," he said. "I have to fly to Atlanta immediately. Call Andrews and order a plane, fuel for Charlie Brown Airport, then call Agent Kerry Smith and have him meet me at Andrews." He hung up and wondered what the hell was going on.

BOB KINNEY WAS USHERED into the family quarters of the White House only moments after Kate had arrived. Will offered him a seat, then handed him the envelope.

"Agent Kinney, I'd like you to fly to Atlanta immediately and hand-deliver this letter to Edward Rawls, who is an inmate at the Atlanta Federal Penitentiary."

"Yes, sir," Kinney replied.

"Mr. Rawls says that he knows where to find Theodore Fay. The letter says that if his information is good he will receive a presidential pardon and the reward we are offering for Fay's capture. I want you to interrogate him thoroughly, then act on whatever information he gives you."

"I know who Rawls is, Mr. President, but may I ask, how can he possibly know where Fay is?"

Kate spoke up. "They both worked for the CIA, and they probably worked together at one time. We don't know the details, but Rawls says he knows where to find the man. We have nothing to lose by playing his game. If his information is incorrect, he stays where he is."

"I understand," Kinney said. "I've already ordered an aircraft for the trip."

"Phone me after you've talked with Rawls," Will said. "I'll leave word with the switchboard to put you through." He stood up and shook Kinney's hand. "Good night, and good luck."

"Thank you, sir," Kinney said. "Oh, excuse me. Could you arrange for a car to take me to Andrews Air Force Base? I came here in a cab. My car is at home."

"Of course," Will said, picking up a phone.

KERRY SMITH WAS WAITING when the White House car pulled up to the hangar. A Gulfstream III was sitting on the ramp, its engines running.

"What's up?" Smith yelled over the noise.

"I'll tell you when we're aboard," Kinney shouted back, beckoning for him to follow.

When they were aboard the airplane and the door was sealed, Kinney sank into a large armchair.

"You're not going to believe this," he said, "but we're flying to Atlanta to talk to a convicted traitor who says he knows where Fay is."

"Who's the traitor?"

"Ed Rawls."

Smith shook his head.

"You're too young to remember. He's been inside a long time." Kinney pulled out the envelope. "This is a letter from the president, offering him a pardon if his information is good."

"Now *that* I don't believe," Smith said.

49

Ed Rawls was awakened from a sound sleep by a guard at 10:30 P.M.

"Get up, Ed, and get dressed. The warden wants to see you."

Rawls splashed some water on his face and got into his clothes. He didn't ask what it was about; he knew. He followed the guard downstairs from his tier and through a series of corridors until he came to the warden's suite of offices. The warden was standing outside his office door waiting.

"Some people want to see you, Ed," the warden said. "In my office."

Rawls was ushered into the office, and the door closed behind him. Two men who were sitting at the warden's conference table stood up.

"Mr. Rawls," the bigger one said. "My

name is Robert Kinney and this is Kerry Smith. We're from the FBI." Both men flashed their ID. "Have a seat."

Rawls pulled up a chair to the table and sat down. "Good evening, gentlemen, what can I do for you?"

Kinney took an envelope from his pocket and slid it across the table. "This is a letter for you from the president of the United States."

"For me?" Rawls asked with mock surprise.

"Read it, please."

Rawls took his time. He slid a finger under the flap of the envelope and carefully pried it open, as if he wished to preserve the envelope. He fished out the letter, unfolded it, and put on his reading glasses, which were on a string around his neck. "Well, let's see what the president has to say to me."

He read the letter twice, carefully. "Well, gentlemen, you can tell the president that this isn't going to do it."

Kinney blinked. "Do you mind if I read the letter?"

Rawls handed it over.

Kinney read the letter and looked up at

Rawls. "This is a get-out-of-jail-free card," he said. "What's the matter with that?"

"It isn't a pardon," Rawls said.

"As I read it, and I'm an attorney, it's a firm promise of a pardon, providing you give us good information."

"It's not a pardon," Rawls repeated.

"You expect the president to hand you a pardon—signed, sealed, and delivered—without hearing a word from you?"

"That's what I expect," Rawls said.

"Well, Mr. Rawls, you're a fool," Kinney replied, standing up. Smith stood up, too.

"I'll convey your message to the president, but I can tell you from my conversation with him on this matter that this is a letter he was very reluctant to sign, and he's certainly not going to send me or anyone else down here with a full pardon that you haven't paid for." Kinney put the letter in his pocket and started for the door, followed by Smith.

"All right, all right," Rawls said. "Sit down and let's get this done."

The two agents sat down again and waited for Rawls to speak.

"Can I have the letter back, please?"

Kinney took the letter out of his pocket and handed it to Rawls. "I'm taking it back in thirty seconds if you haven't started talking."

"I'm going to need some money and some transportation," Rawls said.

"There's a reward of a million dollars up for grabs. You can buy your own transportation. Now stop wasting my time."

"The guy you want is Teddy Fay."

"Tell me something I don't know."

"Teddy was the tech guy on an operation I ran a long time ago. He made a car bomb for me that was a beaut—small, powerful, and set to go off when the guy got out of the car, not into it."

"Like the Vandervelt bomb."

"Exactly like the Vandervelt bomb. At the time, the Agency was short of space, and Teddy and some of his people were working in a rented hangar at a small airport south of Washington."

"Go on."

"I remember Teddy telling me that he was moving his people to Langley in a few weeks, and that he was really going to miss his hangar. He was very fond of it."

Kinney stared at Rawls. "That's it? He was fond of his hangar?"

"I think Teddy bought or rented the hangar after he moved his people out."

"Why do you think that?"

"Call it a hunch."

"A hunch," Kinney repeated tonelessly.

"I'm very good with hunches," Rawls said. "Something about the way he talked about the hangar made me think he wanted it for himself."

Kinney turned to Smith. "Do you believe this?"

"No," Smith replied, "I don't."

"Now wait a minute, guys," Rawls said. "Think about this: The hangar is a nice, cozy place to work, with no interference. It's on the west side of the airport, away from the terminal and the flight school. It's private, and it has the space to hide his RV, plus, it has all the services—power, computer communications, workshop area—that Teddy would need."

"What airport is this?"

"Manassas."

"I know it," Smith said.

"All right, Mr. Rawls, we'll check it out, but I have to tell you, this is a very long shot. If I'd known what you were going to say, I wouldn't have made the trip."

"Wait a minute, fellas," Rawls said. "I'm not through."

"We're listening."

"I have a house—an old family place—on an island in Maine, been in the family for nearly a hundred years."

"Go on."

"The last summer I was up there, the summer before I, ah, ran into difficulties with my freedom, I'm in a little grocery store—it's the only one on the island, so everybody uses it. And who should I see shopping there but Teddy Fay. Now, it's standard operating procedure with Agency people that, if you see a colleague someplace off the campus, you don't go up to him and slap him on the back, because you don't know if he's working. So I said nothing, and Teddy never saw me.

"Next day, I'm at the little post office, getting my mail, and I ask the postmaster if there's somebody on the island named Fay. He says he's never heard of anybody by that name. Now, on the island, the postmaster knows everybody, and I mean absolutely everybody, so I figure Teddy is working.

"Then I go home, and I think about it, and I figure there's no way he's working, because this is not the sort of place to attract any Agency operation, and if it did, I'd know about it, because the Agency knew I had the house and would have informed me that something was happening on my turf. Also, Teddy is Tech Services, not an operational agent, so I think maybe he's renting on the island for a couple of weeks.

"A week or so goes by, and I'm stopping at the post office for my mail, and as I pull up to park, Teddy comes out, gets into an old pickup, and drives away. I go into the post office and say to the postmaster, 'Who's the guy who just left in the pickup?' He says, 'Oh, that's Mr. Keane, Lawrence Keane, just bought himself a place up on the north island.' "

"So what?" Kinney asked. "Don't CIA people use false names all the time?"

"Not when they're not working, and especially not tech people. You see, what Teddy was doing was establishing himself a hidey-hole, a safe house, in a remote place."

"Why?"

"I don't know, but I'll bet if you call the postmaster up there, he'll tell you that Mr. Lawrence Keane is still getting mail, and he'll tell you where that mail is forwarded when Mr. Keane is not in residence."

"What's this island called?"

"It's called Isleboro."

"And where in Maine is it?"

"In Penobscot Bay." Rawls got up and went to the warden's bookcase. "The warden has an atlas somewhere. I've seen him use it." He looked among the books and plucked out an atlas of the United States, brought it back to the table and opened it.

"Here we are—State of Maine. Here's Penobscot Bay, the biggest bay in the state. This long island, here, is Islesboro. You take a ferry from Lincolnsville, on the mainland, just north of Camden, to get there." He pointed to the northern end of the island. "This is North Islesboro, and that's where Teddy's place is."

"Where exactly?"

"I don't know, but the postmaster would. His name is Seth Hotchkiss. He'll be in the book."

"And the ferry is the only way to the island?"

"Well, you can go by boat. The main harbor is here, at Dark Harbor. Oh, and there's an airstrip."

"Where?"

Rawls pointed to a spot on the page. "It's not on this map, but it's right here. It's a paved strip, I think twenty-four-hundred feet. You can get a light airplane in there, or a chopper, of course."

"Where's a bigger airport?"

Rawls tapped the map. "On the mainland, right here at Rockland. I don't know the runway lengths, but you can get just about anything in there."

"What else?"

"That's it. I promise you, he's going to be at one of those two places. I'd try Manassas Airport first. That'll be where he's operating from. Islesboro is where he'll run to when he's done."

"You think he'll finish killing people at some point, then?"

"From what I heard on the news, he's gotten his assets moved somewhere. He wouldn't do that if he was trying to martyr himself."

That coincided with Kinney's thinking. "Okay, Mr. Rawls, we're done here."

"I'll be looking forward to hearing from you," Rawls said. "A cashier's check will be fine, but I'd like a few grand of walking-around money in cash."

Kinney left the room. "He's all yours," he said to the warden and the waiting guard.

In the car, Smith asked, "What do you think?"

"I'd call this a very low order of information," Kinney said, "if we had anything else at all to go on. But we don't."

50

TED WOKE UP in the middle of the night to go to the bathroom, as was his habit, and when he came back to bed, he couldn't sleep. He got up, turned on his laptop, and went to the ACT NOW website. Something had been troubling him. He had passed over a target because he was so obvious and because he would be difficult to kill. Now his conscience was hurting him. He felt he couldn't end his little crusade without knocking off this one man, who had, Ted felt, done so much to harm his country. He stared at the photograph, and his dander rose.

Eft Efton, speaker of the House, had given this administration fits in getting legislation out of the lower house. The president had a slim majority in the Senate, but in the House he was half a dozen votes shy, and he had

had to deal with the speaker to get any legislation through at all.

The speaker had protection, though, and since he was third in line for the presidency, he was guarded by the Secret Service, which had put Ted off. Now Ted reconsidered. The Secret Service detail would be much smaller than the president's, perhaps only three or four guards. He opened his file on the speaker and read the notes he had kept when researching a possible kill. He had decided earlier, on the evidence, that the easiest shot, and one with the greatest chance of escape, would be while the speaker was in a moving car. The car, of course, would be armored, but Ted had a solution for that.

He looked at the routes the speaker's driver took from his house in Georgetown to the Capitol: There were four, but it hardly mattered, if he followed the car from his house.

The time was more important; the speaker left his house at eight o'clock sharp each morning, walked quickly from the front door to the car, and didn't emerge from it until he was safe in the Capitol garage.

Ted stayed up most of the rest of the night planning the killing, and finally, he was satisfied that it would work. He would have to sacrifice the Mercedes, but he had planned to sell it, anyway, and, once clean, it couldn't be traced back to him.

He opened one of his weapons caches in the RV and found the piece that would defeat the glass in the speaker's armored vehicle. It was, essentially, a large, semi-automatic handgun with a folding stock that would fire a .50-caliber, armor-piercing shell, and it had a ten-round magazine. He had made the first one in the Agency's shops and the second one in his home shop, and, as far as he knew, the two examples were the only ones in existence. The weapon would be a nasty surprise for the speaker.

Ted chose a cotton jumpsuit for clothing and a brown wig and a Vandyke beard for a disguise. With his planning done, he wiped down the Mercedes thoroughly, set his alarm clock, and went back to bed.

As soon as the G-III took off, Kinney was on the phone to the duty officer in the Hoover Building.

"I want a twelve-man SWAT team assembled and ready to roll by three A.M.," he said. "Be sure they're equipped with listening equipment. I'll call you back with a destination." He hung up the phone and went forward to talk to the pilots.

"We've just cleared the Atlanta Class B airspace," the pilot said.

"There's a Manassas Regional Airport in Virginia," he said to the pilot. "Can you land there?"

"Just a minute." The pilot picked up an airport guide and checked Manassas. "They have a fifty-seven-hundred-foot runway. We can land there."

Kinney took the book from him and looked at the airport plan. He could see a row of T-hangars on the west side of the field and, behind them a larger single hangar. He picked out a fixed base operator from the list in the manual. "All right," he said, "change our destination to Manassas. We'll stop at Dulles Aviation."

"Will do," the pilot said. He called Atlanta Center, requested the change in destination and was given a new clearance and routing.

"What's our ETA?" Kinney asked when the pilot had entered the new routing into his flight computer.

"Three-thirty-one A.M.," the pilot replied.

Kinney took the reference manual, went back to his seat, and called the duty officer. "When your SWAT team is ready, tell them their destination is the Manassas Regional Airport, in northern Virginia. I will meet them in the parking lot of Dulles Aviation, on the east side of the field. Tell them they are not—repeat, *not*—to drive onto the ramp; I will come to them. I want them in the parking lot no later than four-thirty A.M., armed and ready."

"We're landing at Manassas?" Kerry Smith asked.

"Right. Here's the airport plan."

Smith leaned over and looked at the book. "We're assembling with the SWAT team in the parking lot, here. We'll recce the hangar, here, first, then we'll bring in the team and take it."

"Sounds good to me," Smith said

"Maybe we'll get lucky."

IN THE HANGAR, cozy in his RV, Ted slept on.

51

THE G-III TOUCHED DOWN exactly on schedule and taxied to Dulles Aviation. The engines were shut down, and the copilot opened the airstair door.

Kinney and Smith were out of the airplane in a hurry, jogging toward the FBO. The lights were on inside, and a man sat at the main desk, staring at a television set.

Kinney flashed his ID. "FBI. How long before people start coming into this facility?"

"Usually not until after five A.M.," the man said, "but occasionally somebody will land or turn up for a departure. You guys want fuel?"

"Check with one of the pilots," Kinney said. "We're going to be conducting an operation on this airport shortly." He pointed to the west. "Do you know who owns or rents that big hangar behind the T-hangars?"

"That's Mr. Zane," the man replied. "He bought it a long time ago, I think, but he doesn't seem to have an airplane. At least, we've never sold him any fuel."

"Do you know what he uses it for?"

"A garage, I think. I've seen an RV come and go."

"What kind of RV?"

"Big, white, stripes down the side."

"That sounds like every RV. Do you know the make?"

"No, sir. I don't know anything about RVs, just airplanes."

"All right, now listen to me: I'm going to put a man with a radio in here with you. If anybody arrives, you tell them the airport is closed for an hour or two, and they'll have to wait to go to their aircraft. Then, when we start the operation, I want you and anyone else who arrives to lie on the floor behind your desk. I don't want anybody to catch a stray bullet."

"Yes, sir," the man said.

"Do you have a large plan of the airport?"

The man pointed to a wall, where a framed map about four-by-six feet hung.

Kinney went through the main entrance of the building into the parking lot, where two black vans sat idling. He tapped on the window of one of them, and it slid down.

"I'm Kinney, this is Smith," he said. "Get your men out of there and all of you come inside. Kerry, get the people from the second van."

A MOMENT LATER, they were inside the FBO, gathered around the map.

Kinney borrowed a weapon from an agent and used its laser sight as a pointer. "This is our objective," he said, pointing to the large hangar. "We're looking for one man, Theodore Fay, inside, probably in an RV, certainly heavily armed and a fine shot. We have to do this with the greatest care. I want two men to take some listening equipment and go over there on foot. I want you to attach the equipment to the two side walls, the ones with no doors, and radio back what you hear. You are not, repeat, *not,* to try to detain this man if you see him. If he sees you and runs, you are authorized to fire at him, but aim low. We want him alive, if possible. Any questions?"

Nobody said anything.

Kinney pointed to the SWAT team leader. "Pick two men and get them on their way." He borrowed a two-way radio. "What channel do we use?"

"Three," the team leader said.

"Right."

Kinney paced around the large lounge while he waited for the report.

"Base, this is recce," a voice said.

"This is base," Kinney replied. "Report."

"The building is dark, and there are no sounds from inside. If he has an RV, he could be asleep."

"Hold your positions and wait for backup," Kinney said. He turned to the team leader. "Let's go. Everybody on foot. You can have two men drive your vehicles around to the other side of the airport, but keep your lights off, and stay well back from the hangar. I don't want our man to hear any vehicles coming. When everybody is in place, wait for my command to go in."

"Yes, sir." The team leader barked instructions, and everybody started to carry out his orders. Kinney and Smith followed a few paces behind the main group as they trotted across the runway toward the T-hangars.

"I wish we had body armor," Smith said.

"So do I," Kinney replied.

As they went around the T-hangars, the group began to move with more stealth. Then they were in place.

Smith caught up to the SWAT team leader. "We can't open the big hangar doors from outside, so that"—he pointed to a door in one wall of the hangar—"is going to be the only way in. I want the door opened very quietly, and your men in there with night-vision goggles. Nobody turns on the interior lights until I say so.

"If there's an RV inside, I want it taken without incident, so be very careful how you open the door. I want men on only one side of it—the door side—so that if you shoot through it nobody on the other side will catch a round. Clear?"

"Yes, sir."

"Go."

Using hand signals, the leader ordered his men to don their night-vision goggles and to go in.

Kinney and Smith stood around the corner of the hangar from the door, waiting for it to be opened. It was done in less than thirty seconds, and the men filed through it silently, weapons at the ready. Kinney peeked around the corner through the door, but he could see nothing but dark. A minute passed, then suddenly, all the lights came on in the hangar, and the bifold door began to rise.

"What the hell?" Kinney said. He stepped into the hangar, weapon raised, and looked around. It was empty.

"Everybody hold your place!" Kinney shouted.

The men all froze.

"One man, open the door of the office, over there."

One man did so. "Clear!" he shouted.

Kinney trotted over to the office and went inside. There was some furniture and a big TV set, and there was an empty workbench in one corner. "Put some gloves on," he said, donning a pair himself. "Now, call headquarters and get a criminalist team out here. I want prints, if there are any."

Smith produced a cell phone and made the call.

Kinney walked around the office, looking

for any obvious evidence of the man who had been there. He could see nothing.

TEN MINUTES BEFORE Kinney's first men had arrived, Ted had driven out the back gate of the airport in the RV, towing the Mercedes. He was headed toward Washington and a rendezvous with the speaker of the House.

52

TED TURNED INTO a parking garage that he had selected long ago, because he could drive in and park while towing the Mercedes. He stopped the RV, got out, unfastened the tow bar and stowed it under the rear bumper, where a bracket had been welded, then he donned a pair of latex gloves, got into the Mercedes, and drove to Georgetown.

THE SPEAKER of the House was wakened by his wife at 6:30 A.M., and not gently.

"Eft," she said, "you'd better get your ass out of that bed right now, or you're going to miss the meeting of the leadership."

"Mmmmf," Efton replied, turning over and

staring at the ceiling. "I think I have a hangover."

"And you're surprised? You drank at least half a bottle of Scotch last night. We're going to have to get you into a program."

"Oh, for Christ's sake, girl, leave me alone. It's not as though I drink that much every night. It was a party!" He rolled out of bed and staggered toward the bathroom. "Make me some bacon and eggs, will you?"

"You don't need all that grease in your stomach. What you need is bran cereal, and that's what you'll get."

The shower muted the sounds of Efton's swearing.

TED PARKED nearly two blocks down the Georgetown street from the speaker's house and watched. He could see the front door clearly, but nobody was taking any note of him. He could see the exhaust fumes of the two Suburbans idling outside the house. What he needed most to know was in which car Efton would be riding.

• • •

EFTON FINISHED his bran cereal and resisted the urge to puke it up on the breakfast table. He was shaved, showered, and dressed, and only someone who could look closely into his eyes would have seen the hangover lurking there. He quickly scanned the front pages of the *Post* and both the New York and Washington *Times* for mention of his name, and when he didn't find it, became quickly bored.

"Eft, *please* get going!" his wife begged. She didn't want to be blamed later if he was late to his meeting.

Efton gathered up the newspapers for reading in the car, got his coat and briefcase from the hall closet, and left the house.

Ted watched as Efton emerged, looked up and down the street, then ran down his front steps and got into the second Suburban. No way to tell how many agents there were in each car, but probably two, one driving and one riding shotgun, while Efton had the rear seat to himself. As the two Suburbans left the curb, he pulled out and followed them, staying two blocks behind. They made a right turn, and from that, Ted guessed that they would be taking route number one, the most direct. Efton was probably running late.

The two trucks turned left onto Pennsylvania Avenue and proceeded toward the Capitol. Ted was caught at a light and waited impatiently for it to change. Once it did, the massive acceleration at his disposal quickly caught him up. Now he moved into the right lane and closed the distance between his car and the two Suburbans. A block ahead, he saw a traffic light turn to red. There was nothing between his car and the light, so he could stop next to the trucks. His windows were blackened, like those of the Suburbans, so they could see him no better than he could see them. Ted stopped next to the Suburbans, carefully choosing his position between the two trucks. He had only until the light changed. He picked up the weapon and worked the action, chambering the first round; he checked the cross-street traffic, then he pressed the down switch on his window. From his position a little ahead of the second Suburban, he could see through the windshield into the car, could see both the driver and Efton. There was only one agent in the car. He fired the first round before his window was fully down, killing the driver, then he turned the weapon toward Efton and began emptying the magazine, first at the man, then at the front passenger seat as Efton ducked behind it.

The front passenger door of the first Suburban suddenly opened, and an agent came out, drawing his weapon. Ted floored the Mercedes, striking the agent and taking off the Suburban's door, then he hung a sharp right, drove across two lanes of traffic, and headed down the street. He knew the driver of the first Suburban would have to check on the state of the second truck before pursuing, so he would have a good head start.

He whipped the car down an alleyway, drove a block, then turned left on Pennsylvania, headed back the way he had come. Now he slowed his progress, so as not to attract attention. The garage where he had parked the RV was in sight now, down the street a couple of blocks on his left. He pulled into a parking lot on his right, took a ticket from the machine, and found a spot. He took off the jumpsuit, the beard and the wig, put on a baseball cap and packed the weapon and the wig into a canvas bag; he got out of the car, locked it, and began walking down the street toward the garage where he had left the RV. Halfway there, he tossed the Mercedes's keys into a trash can.

KINNEY HAD BEEN in his office for an hour when the first news came in; typically, it was from CNN.

"There has been a shooting incident in downtown Washington, D.C.," the announcer said. "A black GMC Surburban with D.C. license plates was fired into several times from another car, and a second Suburban lost a door in the incident. We expect to have further details momentarily, but these vehicles are typical of those used by the government to transport VIPs around the city." Kinney pressed the intercom. "Get me the chief of police." A moment later he was buzzed; he picked up the phone. "Good morning, Chief," he said.

"Not really," the chief replied. "We've got three men down in a shooting on Pennsylvania Avenue."

"Any ID?"

"I'm waiting for that, now. Hang on a minute."

Kinney was placed on hold, and he waited impatiently, tapping a foot and drumming his fingers on his desk.

The chief came back on. “It’s bad, Bob,” he said. “Speaker Efton has been shot twice and is being transported to Walter Reed Hospital as we speak. One Secret Service agent is dead and another down.”

“Any suspects?”

“We’re looking for a silver Mercedes that left the scene at high speed,” the chief replied. “That’s all I’ve got at the moment. I’ll get back to you when I have more.”

Kinney had barely hung up the phone when his secretary buzzed him. “It’s the president,” she said.

Kinney didn’t want to talk to the man, but he had to.

53

Kinney took a few deep breaths while he waited for the president to come on the line.

"Bob?"

"Yes, Mr. President."

"Tell me about your trip to Atlanta."

"First, Mr. President, I have to tell you that I've just learned from the D.C. police chief that the speaker of the House has been shot on Pennsylvania Avenue, on his way to the Capitol."

"Good God! Is he dead?"

"He's on his way to Walter Reed, sir. A Secret Service agent is dead and another wounded."

"Was it Fay?"

"I have no evidence to that effect yet, sir, but I have no doubt that it is."

"Was Rawls of any help?"

"Yes, sir. He told us that Fay might be using a hangar at Manassas Regional Airport, south of Washington. I landed there on the way back, and we raided it at the earliest possible moment."

"And . . . ?"

"The hangar was empty, but my crime scene team found a wristwatch that had apparently been run over by a car or truck. It had stopped four minutes before my SWAT team arrived."

"And it was Fay's?"

"I believe so, sir, but he had cleared the hangar of any evidence that he might have been there."

"What's your next move?"

"Rawls also told us that he believed Fay had bought a cottage on an island in Maine, Islesboro."

"I know the place. My wife has spent some time on the island."

"We've checked with the local postmaster and located the house. I have a team on the way to the island as we speak, and I had planned to leave myself almost immediately, until I heard about the Efton shooting. I want to look into that before I leave. I've also alerted every state police department between Washington and Maine to be on the lookout for Fay. We believe he's driving an RV."

"All right, keep me posted. I have to call Walter Reed now, and find out how the speaker is doing."

"I'll be in touch, sir." He hung up.

Kerry Smith had come into his office while he was talking. "Are we on for Maine?"

"Yes, but first I want to check out the scene on Pennsylvania Avenue."

"I talked to the ER at Walter Reed. The speaker is hanging on, but he's gravely wounded. He took two fifty-caliber, armor-piercing slugs."

"Christ, that's machine gun ammo."

"Right. It's hard to know how Fay could have used such a large weapon in such a confined space as a car."

"Let's get out of here," Kinney said.

TED SAT IN the garage, in his RV, watching the story unfold on CNN, switching now and then to MSNBC, to see if they had any further information.

• • •

"THIS JUST IN," the CNN reporter said. "Police have found a silver Mercedes answering the description of the car driven by the shooter of Speaker of the House Eft Efton. The car has a damaged left fender bearing traces of black paint. The first Secret Service vehicle was a black GMC Suburban, and the Mercedes collided with it during its escape, striking a Secret Service agent and taking off the right front door. Crime scene investigators from the D.C. Police Department and the FBI are on their way to the scene now."

The reporter was handed a sheet of paper. "State police units in states along the Eastern seaboard north and south of Washington have been alerted to be on the lookout for the suspect, Theodore Fay, who may be driving a recreational vehicle north on I-95."

The report made him glad he had decided to sit things out for a day before heading for Maine.

KINNEY STOOD beside the silver Mercedes and looked into it. All the doors, the hood, and the trunk were open, and it was crawling with technicians. "Anybody found a print yet?"

"There aren't any prints," a tech replied. "This baby is cleaner than when it left the factory."

"This is no ordinary Mercedes, either," another tech, who was looking into the engine bay, said. "Somebody has shoehorned a big, AMG V8 into it, and the suspension has been reworked, too. You can buy one of these off a lot these days. It's called an E55, but this car was made before they came out with that model. This is a custom job. It must go like a scalded cat."

Kerry Smith looked at his watch. "It's been an hour and a half since the shooting," he said. "He's out of D.C. by now. And we can't even prove it's Fay."

"The lack of evidence is part of his MO now," Kinney said. "Not that that's going to do us any good in court."

"Suppose we caught him right now, Bob? Would we have enough to even hold him?"

"I don't want to think about that at the moment," Kinney said. "I just want to stop the guy from killing anybody else."

"I suppose we could charge him with

some sort of fraud in the faking of his death. We could hold him on that, couldn't we?"

"I haven't seen any evidence that he's defrauded anybody," Kinney said. "He doesn't appear to have gained from faking his death."

"Oh."

"Let's get to the airport. You packed your warm clothes?"

"Yes, sir."

WILL WAS AT his desk when an aide came into the Oval Office. "Excuse me, Mr. President," he said, "but we've just had word from Walter Reed that Speaker Efton has died from his wounds."

"Ask the chief telephone operator to find Mrs. Efton and get her on the phone. She's probably at the hospital by now."

"Yes, sir."

"And order the flags on all federal buildings to be flown at half-staff."

"Yes, sir."

Now he had another grim funeral to look forward to.

54

Bob Kinney's airplane landed at Rockland Airport in the late afternoon. He was met by an FBI agent driving a gray Explorer, and he and Kerry Smith were driven to a boatyard in Camden, a few miles north of Rockland, on the western shore of Penobscot Bay, where a shed had been rented as a rallying point for Kinney's team.

A potbellied stove warmed the shed, with the aid of a large gas heater blowing hot air around. Masts from a couple of dozen yachts were stored in racks along the walls, and the only furniture was a large picnic table and some folding chairs. An easel held a large-scale map of Penobscot Bay. Everyone gathered around.

"All right," Kinney said, "we've got to take

this guy here, because if we don't, we might never find him again."

"Maybe some state trooper will take him on his drive up here," an agent said.

"I don't think he's dumb enough to drive an RV from Washington to Maine," Kinney replied. "He has to have heard the news reports that we've alerted the state police along I-95. Anybody want to take responsibility for that leak?"

Silence prevailed.

"I didn't think so." Kinney pointed at the map. "You've all had an opportunity to look at this while you were waiting for me. The house is here, on North Islesboro, directly on the water. There's no cove, no anchorage, just a rocky beach. The airstrip is here, south of the house. We will not be using that, so get it out of your minds. This island is a sparsely populated place, especially in winter, where there are fewer than a hundred people in residence. If anybody sees anything, it'll be all over the island in a flash. The only person who knows of our interest in Mr. Lawrence Keane is the postmaster, and it's been stressed to him that he is a federal employee and is sworn to secrecy.

"Tonight, we're going to put a team ashore about half a mile north of the cottage, where the beach is near the road. The team will go in civvies, and backpacks, warmly dressed, and try to be indistinguishable from hikers. We will not send any vehicle over on the ferry, since note might be taken of it. We will not use a Coast Guard cutter to get our people ashore for the same reason. We've chartered a lobster boat for that purpose, and the team will go ashore in a rubber boat and stow it in the woods.

"Something I want to stress to those of you on tonight's team. This is a recce, not a capture mission. We don't even know if he's there. That's one of the reasons for the recce. Please keep in mind that Theodore Fay is probably the most technically accomplished fugitive you will ever encounter. You must expect a super-duper alarm system, and I don't want you to try to defeat it. I don't even want you to approach the house until you've electronically swept the area around it. We don't want to set off alarms.

"The sole reason for this mission is to establish whether Fay is in residence. Look and listen, find out what you need to effect a swift and decisive entrance, don't trip any alarms. Any questions?"

"Suppose Fay is in residence and we have an opportunity to take him?"

"You will not do so, until I have cleared it, personally, by cell phone. We will not use radios, because Fay could very well have a scanner. You'll be given a list of cell phone numbers for your commanders. Try to sound like a normal person when you call. Avoid jargon or any reference to the names Fay or Keane. Code name for Fay will be 'Buddy'; I will be 'Jack'; Agent Smith will be 'Barney'; your swat team leader will be 'Charlie.'"

"How do we leave the island?" somebody asked.

"If we effect a capture or a kill, a chopper will land at the Islesboro strip, for a quick evacuation, and vehicles will take the ferry over with evidence-gathering equipment. Once you're in the house, take extreme care not to disturb any part of it. Do what you have to do and get out clean."

"If he's not there, how long do we wait?"

"As long as I think is advisable. If Fay isn't there, the recce team becomes a surveillance team. You'll find a place to camp and wait him out, with two men watching the house at all times."

"Something I've never understood," somebody said. "Where did Fay get the money to buy all this stuff—the RV, the Mercedes, the house on Islesboro?"

"A combination of sources: He held patents on a number of small inventions that paid regular royalties, he saved his money, and he has a pension. He moved just over a million dollars in cash out of the country when he faked his death. Any other questions?"

Silence.

"All right, the lobster boat leaves at eleven P.M. It's a good hour and a half out to and around Islesboro and to the area of the cottage. First, we'll make a pass or two up and down the shore to see if there are any signs of life at the cottage, then we'll put the team ashore. In the meantime, get some dinner and some rest."

JUST AFTER MIDNIGHT, Kinney stood in the big cockpit of the lobster boat and slowly swept the eastern coastline of North Islesboro with night binoculars. He found the cottage, and his pulse quickened: There were lights on. Then, as he watched, the lights went off, one at a time.

"He's there, and he's going to bed," Smith said to Kinney.

"He may have the lights on a timer; let the team know."

Smith went below and spoke for a moment to the half-dozen men huddled in the cramped forepeak, then came back on deck. "They're briefed," he said.

"We'll put them ashore as soon as we're around that point," Kinney said, indicating a finger of land illuminated by starlight. "God, I hope this is an end to it."

"So do I," Smith said. "One way or another."

55

TED'S ALARM WENT OFF AT 3 A.M., and he sleepily put both feet on the floor and looked at his watch, which wasn't there. He'd misplaced it, somehow, and that annoyed him.

He showered, shaved, and, as an afterthought, flipped up the clipper head on his electric shaver and shaved his head, giving himself one more disguise and making it easier to use the wigs.

He had some breakfast, and by 3:45 A.M. he was on his way south; he avoided interstates, sticking to surface roads. He switched on the built-in, hands-free cell phone and dialed 1-800-WXBRIEF. "You have reached Richmond, Virginia, Flight Services. To speak with a briefer, press one."

Ted pressed one.

"Good morning, may I help you?"

"Good morning. This is November one, two, three, tango, foxtrot. Will you please brief me for an IFR Flight from Manassas, Virginia, to Manchester, New Hampshire, departing in one hour? I'd like winds for twelve thousand feet."

"Well, it's pretty simple today. We've got a large high-pressure area dominating your route, ceiling and visibility unlimited all the way. Manassas weather is clear below twelve thousand, winds light and variable, no notams. Forecast at Manchester is for clear below twelve thousand, winds zero ninety at eight knots. Winds at twelve thousand along your route, two four zero at thirty knots, pretty much all the way. One notam, unmarked crane one mile west of the airport at two hundred AGL. That's about it."

"I'll file."

"Go ahead."

"IFR, November one, two, three, tango, foxtrot. I'm a Charlie one eight two Romeo, stroke Golf. Departing hotel, echo, foxtrot at five A.M. local ten hundred zulu, at twelve thousand feet. My route of flight will be direct. Time en route, two hours, twenty minutes. I'll have four hours of fuel. My name is Kenneth Wills, based at Manassas. My phone number is 202-555-6189. The airplane is white over green. There'll be one soul aboard."

The controller repeated the plan. "You know you're never going to get direct along that route, don't you?"

"Yeah, whatever I give them, the computer will give me something else."

"Right. Have a good flight."

"Bye."

Ted was at Manassas Airport by five o'clock, and he entered, as usual, through the back gate, using his card. He drove not to his usual hangar, but to a T-hangar in the row next to the runway. He parked the RV, opened the hangar door, disconnected the battery charger, and, using a tow bar, moved the Cessna 182RG out of the hangar. He drove the RV into the hangar, then moved a lot of gear from the RV to the airplane and closed the hangar door. The monthly rental for the hangar was paid by an automatic bank draft, so it would be years before anybody found the RV. He might even be able to come back for it, eventually.

Using a flashlight, he carefully performed

a preflight inspection, then got into the airplane and started the engine. He called clearance delivery and got a better clearance than he would have thought possible, up to New York, across LaGuardia, then Connecticut, and on to Manchester. Ten minutes later he was rolling down runway 34 left.

The flight was wonderful, and he felt as if he were leaving one life and finding another. He landed at Manchester, and while the Cessna was being refueled, engaged the girl at the counter in the FBO in conversation long enough to plant in her mind the information that he had flown up from Georgia and was on his way to Canada. Then he took off again, without filing a flight plan and with his transponder off.

He flew north at three thousand feet, until he was sure that no one could see him from Manchester Airport, then he turned northeast and flew toward the Kennebunk VOR, then, after that, direct toward five, seven, bravo—Islesboro Airport. His route took him along the coast in bright sunshine, the last of the autumn color showing bright gold below him. Toward the end of his trip he detoured over Owl's Head Airport, at Rockland, and had a good look for government helicopters or airplanes. All he saw was a single corporate jet and a lot of light aircraft tied down. He then flew up the coast past Camden, low, at a thousand feet, to Lincolnsville, where he checked out the ferry parking lot for black Suburbans, Humvees, or other government-type vehicles. There were only three vehicles in the lot, all ordinary-looking, and they were waiting for the ferry, which was just leaving Islesboro for Lincolnsville, on its winter half-schedule.

He picked up a little altitude, then flew over to Islesboro at two thousand feet, first checking out the harbor and the coastline for a Coast Guard cutter. There were few boats moored or docked and none that were threatening. He then flew up the eastern coast toward North Islesboro, checking for anything supicious. There was one lobster boat motoring up the coast, with two men in the cockpit besides the driver, and he took note of that, but wasn't worried about it. He flew past his house and saw nothing that alarmed him. Somebody was camping in the woods a few hundred yards from the cottage, but, even though it wasn't the best time of the year for it, it wasn't all that unusual. He saw no vehicles, which meant they must have hiked over from the ferry.

His inspection completed, he flew away to the northeast toward the Bar Harbor airport.

KINNEY'S CELL PHONE RANG. "This is Jack."

"Jack, we're calling from camp. If anybody's in the barn, he's sleeping late. We've been listening and haven't heard so much as anybody breathing."

"Keep listening."

"Another thing, an airplane, a Cessna, flew over a couple of minutes ago and had a look at our camp."

"Yeah, I saw him. He had a look at us, too, then he flew away to the northeast. I don't think it's anything, unless he comes back."

"Right. I'll call you back if we hear anything."

Kinney hung up the phone and thought about the airplane, then he turned to Kerry Smith. "Call Washington Center at Dulles and find out if any Cessna light airplanes left the D.C. area since yesterday with a flight plan filed for Maine."

"Will do," Smith said and got on the

phone. He was back in a few minutes. "A Cessna 182RG took off from Manassas at about five-thirty this morning and flew to Manchester, New Hampshire, on an IFR flight plan. I spoke to the FBO there, and she confirmed that they refueled the airplane. The pilot was in his fifties, heavyset, dark hair and a beard. He said he was flying from Georgia up to Canada, and he paid cash and took off heading north. I talked to the tower there. He didn't file a flight plan. He didn't turn on his transponder, either, because Boston Center didn't track anybody out of Manchester toward Canada. Center is checking to see if any Cessna 182s left any airport in Georgia in the past couple of days, headed north."

"Did that airplane we saw have retractable gear?" Kinney asked.

"Yes, I think so. Normally, a Cessna 182 straight-leg would be obvious, because it has aerodynamic wheel pants."

"Did you get a tail number?"

"No, but the aircraft that flew from Manassas had a tail number of November, one, two, three, tango, foxtrot."

Kinney made a note of the tail number.

"I'm going ashore," he said. "Do we have a vehicle on the island?"

"No, but we have four in Lincolnsville."

"Where are they parked?"

"In front of a row of stores, across the road from the ferry."

They were around the northern tip of the island now. "You see that private dock over there, with the shingled house behind it?"

"Yes."

"I'm going ashore there. Call Lincolnsville and have the gray Explorer take the ferry and meet me there."

"It could be quite some time," Smith said. "The ferry is on a winter schedule."

"If it's not leaving right away, tell them to identify themselves and press the ferry to return immediately."

"Will do," Smith replied and got on the phone, while the lobster boat turned for the dock.

TED LANDED AT Bar Harbor, then he taxied to a remote part of the field and retrieved a roll of plastic sheets from the luggage compartment. He unrolled the two sheets, stripped the paper off the back side and fixed new numbers to both sides of the aircraft. The sheets had been carefully made to blend with the striping on each side, and, except from up close, the numbers looked as if they had been professionally painted on. The new number was November, three, six, six, nine, charlie, and if anybody checked, they'd find a Cessna 182RG registered with that number to a flight school in Atlanta.

He got back into the airplane, started the engine, and took off, then headed toward the northern end of Penobscot Bay at five hundred feet. That lobster boat worried him, and he was going to be very careful.

56

KINNEY WAITED IMPATIENTLY on the road in front of the house at whose dock he had recently landed, sending the lobster boat on to Dark Harbor, to await further instructions. His cell phone rang.

"Jack."

"It's Barney. They dropped me off at the ferry, which should be docking in a few minutes. Our car is aboard, and we'll pick you up in, say, fifteen minutes."

"You'll have to drive past the barn on your way. Don't look like you're in a hurry." Kinney hung up and stamped his feet to warm them.

TED STAYED AT five hundred feet as he flew around the northern end of Penobscot Bay, enjoying the view. Once, he cut the engine and glided for a minute; he could hear children laughing and a dog barking at a house below. He restarted the engine and began to climb, flying inland past the western shore of the bay, then turning back, so as to look as if he had taken off from Augusta. He climbed to five thousand feet and leveled off as he turned east between Camden and Lincolnsville, and when the GPS told him he was five miles from Islesboro Airport, he pulled the throttle slowly to idle, then pulled out the mixture control until the engine stopped. Finally, he pulled the propeller lever all the way back, feathering the prop and turning the Cessna into a glider. He had done this before, practicing emergency landings, and he was sure he could do it again. The airplane was silent now, and nobody looked up at an airplane that made no noise.

Once over the island, he turned for his final approach to the airport, still three miles out, noting with satisfaction that the lobster boat he had seen was now docked in Dark Harbor. He fixed the short runway at a point in the middle of his windshield and kept it there, adjusting his glide path occasionally to keep his airspeed at ninety knots. The runway remained in the middle of his windshield, meaning that he had the correct combination of descent and airspeed. When he was sure he could make the runway, he dropped the landing gear and put in some flaps, aiming about a third of the way down the runway. He touched down, but did not brake, letting the airplane roll. When he was near the end of the runway, he turned off onto the parking ramp and made a very nice turn into a tiedown. Only then did he use the brakes. Perfect.

He tied down the airplane, then walked a hundred yards to a shed he had rented that belonged to a nearby house. He opened the padlock with the correct combination, unhooked the battery charger, and started the pickup on the first try. Then he drove back to the airplane and unloaded the gear he had brought with him from the airplane into the pickup.

With the heater now blowing warm air, he drove off the airfield to the road, which ran from the ferry past his house, and headed for home. His only other concern now was the campers who had set up a tent near the cottage. He could not see them from the road as he drove past, but he did see a wisp of smoke from their campfire.

He drove past his cottage at an easy thirty miles per hour, checking the place as he passed. Then he drove on down the road for a couple of miles before making a U-turn and starting back. A mile from his place he passed a gray Explorer going the other way with two men in the front seat, both wearing parkas and winter caps. He checked his rearview mirror and saw that the car had Maine plates. At least they were going the right way.

KINNEY WATCHED as the Explorer approached, then jumped in. "Turn up the heater," he said as the driver turned the car around.

"Did you see the pickup?" Smith asked.

"What pickup?"

"We passed a pickup going the other way, about a mile back. Didn't you say Fay had a pickup when Rawls saw him on the island?"

"What kind of pickup?"

"Old. Mid-fifties, probably, but in nice shape. A real gem."

"Drive slower," Kinney said.

• • •

TED TRIED HIS gliding trick with the truck now. He shifted into neutral, switched off the engine, and coasted down a little hill as he approached the cottage. He started pressing the button on the remote control as he coasted, and after two or three tries, the garage door opened. He turned and coasted into the garage, employing the brakes only at the last minute, then he pressed the remote again, and the garage door closed behind him, leaving the overhead light on. He hopped out of the truck, went to a keypad just inside the garage door, and tapped in the security code. The light on the box flashed green, then went out.

SMITH SAW THE HOUSE as they came down the hill. "I don't see anybody. Speed up, and let's see who was in the pickup. There's only the one road."

The driver sped up as they passed the house.

• • •

TED WATCHED FROM INSIDE as the Explorer went past; now there were three men inside.

Kinney's phone rang. "This is Jack."

"Camper here. Did you see the pickup?"

"Yes, we're checking it out now."

"How? You've already passed it."

"What are you talking about?"

"The pickup came down the hill with the engine off, the garage door opened, and it coasted right inside. Our Buddy is home."

"Shit!" Kinney exploded. "Turn this thing around and let's get back to the campsite. Kerry, get on the phone and get our SWAT team over here, but tell them not to use the chopper from Augusta. Tell them to come over by boat, and the Explorer will meet them at the ferry terminal."

"We're coming up on the campsite, now," the driver said.

"Let Smith and me out here. You make a U-turn, go back to the ferry terminal, and wait for the SWAT team. Phone me when you're on the way back."

"Roger," the driver said.

Kinney and Smith hopped out of the SUV and ran into the woods, still out of sight of the house, aiming at the wisp of wood-smoke above the trees. They emerged in a little clearing, where two agents stood, warming themselves by the fire. Both were startled by their approach.

TED MOVED HIS THINGS from the pickup into the house. He checked the freezer and took out a steak to thaw, then he turned on the furnace to get some heat into the place. He looked around. Everything was exactly as he had left it. He went to the front and kitchen doors and checked the markers he had left there on each door—two inches of cellophane tape, joining them to the jamb. They were undisturbed; no one had entered the house. He began to relax, and he stood over a grate and let the warm air blow up his trousers.

"OUR MAN IS IN the house," an agent said, holding the earphones more tightly to his head. "The furnace is on, and he opened the fridge once. When do we go in?"

"Not until dark," Kinney said. "We'll wait for the rest of our team to arrive and for Buddy to get comfortable. When he's settled down for the night, we'll go in."

57

KINNEY AND SIX OF HIS SWAT team gathered around the campfire; he had sent the Explorer back to the ferry terminal for the rest of them.

"Okay, here's where we are," he said. "Buddy is in the house, rummaging around, cooking dinner. All seems normal. We're going to wait until he settles in for the night, then we're going to take him." His cell phone rang, and he opened it. "Jack."

"I've got the rest of the team," a voice said, "and we're on the way back from the ferry terminal. Where do you want them?"

"Drive past the house and up the little hill and around the bend. When you're out of sight of the house, let them out and tell them to take up positions on the north side. Use no lights. They have night vision, after all. Tell them it will be at least a couple of hours before we go in." He looked up at the rest of the SWAT team, gathered around the fire. "All of you listen to this." He spoke into the phone again. "This will be a quiet entry through the front door. Pick the lock. If he has an alarm system, you'll have thirty seconds before it goes off, so make the most of them. No flashlights inside, just your night-vision goggles. Locate and subdue Buddy. Do not fire unless he fires first. When he's down, frisked, and cuffed, call me, and we'll take him home. I'll be in touch." He closed the phone.

TED FINISHED HIS STEAK while watching CNN.

"Word from the FBI is that they are now watching I-95 north and south of Washington, D.C., for an RV driven by Theodore Fay, known as the right-wing shooter. With the death of Speaker of the House Eft Efton, the number of his victims has risen to five, four fatalities. We'll keep you posted on the manhunt as news comes in."

Ted sat back in his recliner and heaved a deep sigh of relief. He had pulled it off. Now all he had to do was enjoy his retirement. He had prepared well, buying this house more than sixteen years before, and the hangar at about the same time. If he had learned anything at the Agency it was that preparation was nearly everything. He had fooled them and the FBI from day one, stealing materials from Tech Services and building identities that could be penetrated only by accident. He still had three left, should he need them, but he didn't expect to. He was now hunkered down in his Maine island cottage with everything he needed to live—and the airplane, if he needed to escape. He had, he believed, thought of everything.

He began to grow sleepy; he had, after all, been up since three-thirty that morning, and it had been a tense day. He went over the events of the day once more, to be sure he had not forgotten something, some threat, however small. He was confident that he had not.

He washed his dishes, turned off the TV and the kitchen light, went to his bedroom, and began unpacking the bags he had brought. Everything had been bought in Maine, much of it from the L.L. Bean catalogue. He put his things away, and as he opened a cupboard to stow some wool shirts he came upon an instrument he had nearly forgotten.

That first summer so many years ago, he had staked out a perimeter about seventy-five yards from the house, trenching the soil and laying wire for a triangulating sensor system. In an emergency, he could switch on the system and, on a small cathode ray tube, see any spot where the perimeter had been breached and track any living thing bigger than a cat as it approached the house. For the fun of it, he switched it on; maybe he would spot a deer coming his way. The unit warmed up, and the screen came up blank of intruders.

TO THE NORTH of the house, the SWAT team leader watched as the kitchen lights went off, and the bedroom light came on. He called Jack. "Looks like Buddy is turning in," he said. "He's left the kitchen and gone to the bedroom."

"I can confirm that from our ears," Kinney replied. "We hear him moving around the bedroom now, apparently unpacking. Let's move a couple of men up now on each side of the house for eyeball surveillance. We'll wait an hour after the bedroom lights go off and we hear deep breathing."

"Roger that."

TED LOOKED AGAIN at the CRT and still saw a blank screen. He left the cupboard door open, turned down the bed, and got out a pair of flannel pajamas from a drawer. As he began to unbutton his shirt, he heard a soft beep from the cupboard; he looked at the CRT and saw a blip on the north side of the house. A deer, he thought, or maybe a raccoon; he continued to unbutton his shirt. Then the instrument beeped again. This time the blip was on the south side of the house. Was he being surrounded by deer? Both blips remained absolutely stationary, but they were still there. Was somebody watching the house? Was somebody, maybe, listening? He switched on the bedside radio, which was already tuned to Bay Radio, which played the old, big band music he loved. He moved quietly around the room, putting a few things into a small duffel, things he might need.

• • •

SMITH TOOK the headphones off. "He's playing music," he said to Kinney.

"Music?"

"Big band stuff, fairly loudly."

"There's a radio station up here that plays big band," an agent said. "I had it earlier on my Walkman."

"Maybe it helps him sleep," Smith said.

"Maybe it's to cover up other noise," Kinney replied.

"Hang on, I just heard a toilet flush," Smith said. "He just sat on the bed, too. The springs squeaked."

Kinney's cell phone rang. "Jack here."

"The bedroom light went off. The house is dark."

"Right, we hear him in bed, but there's radio music playing, so we can't hear his breathing. Check back in an hour if there's no change."

THE MUSIC STOPPED, and an announcer spoke. "We now pause for a test of the national alert system," he said. "We'll return to Bay Radio in sixty seconds." Ted reached out and turned up the radio. A glance at the CRT across the room showed two more blips moving in. Now.

SMITH PULLED OFF the earphones again. "The radio is playing that national alert test that drives everybody crazy. I can't even listen."

"It only lasts one minute," Kinney said.

Smith looked at his watch and waited. Finally, he listened again. "We're back to music, but it's louder than before. Why would he turn up the radio as he was going to bed?"

Kinney winced. "He's on to us. We have to go in right now." He pressed a button on his cell phone, and the SWAT team leader answered. "We have to go in right now. Position your people to enter in sixty seconds from my mark. Ready . . . mark!" Kinney snapped the phone shut and punched a button on his wrist chronograph, starting the second hand.

"Everybody in position; we go in one minute."

58

KINNEY LOOKED AT HIS WATCH, then pressed the button on his cell phone.

"Yeah?" the team leader said.

"Go," he said, and he waved his half of the SWAT team forward. They were all running toward the house now.

INSIDE THE BEDROOM CUPBOARD, more than a dozen blips were converging on the cottage. Ted had already tiptoed out of the bedroom with the duffel, grabbed his parka, and was moving slowly down the stairs to the basement. He was pretty sure they couldn't hear him down here. He got into his warm clothes, went to a large cupboard against the west wall, took hold of it and shifted it away from the wall a couple of feet.

Behind the cupboard was a heavy wooden door. He pushed it open and tossed his duffel through the opening, then he backed through the opening on his knees, and reached out and dragged the cupboard back against the wall, hiding the door. He shut the thick door and double-bolted it from the inside, then he turned around in the tunnel, slipped on his night-vision goggles, and waited for his eyes to adjust.

THE SWAT TEAM had the doors open in a few seconds, and the black-clad men, wearing night-vision goggles, moved through the house, searching each room, each closet, each cupboard. "Okay," the team leader shouted, "goggles off, lights on!"

People began switching on the house lights in each room.

Kinney burst through the front door, followed closely by Kerry Smith. "You got him?" he yelled.

The team leader came out of the bedroom. "He's not here," he said, "but come look at this."

Kinney followed him into the bedroom and saw the CRT in the cupboard. He could see a couple of blips moving around the house; his men were searching the perimeter. "He saw us coming," he said.

"Basement door!" somebody shouted from the hall.

"Go get him!" Kinney said to the team leader. He followed the man into the hallway; SWAT team members were already swarming down the stairs, guns at the ready.

Kinney was right behind them. When he got to the bottom of the stairs, the lights were on, and he looked around. Workbench, hot water heater, furnace, all the usual basement stuff. He opened a large cupboard and found an assortment of tools neatly laid out. "He's in this house somewhere," Kinney said. "Find him." He could already hear the noise of team members taking the upstairs apart, and the men in the basement started up the stairs to help.

"Wait a minute!" Kinney said. Everybody stopped.

TED COULD SEE the tunnel ahead. He began crawling along the plank floor, dragging the duffel. It had taken him three summer vacations to dig this thing and shore it up. He hoped he was crazy, paranoid, that the blips were really deer, but he wasn't going to take the chance. Then he heard the burglar alarm go off upstairs.

He reached another door, opened it, and slipped through into the concrete culvert. Closing and bolting the door behind him, he began to move down the culvert, which was larger in diameter than his tunnel. He was now on his feet in a half crouch, moving quickly. A minute later, the culvert had passed under the road, and he emerged into starlight. He waded as quietly as he could through the shallow end of a small pond, into which the culvert emptied, and made dry land.

He looked up, checked the stars, and began jogging overland, keeping roughly parallel to the road.

He had, maybe, three-quarters of a mile to go, about twelve minutes. He paced himself, breathing deeply. Five minutes later he was loosening clothing to cool down.

"WHAT?" the SWAT team leader asked.

"Is anything in this basement movable,

except that cupboard?" Kinney pointed at the large piece of furniture.

"No, sir, I don't think so," the man replied.

"Have a couple of your men move it away from the wall," Kinney said.

The leader made a motion, and two large men got hold of the cupboard and moved it out.

"There," Kinney said, pointing at the door. "Get it open."

The two men tried and failed to open it.

"Use a door charge," Kinney said.

"Do it," the team leader said to his men. "Everybody upstairs. The concussion will kill your ears in this basement."

Everybody clambered up the stairs. The last man up held a remote control in his hand. He closed the door behind him.

"Blow it," the leader said. Everybody stepped back.

The man pressed a button, and the door flew off its hinges into the hallway, followed by noise.

The team leader was first down the stairs, with Kinney right behind him. The explosion had blown out the lightbulbs, so flashlights came on.

The team leader shone his light past the

splintered door. “We’ve got a tunnel.” Without another word, he knelt down and started crawling.

Kinney followed, and there were more men behind him. He had no night-vision goggles, but everybody was using flashlights.

“We’ve got another door,” the leader hollered. “Hold up!” He tried the door. “It’s like the other one. We’re going to have to blow it. Everybody out of the tunnel!”

There was barely enough room to turn around, but gradually, the tunnel emptied.

Kinney was half out of breath. “Blow it. I’m going to take some men and see if I can figure out where it comes out.” He motioned for Smith and three SWAT team members to follow him, then he ran up the stairs and out of the house. “All right, stop,” he said. “Look around. See where you’d have a tunnel come out if you built it.”

Everybody stood in the front yard and looked around.

“The beach,” Smith said. “That’s where I’d have it come out.”

“Everybody to the beach,” Kinney said, then started jogging. They were there in less than a minute. "Look for an opening. It's probably behind something."

"There's a culvert," Smith said, shining his light on it. "A good-sized one."

"Everybody shut up," Kinney said. He knelt at the culvert and listened. He was nearly blown off his feet by a rush of air and noise from the pipe.

"They blew the door," Smith said. "The tunnel leads into the culvert."

Kinney grabbed a team member. "You go down the culvert as far as you can. Watch out, you might meet Buddy coming the other way. Kerry, you take a man and go down the beach that way," he said, pointing. "I'll take a man and go the other way."

TED CUT ACROSS the road past a farmhouse and ran toward the airstrip. Finally, he had to walk, for fear of having a heart attack; he was fit, but he had just run three-quarters of a mile, carrying a heavy bag. He made the airplane, unlocked it, and tossed his bag into the passenger seat, then released the tiedown ropes. No time for a preflight; he climbed in and started flipping switches. He primed the engine, then turned the key to the starter position. The prop began to swing, and a moment later, the engine caught and started. There was no wind to speak of, so Ted knew he could use either end of the runway.

He started taxiing, then put in twenty degrees of flaps. He stopped at the end of the runway, ran the engine up to full power, paused a moment to make sure it was going to keep running while cold, then released the brakes.

KINNEY RAN for a few hundred yards, then turned back. He met Kerry Smith back at the culvert.

"Hey!" a voice shouted from a distance. "Over here!"

It came from the other side of the house.

Kinney led the group back to the house, past it, and across the road, where the shouts were coming from. Finally, they came across a SWAT team member, standing knee deep in a pond.

"The culvert ended here," he said.

"Where is the guy going to go?" Kinney asked. "He can't get off the island without a boat."

The team leader rushed up.

"Get some men down to Dark Harbor and make sure nobody leaves by boat," Kinney said.

"Listen," Kerry Smith said.

"We've got to get the chopper in here from Augusta with more men," Kinney was saying.

"Shut up and listen!" Smith shouted.

Everybody got quiet.

"Do you hear that?"

"What is it?" Kinney asked.

"An airplane engine. Look!"

Just for a moment they caught a flash of moonlight on something climbing away from the island, something with no lights.

"Oh, shit," Kinney said.

59

KERRY SMITH LOOKED UP in the direction of the parting airplane; it seemed to be making a turn.

"We're fucked," he said. "A Cessna 182RG will make a hundred and fifty knots. That's faster than the helicopter."

"What direction would you say he's flying?" Kinney asked.

"I'd say he's headed southwest, along the coast."

Kinney thought about his options and realized there was only one. He got out his cell phone and dialed a Washington number.

"White House," an operator said.

"This is Deputy Director Robert Kinney of the FBI. Please let me speak to the president at once."

"He's asleep, Mr. Kinney. Do you know the hour?"

"He asked me to call. This is an emergency. Please wake him immediately."

"Hold, please."

Kinney waited, tapping his foot, while Smith and the others stared at him.

"This is Will Lee," the voice said, sounding remarkably awake.

"This is Bob Kinney, Mr. President. Please listen carefully. Rawls was right about Fay having a Maine hideaway. My men and I are there now, and Fay has escaped the island in a light airplane, a Cessna 182RG."

"I used to fly one of those," the president said.

"We now have only one means of catching him, and if we don't get him tonight, I don't think we ever will."

"What means do we have, Bob?"

"You need to call the Pentagon and scramble a couple of jets out of the Brunswick, Maine, Naval Air Station. Maybe they can force him down, but more likely, they'll have to shoot him down."

The president was silent for a moment. "Hold on for a minute."

Smith looked at Kinney. "Are you on hold?"

"Yes."

"What did he say?"

"Not much."

"Is he going to do it?"

"How do I know? I'm on hold."

After perhaps two minutes, the president came back on the line. "Bob, I'm going to conference you with the duty officer in the office of the chief of naval operations."

"All right, sir."

"Just a minute." There was a click, then the president said, "Captain, are you there?"

"Yes, Mr. President."

"I have Deputy Director Robert Kinney of the FBI on the line."

"Good evening, Mr. Kinney."

"Kinney is going to give you instructions on what and where this airplane is. I want you to scramble as many jets as you think it will take from the Brunswick, Maine, Naval Air Station with orders to force down this airplane, and if that is not possible, to shoot it down. Is that order clear?"

"Yes, Mr. President."

"Tell him what he needs to know, Mr. Kinney."

"Captain, a Cessna 182 retractable took off from Islesboro Airport, in Penobscot Bay, Maine, about ten minutes ago. I'm told the airplane can do a hundred and fifty knots."

The president interrupted. "A hundred and sixty, if it's lightly loaded."

"Thank you, sir," Kinney said. "We believe the aircraft is headed southwest, down the Maine coast. If so, it will pass nearly directly over Brunswick. It's not wearing any lights, and I doubt if it has its transponder turned on, but Brunswick ground radar may be able to pick it up as a primary target."

"How many aboard?"

"I believe there to be one man aboard."

"Fuel?"

"As far as I know, the airplane was last refueled at Manchester, New Hampshire, yesterday, before flying to Islesboro."

The president broke in again. "It will carry eighty or ninety gallons of usable fuel, depending on what year it was built, and it uses about thirteen gallons an hour in cruise."

"Thank you, Mr. President," the captain said. "Is there anything else you can tell me?"

"Not I," the president said. "Mr. Kinney?"

Kinney thought for a moment. "The pilot is desperate, I believe. He'll do anything not to get caught. You might inform your pilots of that."

"Thank you, Mr. Kinney," the captain said. "Mr. President, I should inform you that this is going to be a very difficult job for these pilots, because of the difference in airspeed between their jets and a light piston airplane, and I'm not sure offhand whether his engine generates enough heat for a heat-seeking missile to home in on. If they fire, I'll have them fire toward the sea, since we don't want any stray rounds impacting the coast."

"I know they'll do the best they can, Captain. Good night. Please report back to me directly when you have news."

"Good night, Mr. President." The captain hung up.

"Bob, you still there?"

"Yes, Mr. President."

"Am I doing the right thing, here?"

"I believe so, sir. There isn't anything else left to do. He can land that airplane in any farmer's field and be on his way."

"You heard the speaker died?"

"Yes, sir."

"I don't want Fay to still be at large when his funeral is held."

"Neither do I, sir."

"Can I reach you on your cell phone, if I need to?"

"Yes, sir. The White House operator has the number."

"Whoever hears first should call the other, then. Good night."

"Good night, Mr. President." Kinney closed his cell phone and put it into his pocket.

"He's going to do it?" Smith asked, incredulous.

"He's already done it," Kinney replied. "All we can do now is wait. You go back and secure the house until we can get a crime scene team up here. I guess that'll be sometime tomorrow."

"Right."

The men melted away from Kinney, leaving him standing in the road. He looked to the southwest and was glad he wasn't Teddy Fay.

TED HAD BEEN in the air an hour now, and he was approaching the Kennebunk VOR. He checked his fuel: He had been flying the day before at low altitudes and, thus, at a full rich-mixture setting, burning a lot of fuel. He was down to nineteen gallons now, and using thirteen an hour. He couldn't land at any airport, because the airplane would be discovered when the sun came up, and the FBI would know where to start looking. He needed to ditch the Cessna where it wouldn't be found. Where would that be?

He looked down at the Maine coast in the moonlight, and as he did, something roared past him on either side, rocking the little airplane in the resulting turbulence. What the hell was that?

He switched on a radio and tuned it to the emergency frequency.

"Cessna 182 retractable," a young man's voice said. "Do you read me?"

Ted thought for a moment, then he answered. "I read you loud and clear."

"You are instructed to turn on your transponder, your navigation lights, and your strobes, if any, then to make a one-hundred-eighty-degree turn and fly a heading of zero-six-zero degrees until you have the beacon at the Brunswick Naval Air Station in sight, then to land there on runway two. Do you read?"

"Negative, can't do it. I don't have the fuel."

"Then you can land at Portland International on the same heading. You'll be met there."

"Negative, Navy. Can't do it."

"Listen, pal," the young voice said. "I don't give a fuck if you dump that thing in the Atlantic. My instructions are to force you to land or shoot you out of the sky, and those are my intentions. What's it going to be?"

An excellent question, Ted thought.

60

LIEUTENANT J/G HARRIS CONOVER watched his radar screen as his jet approached the target. He had slowed to two hundred knots and, as a result, he was having to fly at a high angle of attack in the swept-wing aircraft, making visual contact with the light airplane difficult.

Then, suddenly in his peripheral vision, the lights of a small airplane appeared, navs and strobes. He saw it for only a moment as he swept past the target, flying at least fifty knots faster than the light airplane.

"Navy, do you read me?" a voice said in his headset.

"I read you, and I have a visual," Conover said, though that was no longer true. "Wingman, left one-eighty." He banked the jet sharply and started back.

"I'm afraid I can't fly back with you, and it would be best if you stay well clear of me."

Conover was flying a reciprocal course now, and he saw the airplane again. This time its landing and taxi lights were on, too. "Don't worry, little guy, I'm not going to bump into you. Wingman, ninety right." He started the turn. He had orders to make his run from the landward side of the light aircraft, so that any stray rounds would land at sea.

"That's not what I mean," Ted said. He started a turn to the right. "Just stay well clear." He looked down at the coast as he crossed it. A tailwind was moving him rapidly out over the water. He reached into the duffel next to him and took out a package about the size of a hardcover book.

Conover still had the airplane on radar, and it had made a turn from its prescribed course. "Listen to me, pal. You're off course, and you'd better make a left turn right now. I'm locked and loaded."

"I'm sure you are," Ted responded. "Good night and good luck." He turned a timer switch on the object in his hand and set it at thirty seconds. There was nothing to think about now. He punched the autopilot on. He thought about his wife.

"Jesus!" Conover screamed as the fireball flared in front of him. "Break right!" He started the turn. "Billy, did you fire?"

"Not me, Harry," his wingman said. "I think the guy did the firing himself."

Conover held the turn until he had made a three-sixty, then he banked left for a view below him.

Small, burning pieces of the Cessna were striking the water. "Okay, Billy, let's go home." He swung on course for Brunswick and changed frequencies. "Brunswick, this is hardhat one."

"Hardhat one, Brunswick."

"Wingman and I are returning to base."

"What was your result?"

"Tell the old man we didn't have to fire. The guy pulled the plug himself. Big explosion."

"Roger that, hardhat one. You're cleared to land on two."

"Wilco."

THE BEDSIDE PHONE RANG, and he picked it up. "Will Lee."

"Mr. President, this is Captain Mason, CNO's office, the Pentagon."

"Yes, Captain."

"Our aircraft made contact with the Cessna and instructed him to turn for Brunswick and land. The pilot declined to do so. Our pilot warned him to land or be shot down, and he declined again, but he turned on all his lights and his transponder. Our pilots were lining up for a shot when the Cessna exploded."

"You mean the man committed suicide?"

"It would appear so, Mr. President. He headed his airplane out to sea, and our pilots saw the burning wreckage fall into the water."

"I see."

"Is this what you anticipated, sir?"

"No, but the man saved us a lot of trouble. Please phone Coast Guard command for me, give them the coordinates of the crash, and tell them I want a search for wreckage and a body to commence at dawn."

"Yes, Mr. President. Is there anything else I can do for you?"

"No, thank you, Captain. Good night." Will hung up and punched another line for an operator.

"Yes, Mr. President?"

"Please get me Deputy Director Kinney of the FBI on his cell phone."

"Yes, sir. Please hold."

KINNEY WAS STANDING in the living room of Teddy Fay's house when his cell phone vibrated in his pocket. He dug it out and opened it. "This is Bob Kinney."

"Hold for the president, please."

"Hello, Bob?"

"Yes, Mr. President."

"The CNO's office just called. The Brunswick jets intercepted Fay's airplane. After some conversation back and forth, he turned on the airplane's lights and transponder, then blew himself up over the water."

"Holy shit," Kinney said involuntarily. "Excuse me, Mr. President."

"I had pretty much the same reaction," the president said. "Bob, you've done a fine job in impossible circumstances, and I won't forget it."

"Thank you, Mr. President, but it was Rawls's tip that made a resolution possible."

"Yes, I guess he's earned his pardon. Well, I'll leave it to you to wrap this thing up. Don't make any announcements about this. I'm going to hold a press conference at the White House at noon tomorrow, and I'd like you to be there."

"Thank you, sir."

"It's snowing in Washington, Bob, the first of the season. Looks like we might have a white Christmas."

"I like the snow, sir. I'll look forward to seeing it."

"Good night, Bob. I hope you can get some sleep on the way home."

"Good night, Mr. President." Kinney hung up the phone. "Kerry," he said to the agent, who was across the room, "get the chopper into Islesboro Airport and have them get the jet ready at Rockland. You and I have a date in Washington in less than twelve hours."

"With the director?" Smith asked.

"I don't think he'll be there," Kinney said.

61

KINNEY AND SMITH STOOD at the president's side in the White House press briefing room and waited for the clock to show 12:01 P.M., which was when control rooms all over the country would insert the live press conference into their noon news.

The press secretary stepped to the microphone fifteen seconds before that. "The president will have a statement, and he will not take questions at this time. A later briefing, to be announced, will be held to provide details." The clock hands moved to 12:01. "Ladies and gentlemen, the president of the United States."

The president stepped to the microphone. "Ladies and gentlemen, my fellow Americans, I have an announcement regarding the series of murders of political figures that have taken place over the past weeks. Last night, the FBI raided a house on a Maine island where the fugitive suspect, Theodore Fay, had fled. Mr. Fay escaped through a tunnel which led out of the house's basement and managed to get to an airfield on the island, where he took off in a light airplane.

"On my orders, two jet fighters were scrambled from the Brunswick, Maine, Naval Air Station, and these aircraft intercepted the smaller airplane, with orders to force it to land or to shoot it down. Mr. Fay refused to follow their instructions, but before the Navy aircraft could position themselves to fire, Mr. Fay caused his own airplane to explode. The wreckage landed in the sea, between Kennebunkport and Portland, and the Coast Guard began a search at dawn for the wreckage and Mr. Fay's body.

"Less than an hour ago, the commandant of the Coast Guard informed me that wreckage of an aircraft bearing the registration number of Mr. Fay's airplane had been found, and they hope to find remains soon.

"I want to express my personal gratitude to Deputy Director Robert Kinney of the FBI and his associate, Special Agent Kerry

Smith, who have been on this case from the beginning and who have pursued it to its conclusion. I want to thank, as well, Lieutenants J/G Harris Conover and William Banks for their fine work in locating Mr. Fay's aircraft in the skies over Maine. All concerned have done good work, and their country should be proud of them.

"Our country can breathe easier, now that this terrible episode in our history has been brought to an end. Mr. Fay, I'm afraid, is all too typical of those, of whatever nationality, who believe that they are right and others are wrong and that violence can move others to their point of view. This never works, at home or abroad, and our nation is poorer for those who have been lost. I wish, once again, to extend my profound sympathy to their families and friends. Thank you."

JUSTICE THOMAS GRAYDON watched the press conference with his wife in their cabin in the Maryland mountains. "Well, that's a relief," his wife said, turning off the TV.

A U.S. Marshal came into the room. "Judge, the plowing is done, and the road is clear now. Are you ready to go?"

"Thanks, Bill, I guess we are." Graydon and his wife got into their coats and followed the marshal out to the judge's black SUV.

"Better let me drive, Judge," the marshal said. "There's still ice, and we're trained for this sort of thing."

Graydon, who preferred to drive himself, reluctantly handed over the keys and got into the front passenger seat, while the marshal assisted his wife into the rear. After a moment, they were headed down the mountainside, followed by another car carrying two marshals.

Graydon instinctively grabbed for the dashboard as the car hit a slippery spot and skidded a little. "Watch it, Bill," he said.

"Judge, please fasten your seat belt," the marshal said.

Graydon, who detested seat belts and felt they were an infringement on his civil rights, grudgingly reached for his seat belt.

At that moment, the car began to skid again.

"Hang on, Judge," the marshal said. "It's going to be all right."

But then the SUV was suddenly traveling sideways.

"What the hell?" the marshal was able to say before they crashed through the guard rail.

Justice Graydon saw the river far below rushing up at him. He was not able to fasten his seat belt before they crashed.

ED RAWLS WATCHED the press conference in the warden's office.

"Why were you so interested in that, Ed?"

"Just curious," Rawls replied. He hadn't expected to be mentioned, but still, he was disappointed.

"All right, Ed," the warden said, standing up and extending two envelopes. "Here's your pardon; it was delivered by messenger a few minutes ago, along with an envelope from the FBI."

Rawls stuck both in a pocket of his old civilian suit without opening them.

The warden offered his hand. "Good luck, Ed," he said. "Try to stay out of trouble."

"You bet, Warden," Rawls replied, shaking the hand. He followed the guard out of the office, through the prison and to the front gate, where a taxi was waiting. He shook hands with the guard and got into the cab. "Atlanta Airport," he said.

As the taxi drove away, Rawls opened the first envelope and read over the pardon. "Very satisfactory," he said aloud.

"What?" the cabdriver asked.

"Just talking to myself," Rawls replied. He opened the other envelope and found $10,000 in hundred-dollar bills and a cashier's check for $990,000.

"Very, *very* satisfactory," he said.

KINNEY AND SMITH were driven away from the White House by an FBI car and driver.

"Bob," Smith said, "I'll bet you're going to be the next director."

"Oh, shut up, Kerry," Kinney said. He wanted to get back to his office to call Nancy Kimble.

They rode along in silence for a while, then Smith spoke again. "The Coast Guard still hasn't found Fay's body, have they?"

"Not the last I heard," Kinney said.

"Jesus," Smith said. "I hope the son of a bitch didn't have a parachute."

Kinney made a groaning noise. "Kerry, I told you to shut up."

ACKNOWLEDGMENTS

I am grateful to my editor at Putnam, David Highfill, for his continuing fine work on my manuscripts and his shepherding of my books inside the publishing house, as I am to all the people behind the scenes at Putnam who do so much to make my work a success.

I am grateful, too, to my literary agents, Morton Janklow and Anne Sibbald, for all their work in the management of my career over the past twenty-two years, and all the people at Janklow and Nesbit. They have always made me feel I am in good hands.

AUTHOR'S NOTE

I am happy to hear from readers, but you should know that if you write to me in care of my publisher, three to six months will pass before I receive your letter, and when it finally arrives it will be one among many, and I will not be able to reply.

However, if you have access to the Internet, you may visit my website at www.stuartwoods.com, where there is a button for sending me email. So far, I have been able to reply to all of my email, and I will continue to try to do so.

If you send me an email and do not receive a reply, it is because you are among an alarming number of people who have entered their email address incorrectly in their mail software. I have many of my replies returned as undeliverable.

Remember: email, reply; snail mail, no reply.

When you email, please do not send attachments, as I *never* open these. They can take twenty minutes to download, and they often contain viruses.

Please do not place me on your mailing lists for funny stories, prayers, political causes, charitable fund-raising, petitions, or sentimental claptrap. I get enough of that from people I already know. Generally speaking, when I get email addressed to a large number of people, I immediately delete it without reading it.

Please do not send me your ideas for a book, as I have a policy of writing only what I myself invent. If you send me story ideas, I will immediately delete them without reading them. If you have a good idea for a book, write it yourself, but I will not be able to advise you on how to get it published. Buy a copy of Writer's Market at any bookstore; that will tell you how.

Anyone with a request concerning events or appearances may email it to me or send it to: Publicity Department, G. P. Putnam's Sons, *375* Hudson Street, New York, NY 10014.

Those ambitious folk who wish to buy film, dramatic, or television rights to my books should contact Matthew Snyder, Creative Artists Agency, 9830 Wilshire Boulevard, Beverly Hills, CA 90212-1825.

Those who wish to conduct business of a more literary nature should contact Anne Sibbald, Janklow & Nesbit, 445 Park Avenue, New York, NY 10022.

If you want to know if I will be signing books in your city, please visit my website, www.stuartwoods.com, where the tour schedule will be published a month or so in advance. If you wish me to do a book signing in your locality, ask your favorite bookseller to contact his Putnam representative or the G. P. Putnam's Sons Publicity Department with the request.

If you find typographical or editorial errors in my book and feel an irresistible urge to tell someone, please write to David Highfill at Putnam, address above. Do not email your discoveries to me, as I will already have learned about them from others.

A list of all my published works appears in the front of this book. All the novels are still in print in paperback and can be found at or ordered from any bookstore. If you wish to obtain hardcover copies of earlier novels or of the two nonfiction books, a good used-book store or one of the online bookstores can help you find them. Otherwise, you will have to go to a great many garage sales.